When They Weren't Looking

The Wardham Series
Book No. 3

ZOE YORK

Copyright © 2014 Zoe York

All rights reserved.

ISBN-13: 978-0993667527 (RRKY)
ISBN-10: 099366752X

OTHER WORKS BY THIS AUTHOR

The Wardham Series
Between Then and Now (a Wardham Novella)
What Once Was Perfect
Where Their Hearts Collide

Boxed Sets and Anthologies
Shades of Pink
Love for the Holidays

Zoe York

DEDICATION

because life is too short to not be yourself

For all women who have had the courage to start over

Zoe York

CHAPTER ONE

The only thing that would make Evie Calhoun's weekend away in the city better would be an orgasm or two. In an ideal world, served up on a platter by a pool boy or a lumberjack.

But even though that wasn't going to happen, she couldn't keep a smile off her face. It had been a near-perfect day, and now she was walking back to her hotel after witnessing a world-class dance performance. A gorgeous lake on one side of her and the city on the other. The sun, setting behind her in the west, lit up the glass towers of Toronto's central business district and what might be an everyday view for others struck her as magical and sophisticated.

No wonder the condos advertised along Lakeshore Driver were so expensive—it was the best of both worlds in one perfect location. Man, what an exciting place to call home.

Evie never would, of course, but she could pretend for a night or two. Her mother had surprised her with a much needed break. Away from Wardham, and her ex-husband, and even her much-loved life with her boys.

Claire Calhoun had given her daughter a train ticket to the city and five hundred dollars, with an order that none of it was to be spent on anything even remotely like a bill or clothes for the kids. Evie was to spoil herself.

And she had: conveyor-belt sushi for dinner the night

before, a gorgeous room at the Westin Harbour Castle hotel, a few splurges at Sephora and Victoria's Secret this afternoon, and a front row ticket to see The Mitchell Raz Collective at the Harbourfront Centre.

In another life, Evie might have moved to the city and auditioned for similar companies. Shared a flat uptown with three other girls and bartended all night so she'd be free to dance during the day. But she'd been scared of the odds against her, and her few visits to the city to see Evan in those halcyon early days after graduation had left her underwhelmed. Loud, expensive, dirty. Wardham, with its sleepy beach and zero competition for anything was the more comfortable choice.

And she wouldn't do it any differently, given the chance, because whatever other costs her choices had, she had two beautiful sons who made her world right. Her family, for all the bumps and bruises it had sustained over the last two years, was a wonderful unit. Connor was rapidly turning into a young man, careful and studious, but always staying on the cute side of bossy. Max, two years younger, had finally figured out how to stick a punch-line and used it to maximum advantage in his natural calling as an entertainer. His teacher danced around the term class clown, but grade one had been a hard transition for him, and she expected more of the same in the fall.

But Evie... Somewhere in the mix, she'd let herself be compressed to mother, community member, daughter, and sister. All good, but all giving. This was the first time in years she'd allowed herself to truly indulge. Sleeping in, shopping, dance. She'd joked with her girlfriends about adding sex into the mix, but the closest to that she was going to get this weekend was being able to spread out on the hotel bed and read an erotic romance novel without worrying about hiding it from prying eyes.

Sex.

It had been so long, she might actually have forgotten how to do it.

Two years since she and Dale last made love, although there hadn't been much love in that coupling. Or the infrequent times in the year before that. No love, and even less passion.

Deep down, she yearned for that passion. If she was being honest with herself, what she really wanted was an awesome romp. With someone who didn't lose their erection if she moved in the wrong direction. Someone who wanted her for who she was right now, stretch marks and old lady hands included. Who didn't have a pathetic Madonna/whore complex.

A flash of anger at her ex-husband pulsed through her. She glanced down at her bare fingers, glad to be rid of the rings that hadn't guaranteed the forever they were supposed to.

But she was thirty-five, and a mother, and it had been fifteen years since she'd last had sex for sex's sake. She wouldn't even know where to start in the city, and the thought of actually picking up a stranger...that was an awesome fantasy, and a terrifying reality.

A hot bath and a blush-inducing book would have to be enough.

But first, a drink. Maybe two, because she could sleep in tomorrow.

The hotel bar was empty, but the friendly bartender gestured for her to take a seat. "What can I get you?"

"Something fancy." Wardham's only bar, Danny's, was known for cheap beer and straight shots.

"Do you like peaches?" She nodded, and he began assembling a bellini in front of her. She slid some cash toward him when he finished, and after taking a sip, let her thoughts wander down an imaginary path. If she had come to the city to be a dancer, what would she be doing now? Choreography? Married or single? Still on the audition circuit?

She nursed her drink, lost in a tangled web of what-ifs, and was just about to head upstairs when the bartender placed another bellini in front of her. She shook her head. "Oh, no, I'm sorry, I didn't—"

"It's from the man in the corner," he said.

Evie twisted in her seat to see where he was pointing. Her breath caught in her throat as her gaze collided with dark, unvarnished interest. There were six of them, four men and two women, all in suits, but only one was staring at her like he wanted to eat her up. And as heat sparked in various places throughout her body, being devoured by a perfect stranger suddenly sounded like an excellent idea. Hot damn...

No. What kind of hussy would that make her?

A satisfied one, probably, if he could deliver on the promise in his eyes.

She smiled, enjoying the moment of attention, and nodded her head in thanks. A warm blush crawled up her neck and she spun back to the bar, but a minute later she glanced back over her shoulder. There was something unbelievably tempting about the man. Long and lean, with dark hair and refined features. Quietly handsome, but overtly sexy. Urbane and sophisticated, like he wouldn't blink to discover her Brazilian bikini wax. Like he'd understand the implicit request of it, and dive in for a feast.

It didn't take him long to make his way over to her.

"Can I join you?" His voice was rich and warm with a shiver-inducing edge, like chocolate syrup on vanilla ice cream. Up close he was younger than she first thought. Definitely younger than her, and not just by a few months.

"I suppose it's the least I can do, since you bought me a drink." She glanced up at him from under her eye lashes. God, she had no clue how to flirt. She didn't want to lead him on, but every fibre of her being wanted him to keep talking.

Instead of sitting, he leaned sideways against the bar. "That's not a ringing invitation, but I'll take it." He flashed a crooked smile, the left side of his face curling up in a wink, and butterflies took flight from the pit of her stomach.

"I'm out of practice, I promise it's not personal. I'm Evie." She held out her hand, and something bright sparked in his eyes. Everything around them faded to nothing as he wrapped his hand around hers and she swallowed hard against something that felt suspiciously like a giggle trying to fly out of her mouth.

"Liam." Another smile, and her panties started peeling themselves down her hips. "And I don't have a ton of practice at this either."

"I find that really hard to believe," she admitted, kicking herself momentarily for the honesty, but he just chuckled.

"Where are you from?"

"Out of town." He lifted one eyebrow at the coy response, and a warmth spilled across her chest. This was fun.

"Would you like to join us?" He nodded his head toward his friends. "We've just written our final exams—"

A dull roar filled her ears, and her face must have fallen, because he leaned in and touched her forearm. "You okay?"

"Exams?" Her voice came out as a squeak. Holy shit, he was a college student. An incredibly mature, sexy, masculine…kid. She narrowed her eyes at him, then glanced over to his friends. None of them looked like teenagers. Maybe they were grad students. But still.

"Business school. Two years of grueling hell completed. We're heading up to Koreatown next for some karaoke."

Business school. Not babies, just…younger than her. A fun kind of young. Yeah, she could still do this. "Sounds intriguing."

He laughed at the obvious doubt in her voice. "It is, I promise."

Something about the dip in his voice, the private pause, made her come undone, and the giggle snuck out, followed by another. He raised his eyebrows, but he didn't seem concerned by her bizarre behaviour, just amused. "And just how can I trust your judgment on such matters?"

He leaned in close enough for his cologne to faintly

imprint on her senses. He smelled yummy and expensive and not really too young at all. She was clearly drunk, which would explain why she licked her lips and tilted her head just so, a move he definitely didn't miss. He paused a few inches away from her face, naked appreciation zinging between them, then shifted his approach and brushed his lips against her ear. "Come with us, I'll sing you a song."

"Okay, that definitely sounded practiced," she breathed.

"I promise, I've never invited a woman to karaoke before." He pulled back just enough to ease out of her personal space, but his hand lingered on the back of her upper arm, and she was painfully aware of his fingertips brushing the side of her bra. Which didn't match her panties. Which shouldn't matter, but she had a sneaky suspicion if she accepted the invitation, it just might.

"My choice?" Evie's voice wavered as she realized she was seriously considering karaoke—and whatever else Liam was offering.

"For you, Evie, I'd sing just about anything." He chuckled and eased himself back against the bar.

She wobbled on her stool and took a steading breath. She needed a second to think this through…

"Tell you what." He glanced at his watch, a shiny thing that looked expensive and functional at the same time. "I'm going to get another round of drinks for my colleagues, so you've got some time to make up your mind. Finish your bellini and come up with a short list of tragic song choices."

"I might just head up to my room for a minute and change," she whispered. He glanced down at her skirt with appreciation, and she flushed.

"I hope you come back down." He brushed his fingertips over her knuckles as he stepped away from the bar, breaking that contact only when his body carried him too far away. "We're going to have fun tonight."

"Pick up, pick up, pick up…" Evie hopped around her hotel room, juggling her phone in one hand and a brand new pair of red lace panties in the other. Thank goodness for her earlier visit to Victoria's Secret.

"Hello?" Her sister answered on the fourth ring, her voice full of sleep and confusion.

"Laney, it's nine o'clock on a Saturday night, why are you in bed?"

"I was in the OR all last night and Kyle sent me to three open houses today." She yawned. "What's up?"

"Would it be wrong to have a one-night stand?"

Dead silence was not a reassuring response.

"What's the deal with safe sex? Do I need anything other than condoms?" Goddamnit, she needed to get her voice under control, the warbling idiot was not a good sound.

"Uhm…" Laney cleared her throat. "I don't have enough information to advise you, really. Are you in Toronto?"

"Uh huh. And a guy, a really, really cute guy, approached me in the bar downstairs. Laney, his voice…and his eyes. And his smile. I don't think he's an ax-murderer, and if I ask him to leave something valuable with the bartender he would, I'm sure of it. Laney, he's hot, and possibly too young for me, but I think he just might be what I need right now."

"You don't need permission, Evie. Just be safe. Condoms, for all sex acts, got it?"

"Got it." She took a deep breath. "I might not even do anything, in the end…"

Her sister laughed. "That would be disappointing, after that preamble."

He really was out of practice. Evie wasn't the first woman he'd chatted up in a bar, but his dating over the last two years had been sporadic itch-scratching. Nothing in his recent history compared to ten minutes of flirting with the beautiful blonde.

She'd caught his eye as soon as they entered the bar. Shiny long hair, falling straight down her back, like a beacon calling his attention to her tight round ass perched on that bar stool. Small and slim, but strong. Her bare arms were curvy with subtle definition, and even lost in thought she held herself upright. Not stiff, just…poised. Her natural class took his breath away, like he was looking at a real-life princess.

The irony wasn't lost on him that at first glance, this woman checked every one of his mother's superficial requirements. Qualities he'd always eschewed in the women he'd dated. But there was something else about her that captured his imagination. She was sexy, no doubt about it, but naked feelings danced across her face as she lost herself in her fancy drink, and that raw vulnerability was what sealed the deal. Even though he was there to celebrate the end of their program, he'd abandon his friends in a heartbeat if she'd give him some of her time. And when the bartender ambled over to take their order, Liam quietly asked him to make her another of whatever she was having.

Up close she was even prettier than at first glance. Pale skin, delicate bone structure, lush pink lips with just a hint of lip gloss, like she'd been licking it away for a few hours. Her dark grey eyes flashed with a thousand emotions, and her voice tangled his heart into knots. She was fascinating, and he couldn't wait to discover more of what made Evie tick.

He wasn't sure if she'd come back, and he was kicking himself for not gleaning more identifying information before she glided out of the bar. He was tossing up the idea of sending Jessica to flirt with the front desk clerks and find out Evie's room number when she returned.

She'd changed, all right. Into tight jeans that left nothing to the imagination, a silky blouse, and fresh lip gloss.

It needed to be nibbled off, immediately, and he knew just the man for the task.

Karaoke was a terrible idea. He wanted to stalk across the bar, toss her over his shoulder, and carry her back to her room. He'd sing whatever she wanted while she shimmied out of those jeans. His dick agreed. A private strip tease was definitely the way to go.

But as she drew closer, her eyes wide and her breath shallow and rapid, he shut himself down. She was nervous, and he wasn't a brute. Although she certainly brought out the cro-magnon tendencies, holy shit.

He stood and reached out his hand. When she took it, he tamped down the desire to tug her fingers to his lips, and instead gave her a reassuring squeeze. His voice, husky and raw, more than made up for his restraint. "You decided to join us."

Her sharp intake of breath at his tone, coupled with a blush and a smile, promised that if he played his cards right he'd get a chance to show her his inner caveman. All in good time. He turned to introduce her to the group.

Two hours later, Evie had fallen head over heels in love with the Korean karaoke club, with its private rooms, high-tech sound system, and prompt to-the-door drink service. From the hot glances she kept sliding his way, she was still interested in an even more private party, but for now, he was having fun watching her cut loose. She'd hit it off with Jessica right away, and they were currently tag-teaming "Hit Me Baby One More Time". His closest friend in the program, Jess was in a long-distance relationship that was falling apart, and while he would have abandoned her in a heartbeat for Evie tonight—because Jess was a big girl and Evie was, well, probably one-in-a-million—he was glad she was having fun.

And Evie. She was incredible. By the fourth saucy holler that her loneliness was killing her, he was on his feet, applauding. As Chet took over at the mic, she skipped back to the leatherette bench and flung herself around his neck.

"That was hot," he muttered into her hair, and she flashed him a million watt smile.

"Your turn again soon."

"You haven't chosen one for me." He bit his lip and waggled his eyebrows at her.

She hummed under her breath for a minute, then pushed

him away and grabbed for the song binder. He tried to ease against her, see what page she was looking at, but she gave him a playful elbow to the ribs.

Jess joined them, sitting on the far side of Evie, who after thoughtfully stroking her chin for a minute made a song code note on the pad of paper and passed it to Mike, who'd made himself the de facto DJ.

"Are you torturing my boy there," Jess asked with a wicked gleam in her eye.

"Oh, I don't know. I think he's up for it." Evie reached behind her and laced her fingers into his, and he felt like crowing. Damn straight, he was up for anything tonight. "So Jess, you were saying your boyfriend lives in London?"

His friend nodded. "I'm moving there next month for work. It'll be nice to live in the same city again."

"London's lovely. Some of my friends went there for university." Evie took a sip of her drink. Liam stilled behind her, his heart pounding. A clue to the mystery that was Evie. Ever since she'd demurely told him she was from out of town, he'd been hesitant to ask any more details. This was gold.

"Are you from around there?" Jess clapped her hands. "Maybe we could get together for brunch!"

Evie laughed. "I'm a little far for that, but who knows, maybe. I live in a little town on Lake Erie, not far from Windsor. I'm sure you've never heard of it."

Liam's pulse picked up. What were the odds?

"Is it near Pelee Island? We went there for a getaway a few years ago, it was lovely."

She nodded. "Very close! Wardham…between Kingsville and Colchester Harbour."

Jess cocked head. "That sounds familiar. Liam, isn't—"

"Hey, who chose Journey?"

He took a deep breath. He should probably tell her, but then she turned and beamed at him. "You're up!"

He'd tell her. Right after he knocked her song out of the park. He shrugged out of his jacket and rolled up his sleeves.

Evie and Jess hooted and hollered as he rolled his hips to the opening strains of "Don't Stop Believing", but as he started singing the lyrics, the light-hearted tease became something else. Evie held his gaze, and he knew the song choice was an opening, and damn fucking straight he was going to take it.

And once they'd shared this night, he'd find her again, and they'd share another. It would take some time, but he wasn't about to let Evie go, not when he'd just discovered her.

As the song came to an end, he tossed the microphone to Chet, scooped up his jacket with one hand and pulled Evie off the couch with another. With the scantest of goodbyes to the room, he hustled them out onto the street and hailed a cab.

"You don't mind cutting your celebration with your friends a bit short?" The breathless thrill in Evie's voice pumped adrenaline directly into his veins, and blood straight to his cock.

He pulled her tight against him, his hand firm against her side. He pressed a kiss to the side of her neck. "This is best graduation present I could imagine."

"Kissing on the street?" She laughed gently. "You have low standards, my friend."

"Hearing you laugh, Evie. I've been missing that, and I didn't even know it."

She licked her lips and touched the side of his face. "Want to know a secret?"

He grinned. Her eyes were bright, and he knew his were the same. They were just drunk enough to do something crazy.

"I'm extremely ticklish. Take me back to your place and I promise, I'll laugh all night."

He whipped open the door and guided her into the taxi. She slid into the middle seat, and he pressed himself against her side, his hand on her knee. His fingers lightly touching the inside of her thigh.

"Liam? We're going to need to stop and buy some condoms."

CHAPTER TWO

Her hands shook as she held the plastic stick between her legs.

On the other side of the bathroom door, the thump of feet was followed by a distant, "*Mom!*" The boys were up. Evie cracked the door and hollered that she'd get them breakfast in a few minutes. Another thump as one of them jumped for the TV remote. Great. Cartoons would make a suitably bizarre soundtrack for what she knew was coming next.

Two blue lines.

Goddamn it. More colourful curse words would be appropriate, but almost nine years of motherhood had trained her to keep the F-bomb inside her head. Her mouth, now full of cotton and unable to produce any more saliva, let alone swear, dropped open in shock as the reality of just how stupid she'd been started to sink in.

One night.

One weekend of fun after years of being a responsible mom. Two years without sex. And eight hours of reckless pleasure was her undoing.

How was she going to handle a newborn on her own? She thunked her head against the wall. A wall still primarily owned by the bank. Oh god, her mortgage. Not working wasn't an option. She'd only been in the house three months. There was no way the bank would waive even a single month's payments. And with the new studio renovations still on her credit card…

She could borrow money from Laney. Her sister would share it, no questions asked. How humiliating, to go hat in hand to one's younger, more successful sister, and confess you got knocked up on a one-night stand with a college kid you haven't talked to since.

Oh god. The kid. Who was going to *have* a kid.

No, no, no. Fluttery panic trembled up from her stomach, crowding against what tasted like bile in her throat, and she spun around, folded over the toilet, and let it all out.

Co-parenting the boys with Dale was hard enough, but at least they had history. She knew him, could read his moods, anticipate what he might want, and how she might be able to get what she wanted out of him.

She was going to have to find Liam. Thank god for small miracles, she remembered his name. First one, anyway. The engineer who'd just finished a business degree. Who'd celebrated by going to karaoke in Koreatown with his equally young friends, and somehow, Evie had agreed to tag along.

It was his eyes. And his voice. She was a sucker for a man who could sing. He'd done something to the two syllables in her name, something that should have been illegal. A rolling, teasing pronunciation that had her panting for more.

"Evie from out of town. Come to karaoke with me. Let's celebrate."

Oh, Liam whatever-your-name is, you're going to regret that invitation.

On the other side of the bathroom door, Max was hopping up and down. Connor was with him, whispering something about leaving Mom alone, and her heart broke. She'd been too hard on them the last few days, knowing she needed to pick up a pack of tests. Not wanting to confirm what she already knew in her heart of hearts. She swung the door open.

"Sorry, Mommy. I really gotta pee!" Max bounded past

her. Connor stood in the hallway, looking somehow taller than the day before. Maybe it was look of concern on his nine-year-old face.

"Breakfast, kiddo?" She lightened her tone and gently bumped his shoulder as she stepped past him.

"Are you sick?" He turned and followed her down the tiny corridor to the living room, and the galley kitchen on the other side. Their bungalow was wee, but it was theirs. After living with her mother for eleven months, Evie was happy to have a place all her own. A two-bedroom place.

A baby could sleep in her room for the first few months. Or longer, if he was like Connor. But Max had needed his own room after six months. What if this one was the same?

"Mom?"

She swallowed hard. "No, honey. I'm fine." *For now.*

Hunger won out over curiosity, and Connor turned his attention to the yogurt and granola she set out. Max soon joined them, and then it was a flurry of eating, changing, library book finding, permission slip signing. By the time she'd escorted them across the street and down the block to school, she was ready for a nap.

Too bad she had four classes today, and dinner at her mother's tonight, which was doubling as a planning session for Laney's engagement party. Eleanor Nixon, Laney's future mother-in-law, would also be there. Two smart women who would smell fear a mile away. She had seven hours to pull her shit together and pretend she wasn't knocked up.

And hope that the erroneously named morning sickness didn't choose tonight to make another appearance.

It was too early for that, wasn't it? She'd sold her prenatal books at a garage sale after Max was born. Maybe the internet would have the information she needed, because there was no way she was going to the Wardham Public Library and signing out *What to Expect When You're Expecting*.

First step, figure out a due date. That would be easy. There was only one possible date of conception. The night she lost her mind and slept with a college student. *God.*

Second step, call the midwife and get on the waiting list. And hope to hell that Molly Weisz, the receptionist in the Essex Birthing Co-op, and born and bred Wardhamite, actually respected patient confidentiality.

Holy hell. Molly wasn't going to say anything, but in a few short months, her belly certainly would. Everyone in town would soon know that Evie Calhoun, the one with the plastic surgeon sister, an ex-husband running for town council, and two lovely little boys, was knocked up by a mystery man who was most definitely not in the picture.

Evie was half-way into a panic attack when Carrie Nixon, Laney's future sister-in-law, and owner of A Bun in the Oven, a bakery-coffee shop that was the jewel of downtown Wardham, popped up in front of her. Carrie's daughter was in Max's class, and her son went to the preschool Evie had just walked past.

"Hey, chickadee, what's up?"

"Heading to the studio. You on your way to the store?"

Carrie nodded and fell in step beside her. "Yep. I'm not in a hurry, though. I love having an assistant manager." Carrie had recently promoted one of her part-time staff, giving her some much needed mornings off to take her kids to school. Her husband, Ian, was a farmer. Early summer was a busy time for both of them. "I could grab us some lattes and keep you company at the studio for a bit."

"I...I can't today, sorry. I've got a bunch of calls to make before my first class." Not a lie. She had to call the midwife, and the University of Toronto. See if she could find someone who would help her track down a student by the name of Liam, with dark hair, dark eyes, and a voice that evaporated panties.

That would work, right?

Because she had to tell him. *Maybe he wouldn't want to know*, a little voice piped up from the back of her head. She shook the thought away. Not an option. But she didn't need to tell him right away. The pregnancy might not stick.

"Evie, are you okay?" Carrie pressed a hand to her shoulder and they both slowed to a stop just shy of the main intersection. "You don't just look preoccupied, you look...sad."

That was Carrie. Blunt and to the point. And a good friend, but Evie wasn't ready to confide in anyone just yet. "I've got a lot on my mind, I'm sorry. I'm terrible company right now. Catch ya later?"

She took off without looking back.

Neither Eleanor nor her mother noticed anything over dinner, and discussion of the potluck extravaganza for Laney and Kyle that was just a week away dominated the evening. She was able to duck out early, citing the last few days of school as a reasonable excuse. Connor had to leave early the next morning for a field trip, and Max just needed more sleep in general lately, it seemed.

She'd decided over dinner that she couldn't tell Laney yet. After the party. Her sister was sticking around for a week of vacation, before finally moving her fiancé and their dog to Chicago, where she was a paediatric plastic surgeon.

The sisters couldn't be more different. Instead of going to college, Evie had opted to teach dance part-time and work at a clothing store that had long since closed its doors, then married young. She had Connor, and two years later Max. It had taken another six years to realize that she didn't want to grow old and grey with Dale, who was a good dad, but a shitty husband. Too many issues had cropped up between them that they never dealt with—including Evie's desire for more kids, and Dale hating to share her body. With his children, and her past.

Evie shook her head. It was time for her to get over that.

As she watched her sons brush their teeth, jockeying for position at the tiny sink in the tiny bathroom, she pressed a hand to her flat stomach. *Oh, little bean. I want you. I just don't know how I'm going to manage to give you everything you need.*

And at this rate, it might be just her doing the providing.

The call to the midwife's office had been productive—as a returning client, she was guaranteed care—but as she feared, the calls to the university, and then the Department of Engineering, proved fruitless. No one would give her any information on a student, which of course made sense, but logic and rationality didn't cut her frustration at being blandly told she'd hit another dead end.

Hot tears pricked her eyelids, and she widened her gaze to hold them at bay, willing herself to hold it together until the boys were asleep.

"Dude, you spit on my ear!"

"No, I didn't! You put your head under my mouth! Mommy!" Max spun around, looking for her to intervene. His outrage, fueled by fatigue, wasn't going to go away on its own.

Evie shot Connor a beseeching look and her eldest, always the peacemaker, ruffled his brother's hair. "Sorry for yelling, buddy."

"'Sokay. Sorry for spitting." Max shuffled out of the room with a yawn, and Evie wrapped her arms around Connor for a second before he wrestled away.

In their room, Connor settled into the top bunk with a book and his night light. Evie crawled in with Max on the bottom, and listened with half an ear as he slowly made his way through a Star Wars reader. When he set it down and rolled over, eyes shut already, she got up, patted Connor's leg, and flicked off the light on her way to the kitchen.

No one else was going to do the dishes, and she hated having them there in the morning, so even though sandpaper and sadness were scratching at the inside of her eyelids, she tidied up before making herself a cup of tea to take to bed.

Why now? There was no ready answer. She'd just gotten her life back together. Set aside her hopes for a big family. Made peace with the fact that she'd left her husband because he didn't love her the way she wanted to be loved. Moved forward with an alternate dream, one that was harder and more grueling that she ever thought possible. More humble, too. A tiny two-bedroom bungalow on the modest side of town, although Wardham was small enough that it wasn't far from the quaint main street strip and the public beach on the other side. A rented studio space where she taught Pilates instead of dance, because that's what paid the bills.

And she loved it. All of it. The coupon clipping and the lentil-heavy meals when she only had fifty bucks left in the bank. The quiet nights after the boys went to bed, and the days to herself when they were with Dale.

She'd made peace with where life had dumped her. Started to make something special out of the pieces of her former world. And in a few short months, all of that would be threatened. Unless she asked for a handout. Something she'd avoided so far.

She wasn't too proud to accept help. Her mother had given them a place to stay after she and Dale split the less than impressive proceeds of sale on their old house—which had been on the fancier side of town, but mortgaged to the hilt—and Dale gave her child-support every month, which she was grateful for as well.

But this would be different. This wouldn't be something reasonable and small. If she didn't teach classes for six or eight weeks, maybe more if she had a difficult delivery. The math took her breath away, and she couldn't hold back the tears any longer.

A lot can happen in nine months. The logical part of her brain fought against the list of concerns she'd been developing all day, but the emotional overload won out. And she didn't have anyone to share her fear with. Another couple of weeks, and she'd be able to tell her sister. Her mother, too, and how humiliating would that conversation be? But Claire would be supportive. Too supportive.

Evie curled onto her side, and buried her wet cheeks in the patchwork quilt stretched over her bed. She wouldn't be able to handle her mother's eternal optimism or the immediate leap to finding solutions. Not yet. Not before she'd had a chance to wrap her hand around how drastically her life had changed.

No. For now, she was on her own.

And she still had a big problem in the form of a missing sperm donor. Missing, and probably unwilling. And how would she even explain how this happened? They'd bought a brand-new box of condoms, and to the best of her hazy recollection, none of them malfunctioned.

She fisted her hands into the bedding as a sob wracked her frame. *Pull it together, Calhoun. This wasn't in your master plan, either.* As the wave of emotion ebbed, she hauled herself to a sitting position and reached for the laptop tucked neatly on her bedside table. She did her nightly check-in on her favourite message board, then opened a new tab. The cursor blinked at her, a taunting vertical line. What search words could she use, exactly? Liam + engineering + business + Toronto? As she started typing, the search engine helpfully suggested Liam Hemsworth. *Wouldn't that be nice.* Maybe her Liam was a movie star, too.

Her Liam.

That was a phrase she needed to strike from her lexicon. Whatever co-parenting relationship she managed to sort out with the student, if he was interested in that, it would have to be one that ignored how their connection started. Ignored their night together, when he willingly and repeatedly made love to all of her body with all of his.

Evie's hands flared over her laptop keyboard. Graduating. Maybe there would be photos…but that didn't lead anywhere, either. She tried a few more things, but soon fatigue pushed the computer away. She had some time still.

Nine months, to be exact.

CHAPTER THREE

There were two realty offices in Wardham. Liam's uncle didn't recommend one over the other, and he figured the more time he spent on the main drag, the greater likelihood he might run into Evie, so he planned to visit both. After he did some property browsing, he was going to grab a coffee and take a stroll to look for her studio. Maybe catch a glimpse of her in workout wear.

Evie from Wardham. He hadn't been able to get her out of his mind, but he hadn't tried hard, either. Ever since that night, he'd wanted to make the drive, come and find her and ask her out on a second date. If she hadn't disappeared from his condo in the middle of the night, and checked out of the hotel before he made it down to the waterfront, their second date might have been brunch.

But then he'd gone back to work at Hexwell, trading his crazy school schedule for an even crazier work schedule. He'd found it hardcore when he was a specialist, but leading the project management team was a whole different level of commitment. One he quickly discovered he didn't like. The company had been good to him, giving him a leave of absence for his schooling, and employing him during his summer internship the previous year. He would have stuck it out for a while, for reasons of both loyalty and professionalism, but when another manager returned from maternity leave without a project to lead, he saw an opportunity and seized it. He wasn't cut out for a hundred hour work week. He knew that by the midpoint of his MBA. He was enough of a professional to extricate himself diplomatically, and threw himself into making a small but meaningful contribution before he left. They made noises about a specialist role should he want to return, but he knew he was done.

He had a few months until the sale of his condo closed, and in that time, he was going to help his uncle with the farm, and figure out how he could make himself useful in Wardham.

And hopefully get laid.

Evie. She'd been an unexpected treat after his final exam. Sexy as hell and completely unaware of her appeal. Gorgeous in a shimmery top and jeans. Breathtaking out of them, stretched out on his bed, making a hell of a lot of noise as he made her come, again and again. And more than a little dirty, which he loved.

He loved it so much, he was getting hard just thinking about it. In the middle of a real estate office. Time to focus.

"So you're looking for a duplex, maybe?"

He nodded as the agent returned to the round table with a handful of printed sheets. "Yep. Something I could maybe live in, but also get some rental income out of."

"These are a few recent sales in the area, to give you an idea of the price range." All dead cheap compared to Toronto. This plan might just work out. "I know that Terry Wolton is thinking of selling his triplex. It would probably go for twenty percent more than these properties, although a quick sale might save you some money."

Liam slid his business card across the table. "If you hear any noises in that direction, give me a call. It's a Toronto number for now, but I'll be changing it soon and I'll let you know when I do."

"You're moving to the area permanently, then?" Even this city boy could spot that curious gleam a mile away. It wouldn't be long before the entire town was chattering about Ted's nephew buying some property.

"That's the plan." After sliding the papers into his rucksack, and thanking the agent for her time, he hit the street. He was about the visit the next agency when he saw her, crossing the street a block ahead.

Evie's long blond hair was up in a swingy ponytail on the top of her head, and she was, much to his delight, wearing tight black shorts that made her ass look fantastic and a bright orange tank top, snug all over. She looked like a woman on a mission, her slim legs scissoring quickly as she dashed away.

All thoughts of real estate fled his mind as he made the instantaneous decision to follow her. He glanced at his watch. It was mid-morning. She was probably between classes. He searched his brain. They'd talked about work in the most general of terms, but people didn't exercise at half past ten in the morning, did they?

In the next block, he passed a grocery store, a bakery that smelled like lemons and espresso, and a consignment shop that had a sale table out front brimming with children's toys. A flash of orange disappearing up ahead showed him where Evie's studio was—a simple storefront with a purple sign in the window advertising Pilates classes. A quick perusal through the plate glass showed that she was alone inside.

Perfect. With a grin, he pushed the door open and stepped inside.

"I'll be right with you," she murmured, her head down. She was writing what looked like a weekly schedule on a portable white board. He glanced around at the space. An empty easel at the end of the counter probably held the board when she wasn't carefully printing on it. He stepped closer, intrigued at her alternating use of colours and the flower doodles she used to fill in blank spaces. She bit her lip in concentration, re-reading what she'd written, then straightened up and snapped the cap on the marker in her hand.

"Looks like a busy week of classes."

She jerked her head toward him, noticing for the first

time who was standing on the other side of the counter. The marker slipped from her hand, clattering loudly as it bounced off the board and skittered to the floor. All the colour drained from her face. Not exactly the reaction he was expecting.

"Liam." His name came out in a strained whisper.

"Hi? Is this a bad time?" He was starting to doubt his recollection of their night together. Was he that awful? Had he somehow taken advantage of her?

"You're here." She pinched her lips together and shook her head, like she was trying to focus. "Why are you here?"

"Uhm." He really wasn't sure how his answer would land. "I thought I'd ask you out on a second date."

A hysterical, watery laugh slipped out of her mouth before she clamped a hand over her face, shutting herself up.

"Evie—"

"What's your last name?" She grabbed a piece of paper and a pen. Her hand was shaking noticeably. What the hell was going on?

"McIntosh. Are you okay?" He took a step toward the counter and leaned against it. "You remember me, right?"

"Oh, yeah."

"I was hoping for less panic, more enthusiasm. Is that a no on the second date?"

"I don't think a date would be a good idea. But we should have coffee. How long are you in town?" Evie was talking a mile a minute now, not quite making eye contact with him. "Do you have a phone number and address I could have, as well?"

"Sure...can I ask why?" He reached for the paper, and she tossed the pen at him, as if accidentally touching him would be a nightmare. A second date was most definitely not on the horizon. Well, this might make his move to Wardham awkward, but maybe she was just having a bad day. He jotted down his phone number, and after a beat, added Ted's phone number. "That's my cell and this is the number where I'm staying for now. I'm not sure of the exact address. It's a few roads out of town."

Evie glanced at the paper and frowned. "I know that number." She mouthed the digits silently, thinking. "That's...that's..."

"Do you know Ted?"

"DO I KNOW TED?" The hysteria was back. "How do you know Ted?"

"He's my uncle."

Her gaze flicked to the window, where two women were talking, but from their outfits, he guessed they were on their way into the studio. A tendon in her neck flexed as she pulled herself back to the conversation, lowering her voice to a harsh whisper. "I have a private session right now. Those are my clients. You need to leave." She held up her hand. "Don't go far."

He hadn't been planning on it. Even though she should have been freaking him out, his only thought was that something was seriously wrong and he wanted to help make it right. "I'm going to grab a coffee and take a walk. When's your next break?"

"After these clients, I have a group class at noon. Then nothing until..." She took a deep breath. "Until I pick up my kids from school at three."

He nodded in what he hoped was a cool, reassuring way. He knew she was a single mom. Did she not remember that they'd talked about that? "I'll be back this afternoon, then."

At quarter after one, he arrived back at the studio, prepared to find a locked door and a sign barring all Liams from the premises. Instead, he found a very nervous Evie pacing back and forth.

"I should apologize for being weird earlier," she burst out as soon as he stepped inside. "I'm surprised you came back."

He refrained from pointing out that she was still being weird. She was also beautiful, and with her back straight and her shoulders squared, she looked brave in the face of a fearsome foe. But since he couldn't figure out why, it was weird. The best course of action would be silence. He nodded and took a careful step toward the counter.

"The thing is..." She swallowed hard and paused. "I tried to find you last week."

"But you didn't know my last name." He offered a gentle smile. "Now you do. And two different ways to contact me. I'm very findable now."

Her lips wobbled, like she was trying to return the smile but tears or anger was interfering with her facial muscles' attempts to twitch upward.

He decided to be brave and leaned in. "I'd very much like for you to find me. I really enjoyed our night together."

Liam wouldn't call himself a player, exactly, but he had a decent track record with women. He knew how to be charming and offer a compliment that landed with sincerity. Never before had he made a woman burst into tears like Evie did now.

She spun on her heel and ran for the back of the room. Liam swore under his breath. He turned to the front door and flipped the lock, because he was quite certain whatever was going on didn't need to be for public consumption. Then he moved to follow her, but the sign on the wall about outside shoes caught his attention. One glance at the smooth laminate flooring had him bent over, untying his laces. He didn't want to piss her off for something legitimate, as well.

Are you sure this chick is worth this drama? The voice of rationality asked the obvious question, but the answer was definitely a resounding yes. Whatever her deal was, this wasn't the Evie he met six weeks earlier. This woman was under incredible stress, and he was a part of it.

Six weeks. His pulse picked up, thudding loudly in his ears.

Running water obscured the sound of Evie's sniffling. He found her in the bathroom, patting her face with a towel.

"Evie?"

She glanced at his reflection in the mirror.

"You want to tell me what's going on?"

She shook her head. No.

"Is there something going on?"

A nod. Despite the summer heat, her face was pale and drawn. Still gorgeous. *Fuck me.*

"If I take a wild guess, will you be mad if I'm wrong?"

"Don't," she whispered. "Just give me a minute. This is harder than I thought."

The inkling that had dawned on him was looking more and more likely. Something hard and nasty twisted in his gut. She was gorgeous, and didn't want anything to do with him.

And didn't want him to have anything to do with her. Or her—

"Liam." She was still whispering, and her voice took on a tone of desperation. "Why did you come here today?"

He was having trouble thinking straight, but that answer was easy. "I don't think that matters, now." He wanted to shake her, and punch himself, because they were both handling this pretty poorly. Then he wanted to kiss her, and tell her it was going to be okay, but he didn't actually know that. When it came to this, he didn't know much of anything.

He couldn't remember the last time he'd been in that position. His entire adult life, he'd been in a position of knowledge. An expert, confident in his ability to solve problems and provide solutions.

"How long are you staying at Ted's?" Her voice was less shaky now, and after she cleared her throat, it was stronger again.

"A while." She frowned in confusion, but he wasn't sure elaborating at the moment would be helpful. Two hours ago, she hadn't even known his last name. Sharing that he was moving to her small town would probably be the straw that broke her. No way to make that sound non-creepy. "Long enough to be around to talk."

She nodded. Silence stretched between and around them. In the distance, a single church bell rang. Bottom of the hour. An hour and a half until she needed to pick up her kids. Time enough to rip off the band-aid and deal with the consequences.

"Evie, are you pregnant?" He braced himself for more waterworks, but none came, just a solemn nod and a wary side-eye glance as she turned to dump the towel she was holding in a laundry basket. Fuckity fuck. "And, am I…"

That didn't land well. Cold as ice, she crossed her arms over her chest. "You're the only person I've slept with in the last two years."

He ducked his head, feeling like an ass. He'd known that. But they'd used condoms, for everything. He had a half-empty box in his suitcase that proved they'd been responsible. Flashbacks to grade eight health class thudded through his brain.

"I really did try to find you last week. This isn't how I'd have elected to tell you." She cleared her throat again. "You have a right to know, of course. But I won't expect anything of you."

White hot anger lanced from his core straight up his spine, and he grabbed her gaze with his own. Like hell he wasn't going to be involved. "I have more rights than just to know."

She bristled, but didn't respond right away. Her lips bowed together, like she might be biting the inside of her lip on one side, and he wanted to reach out and touch her face. Rub his thumb against her bottom lip, and see if she made that happy little purring sound when she was sober. Right after he punched the wall. Yeah, his emotions were all over the place. He'd just been dealt a knock-out blow by fate, he should get a pass.

Not a pass to actually punch the wall, although for the first time in his life, he understood how that could happen.

"When would you…" He trailed off, glancing at her flat stomach, bracketed by her trim hips. No sign of anything yet, but it was probably too early. Whatever he'd been planning for the afternoon had just been replaced with prenatal research.

"I'm due in February."

"And do you have doctor's appointments lined up?"

She raised one eyebrow. "My prenatal care will be with a midwife, but yes, I'll have regular appointments. Would you want to attend one?"

"I'll be at all of them."

"Hang on, some of those appointments have physical exams!"

Now it was his turn to cock a brow in her direction. She blushed, but it wasn't cute and flirty. Damn. He didn't want to make her uncomfortable, but he was so far out on the ledge he didn't know what the next right move was. Backing down wasn't an option. "Nothing I haven't seen up close and personal, but I can wait outside. Your body, your care. But—" the next words stuck in his throat, not because he didn't want to say them, but rather the opposite. The realization that he wanted to say them very much struck him hard and swift. "Anything to do with my child? I'm involved."

Her eyes widened, and one hand slid down her chest to rest protectively over her lower belly. Damn it again.

"Evie, I didn't mean—"

"That's probably enough talking for one day, don't you think?"

Hardly. But he could back off for a day or two. "When can we meet again?"

"My sister's arriving in town tomorrow night, and I'm going to be pretty busy with her engagement party this weekend—"

He held up his hand and she bit her lip. "Hang on. Claire from across the road…that's your mother." Well, hell. Now that he thought about it, there was an obvious resemblance.

Evie didn't bother responding, just wrinkled her brow and shrugged, like she'd exhausted all of her conversational ability for the afternoon.

The next thing he had to say wouldn't please her in the least, but he couldn't very well avoid it. "She invited me to the party."

"You can't—" She spluttered out the first part of a command, and then gave up again.

Refusing to accompany his uncle to the party would bring up all sorts of questions, given that he'd already told Claire he looked forward to it. Maybe he could arrange to get thrown from a horse. "No one knows?"

"You, me, my midwife's office."

That admission pleased him in an unexpected way, and loosened some of the knots his guts had twisted into when he found out. It also reminded him that she'd been all alone with this information, and he'd just pushed her from simmering fear to full-blown panic. "We can keep it that way for as long as you want."

"I'll tell my sister after the party, but other than that, I'd like to keep it quiet until the second trimester."

Something to look up later. He nodded. "Okay. If I see you at the party…"

"I'm sure I'll be able to hide from you." She said it without humor, but something about the idea of hunting for Evie made him smile. "But if we're introduced, then it will be…nice to meet you, I suppose." Good thing he hadn't asked Ted about a blond Evie yet. "And then we can talk again next week."

"When is your first appointment?"

"Middle of July."

"Okay. Do you need anything…" She bristled, but he forged ahead anyway. "Are there any costs associated with pregnancy that I should be helping with?"

"Are you currently employed? You said you're staying at Ted's right now."

"No, but—"

"Then don't worry about it."

"Evie, I'm in a position—"

She held her hand, and he let her have his silence. For now. "We have almost nine months to sort that out. Babies aren't expensive, it's going to be okay."

He was pretty sure that babies cost a mint, but there would be time to deal with that later. "Okay. Good luck hiding from me this weekend."

CHAPTER FOUR

She was hiding from him.

Liam had been at the Calhoun farm for almost two hours, and the future mother of his child was like Polkaroo. Ha. At least he was already thinking in terms of children's TV shows.

Except he wanted to find her. He'd had second thoughts about them pretending not to know each other. At some point, the timeline would need to be explained—at the very least, to her sister, the doctor. And probably her collection of friends, most of whom had children and were very familiar with the standard gestational period of the human female.

A group he could now count himself as part of. Not the friend part, not yet, but he'd spent the weekend boning up on all things pregnancy. He was still freaked out, but the horse had left the stable, so what could he do?

And like many other men who'd found themselves in this position, Liam was ready to do the honourable thing. He just needed to find his future bride. Too bad his uncle didn't realize he was on a mission.

Ted had kept him busy, first introducing him to the happy couple, and Liam had done his best to be charming and relaxed and not blurt out that he'd knocked up Laney's sister. After that task was successfully accomplished, the next introductions were to a few people Ted thought might want to sell land privately. Then it was Ty West, a local businessman, because Ted believed in diversification and Liam had an MBA he wasn't currently using.

It was mid-afternoon before he extricated himself and ducked into the farmhouse. Claire Calhoun was in the kitchen, directing a crew of women shuttling the dessert contributions out the door to the buffet tables.

"Excuse me, Mrs. Calhoun? Would you mind if I find a quiet place to make a phone call?" He waved his iPhone in the air.

She waved him in and pointed down the hall to the living room, before grabbing a pie and heading out the door herself. She hollered over her shoulder that he should call her Claire. He probably would have, if he wasn't half-afraid that when she found out what he'd done to her daughter, she just might kill him.

Evie wasn't in the living room, but some of her pictures were. He stepped closer to the wall, glancing from one frame to the next, soaking up her history. Ballet class, swim meets, high school graduation. In the hospital with one of her boys, looking barely old enough to have a baby.

"What are you doing in here?" Evie had slipped into the room quietly, and when he turned around, she was perched on the arm of an overstuffed loveseat.

Might as well go with honesty. "Looking for you."

She glanced down the hall, relaxing visibly as she realized they were alone in the house. "I asked you not to do that."

"Not in so many words." He pushed himself to the full extent of his height, all of a sudden feeling unsure of himself. This was only their third time meeting. He didn't know much of anything about this woman, and yet she carried his child. And there was only one thing to do about that. "Can I see you later? Alone?"

"I thought we'd agreed to talk again next week." She crossed her arms in front of her body, her pale green sundress pulling up a bit on her legs, and he couldn't help but wonder what she was wearing underneath. She was a captivating blend of elegance and practicality, he thought as his gaze drifted down to her feet. Her toes were painted a creamy opaque nude, and the shiny pedicure was like a beacon. He'd never felt strongly about feet before, but he had an overwhelming urge to wrap his hands around her arches and squeeze and stroke until she moaned. His dick twitched at the memory of her throaty vocalizations.

"Is there a reason to wait?" He itched to cross the room and touch her. "I've done a lot of thinking, and reading and—"

The kitchen door slapped open. "Evie!" Claire's voice rang out, and before he could press her for a meeting time, she offered a weak smile and slipped past him. His fingers splayed wide, his arms tense, as he held himself back from grabbing her. The faint whiff of her scent as she dodged out of the room was a punch to the gut. Vanilla perfume. She'd worn it that night in Toronto as well. He'd licked her all over, listing all the baked goods he could think of that included vanilla. He would never look at cookies the same way again.

It was time to push a little. He opened the Yellow Pages app on his phone. Sure enough, Evie was listed. There probably weren't many unlisted numbers in Wardham. He added her details to his address book, and headed back outside, but didn't make it before his phone beeped.

A text message from his mother. Well, that was something new. **Your father would like to hear from you.** And so was that, except it was most certainly fiction, invented by a woman desperate to hold her family together without any of the basic human emotions that generally achieved that goal.

Liam pressed delete. He didn't have time for that. Not now, not ever.

After setting the strawberry pie she'd been handed on the buffet table, Evie went in search of her kids and found them with their father. Only in Wardham would her ex-husband be invited to her sister's engagement party. And her mother had the annoying habit of liking everyone, no matter how much of a douche they might have been to her daughters. Okay, that only applied to one man. Maybe two, if she counted Kyle, but he'd reformed himself, due to being head-over-heels in love with Laney. So Claire's affection there had been warranted.

Dale wasn't horrid. He was diligent about his time with the boys, fair with child-support, and a committed community member, leveraging his position as the Sales Manager at McCullough Ford to give back whenever he could.

But he'd been an absolute shit husband, beyond the providing part. If it weren't for their two amazing boys, Evie would regret the marriage entirely. She'd been looking for something different, someone mature and dependable and a homebody. She got all that, but it came with anger and judgment over her past deeds, none of which she'd felt remotely bad about until Dale began a protracted campaign to make her feel like depraved filth.

The irony that in the two years since they'd last slept together, Dale had gone through a host of affairs, and Evie hadn't slept with anyone until Liam. Well, that would have been sweeter if her single indiscretion wasn't going to be well-documented by a burgeoning midsection in the coming months.

Evie shuddered at the thought of Dale's reaction. *None of his fucking business*, her inner mama bear growled. For a fleeting second, Evie imagined Liam taking on her ex-husband and defending her honour. Not that it needed defending. They hadn't done anything wrong. But the chivalrous fantasy was still compelling.

The two men couldn't be more opposite. Dale, big, blond and brash. Liam, lean, dark and restrained. Also more than a decade younger, a decade which hadn't been kind to Dale. He was still good-looking, in a fading way. He didn't play football much anymore, and he had a small gut that spoke to his love of beer and second helpings. It hadn't bothered Evie at all. She'd wanted to love the man inside, but that man didn't love her, so it was a moot point.

After her night with Liam, she'd been looking forward to exploring her sexuality, in an easy-breezy way. Liam had been such a breath of fresh air. It might have been the alcohol, but she'd never had such a fun night of sex in her entire life. Even with Evan, who she'd been more compatible with than Dale. Evan, who realized after they broke up that he was gay. Except the sex had been really good between them, so that was a shame for the female population of Wardham.

But Liam had taken it to a new level. He'd talked, a lot. Alternatingly hot and funny, he'd wound her up with murmurs of what he wanted to do, what he'd just done, what he was currently doing. He'd touched and teased and licked, until she was out of her mind with a feverish need for him, and then he'd taken his time donning a condom, teasing her some more as he stroked—

Well, there wouldn't be any more of that.

The thought of shuttling a child back and forth to Toronto made her queasy, but hopefully Liam would be busy with whatever recent college grads needed to do in their lives, and wouldn't expect long visits until the baby wasn't a baby anymore.

If he wanted visits at all. He'd said he would be involved, but that had been under duress. He'd had days to think now.

As if on command, the subject of her thoughts stepped out of the house. He paused on her mother's porch, surveying the party that spilled across the green lawn between the gravel drive and the neat wooden fence, freshly painted. Evie wanted to think he looked out of place, an urban boy visiting farm country. But for all of his metrosexual good looks and expensive clothes, Liam fit in. More than that, he looked comfortable. He'd worn leather boots that were only enhanced by gravel dust, and his light blue buttoned down shirt, probably meant to be worn under a suit, paired perfectly with slim cut dark wash jeans. A brown leather belt, capped with a significant buckle, pulled the outfit together. She hadn't noticed how grown up he looked inside. She'd been too distracted by his searching brown eyes, pressing her for more than she'd given him so far, and his deliberately scruffy hair, which she'd wanted to smooth flat with her hand.

She owed him a conversation—more than one, probably—and the man in front of her looked like he could handle whatever she threw at him.

And now he was looking at her. Not moving, or saying anything, just watching. Waiting for her to make her move. Probably expecting her to be skittish and run away again. But he was right—they needed to talk and tonight was the perfect time. The kids were spending the night with Dale.

She looped the long way around the yard, speaking to a few people she hadn't yet greeted, until he was in front of her. Eyebrow cocked, pleased as punch she was coming to him.

He might not be so happy after tonight.

"Liam," she smoothed a pleasant smile across her face, knowing they weren't alone. "Are you having a good time?"

"Thank you, yes." His lips twitched. Standing in the long afternoon shadow of the farmhouse there was no glare to avoid, but she glanced down at her feet all the same. His penetrating gaze was just as bad as the sun—the warmth deceptively inviting.

"Listen, I wanted to introduce you to someone." She placed her hand on his elbow to steer him to a more private conversation spot, but instantly regretted the touch. His shirt was thin, and just above where her fingers rested, his biceps bunched and shifted as they stepped away. The urge to curve her palm northward and caress his muscles was...stupid. It was entirely ridiculous for her to be thinking about sex right now. Or seeing Liam naked, touching him while dressed, or wishing he would kiss her. Trouble was, she had a searingly bright memory of all of that from six weeks earlier, and logic and reason wouldn't dislodge it from her brain.

As they walked, she lowered her voice. "The kids will be with their dad tonight. You could come over if you'd like to talk sooner than next week."

He paused before responding. "What made you change your mind? Never mind, don't answer that. I'll take it."

"I live on Elm, it's the smallest—"

"I know where you live, Evie."

She wanted to think that was creepy, but his warm, low words filled her with an annoying amount of pleasure. *Focus, Calhoun.* This was not the time to want more of the boy wonder.

"I'll be there at eight. Now, shall we find someone for you to introduce me to?"

CHAPTER FIVE

Liam left the party shortly after they spoke. Evie didn't have the same luxury, but as her mother organized a third round of food to be set out around dinner time, she finally begged off. Laney ran interference, and walked her to her car.

"You okay?"

"Just tired."

They stopped at the end of the tree-lined lane and took in the summer evening. A dozen cars remained, but the air was still and quiet around them. Laney took a deep breath, and launched into a staccato, stream-of-consciousness reach-out. "Because if you need anything, anything at all, you know I'm here for you. If you need money, or help at the studio, I mean, I can't do that after this week, but Kyle looks good in a pair of shorts, and while I want him to come home with me, and we close on the new house soon, we could still manage if you want—"

"I'm pregnant."

Laney snapped her lips shut and held them there, questions obviously bouncing around on her tongue, but she was putting her best non-judgmental face forward and waiting.

"It's a long story, and I wanted to wait until after your party—"

"It's technically over, so spill." Laney squeezed her sister's hand. "Are you okay?"

Evie nodded. "It's early still. Happened six weeks ago.

Might not take, you never know."

"But you want to keep it?" Laney knew Evie had always wanted a large family.

She nodded. "Is that stupid? I'm just getting back on my feet…"

"Not stupid. Difficult, maybe, but you'll make it work. When are you due?"

Evie filled her in on all the details. All but one.

"And the father?"

She took a deep breath. "Funny story…" She glanced over at Ted's farm. "That guy? The one in the bar in Toronto. Turns out, his uncle lives across the road."

Laney lost her typical cool and shrieked.

Evie grabbed her sister and dragged her the last few steps to her station wagon.

"Nobody can hear us, settle down." Laney laughed. " So does he know?"

"Of course he knows!" She took a deep breath. "No way could I hide it from him. I acted like a total idiot when he showed up at my studio, actually, and that tipped him off. I guess it wasn't a big leap to the source of my panic."

"Wow. He was a cool cucumber today, then." Laney hesitated. "Is he going to be involved?"

Evie shrugged. "He says he wants to be."

"I gotta ask—did you use protection?"

"Of course we did. We actually stopped and bought the condoms on the way to his condo." She winced. "I guess this is what they mean when they say they're only ninety-nine percent effective."

"You'll want to get tested, both of you, for infections. Just in case. Your midwife will probably give you the same counsel. And Evie—your chance of getting pre-eclampsia again is higher with a new partner." Laney reached out and pulled her into a sisterly hug, complete with a reassuring back rub. "Nothing you can do about that, of course."

On that last point, Evie disagreed with her medically trained sister, but it wasn't worth the debate.

"You'll tell me if Pipsqueak hurts you, right? I'll send Kyle home or we can sic Ian on him. He's cute, but he's no Nixon."

Evie secretly preferred Liam's more refined features to the handsome farm boy look of Laney's fiancé and his brother, and she knew from first-hand experience that under his tailored clothes was a body tightly corded with muscle. He could probably hold his own. But if he was a jerk, she'd happily let the Nixon brothers deal with him.

"I've been calling him the Boy Wonder, not Pipsqueak," she muttered, and Laney joined her in a rueful chuckle. "You know, I don't even know exactly how old he is." Evie groaned. "This is all kinds of embarrassing."

"Don't worry about that. Seriously."

"I can just imagine what Dale's going to say." Something darker than embarrassment unfurled in her chest, a hot, pulsing shame she thought she'd banished permanently with the divorce.

Laney narrowed her gaze. "He doesn't get to say anything."

"It might not stop him." Evie's voice cracked, and she rubbed her neck. "So...I'm hoping I can keep this a secret for a while still. Until we know that everything is progressing well, and..." She touched her stomach. "Well, until it's obvious, I guess."

"You going to tell Mom?"

"Yes. Not this week, though. Soon."

"She'll be supportive." Laney grinned. "This might get her off my back about babies for a while."

Evie smacked her sister's arm lightly before opening her car door. "Whatever I can do to help you out, sis."

With a laughing wave, Laney hopped off the road and Evie headed home.

Smallest house on the block wasn't an understatement.

Evie's tiny cottage sat back from the street, dwarfed not just by the two-story homes on either side, but also the looming maple trees rising majestically from her backyard. The street was a mishmash of brick and siding houses, some renovated, others not. None quite as neat and tidy as the cottage, freshly painted white with a bright blue door.

Liam pulled into the long drive, ignoring the nervous flutter in his chest. Maybe he should have brought flowers. Or chocolate. Definitely should have brought a ring.

But given that Evie was still a stranger, he couldn't pick jewelry for her. They'd go together. Not as romantic as getting down on one knee, but given the circumstances…

"Hey, you coming in?" Evie called out as she strolled toward his SUV on a path from the backyard. She was still wearing the green dress, but she'd ditched the pretty sandals and her bare feet grabbed his attention for a moment. High arches, delicate bone structure. Feet. What was wrong with him? Then they disappeared as she stepped alongside the vehicle. "Having second thoughts?"

Was that even an option? "No." He steeled himself against all the reasons to feel nervous and unsure and pushed the door open. "You have a nice house."

She offered a polite smile that told him she didn't believe the compliment. "I have a house. That's more than I could say six months ago and I'm proud of that fact."

"Evie…" But she was gone with a twist of her slight body, bounding ahead of him like a gazelle. Shouldn't she be full of fatigue right now? The books had promised fatigue. That would be something he could work with. She'd say yes because of a weakened state and a fear of being alone. But the gazelle didn't look weak, or afraid. She was fearless and swift, and far too proud to accept a proposal sprung from a thoroughly unromantic sense of responsibility.

This was a terrible idea, and he was doing it anyway. Because he'd hate himself if he didn't.

Inside, the small living room was empty. A collection of running shoes and flip flops overflowed a black rubber mat next to the entrance. They were all much smaller than his size twelves, and he was reminded again of the different worlds from which he and Evie were coming at this situation.

Her kids were all over the comfortable space—an Xbox sat next to the TV, games piled next to it. A sports bag lay open beside the couch, baseball bats and a glove sticking out. A black hoodie was tossed over the arm of the oversized armchair in the corner.

Liam took a deep breath, exhaling slowly. For all that his life was going to change, he was ready for it. This wasn't the ideal circumstance, maybe, but building a family was the next step for a lot of his friends and colleagues, so why not him? But Evie and the boys...this wasn't their next step. Their lives in this warm little cottage were about to be tossed upside down. He squared his shoulders and followed the sound of clinking dishes and splashing water to the kitchen.

"Evie." She was doing the dishes in a way he'd always imagined mothers would when they were pissed off. He'd never seen his own mother do any dishes, not even at the cottage; that's what housekeeping staff and, if necessary, dishwashers were for. "Hey. Are you mad at me?"

She paused, then finished rinsing the plate in her hand before turning to face him. Her hands were dripping wet, and he looked around for a tea towel. One was draped over the handle on the oven, so he snagged it and stepped close enough to take her wet hands in his, patting them dry with the towel.

Her hands, like the rest of her, were small, but stayed just shy of being delicate. Long, tapered fingers with blunt fingernails, free from polish. Soft, translucent skin, firm and tight. Strong, capable hands.

"I can do it myself," she whispered, pulling away. The loss of her touch was a cold whisper of sadness, and he almost reached for her again.

"Maybe I wanted to do it for you." His voice caught on a gruff note mid-sentence, and he cleared his throat before continuing. It wasn't just his sense of responsibility speaking. "I'm going to want to do a lot for you, Evie. It's just who I am."

She laughed, and again he noticed that she used false humour to hide. "We'll see how that goes."

There was a lot of history weighing down her doubtful words. They needed to back up, get to know each other. But there wasn't really time for that.

"Can we sit down?" She nodded and brushed past him, her hip glancing against his thigh. Goddamn, he wanted her to stop running away from him. Frustration stirred in his gut. He followed her to the couch, where she was sitting stiffly, knees front. He opted for a more inviting pose, casually canting his upper body sidewise against the couch cushions as he folded one leg up onto the couch seat between them. "Let's start at the beginning."

She took a deep breath. "This is going to come out the wrong way, I'm sure, but...how old are you?"

He grinned. "How old you think I am?"

"Liam—" Her brows knitted together, her voice plaintive. It was hard to leave her on the hook, waiting for an answer. Hard, but not impossible.

"Are you worried that you've robbed the cradle in a big way? Made me into a man before my time?"

"Something like that? Jeez, you just graduated." She pressed her lips together. "You're being really good about all of this, but if you aren't ready—"

"I'm almost twenty-nine."

"Oh, thank god." Relief visibly washed over her, but then she squinted at him suspiciously. Damn, she was good. "How close to twenty-nine?"

"Ten more months." He offered a sheepish smile that he hoped drifted toward cute. "Okay, I'm twenty-eight. I went back to school, but I'm no kid."

"We're still not in the same...generation." She chose the word carefully and he looked at her anew. She was gorgeous. Hands down, the most beautiful woman he'd ever been with. Was she worried about their age difference?

"That doesn't matter."

"No, I suppose it doesn't." She offered a small, sad smile that told him they meant the same words in two different ways.

He tried again. "I mean, your age, my age…they weren't an issue when we…" Trailing off seemed like a better option than naming what they'd done. Not for him, but for Evie, who'd stiffened next to him.

"I don't have one-night stands, you should know that."

"Okay. Okay if you did, too, as long as you were safe."

She gave him a curious look, one that he couldn't figure out. Not judgment, but maybe disbelief. Their night together had been fantastically uninhibited—he had trouble reconciling that Evie with the one giving him the wary side-eye right now. A part of him wanted to crow that he wasn't just another notch in her belt, but a bigger part clamped down hard on the celebration. It was likely that he *was* a notch. The first one. He pushed that thought away, and turned the conversation back to the most important topic at hand.

"Tell me whatever you think I need to know about…" He swallowed hard. "Our baby."

Over the next thirty minutes, Liam probed and prodded until she relaxed, and they managed to get some important pieces of information out in the open. Evie wanted him to get some testing done—not a problem—and reiterated that she wanted to keep the pregnancy a secret until the end of the summer. Liam was secretly pleased when Evie appeared startled that he'd read up on pregnancy as much as he had.

"You really aren't freaked out about this, are you?" She'd turned now, mirroring his posture, and the last rays of the summer sun were slanting in the window behind her. She literally glowed, and in that moment, he knew he had to take a chance.

He reached between them and laced his fingers into hers. "I'm only worried about how much this is going to impact your life. Maybe that's naïve of me, I don't know, but over this week, I've never once been freaked out about *you* having my baby. Having a baby, yes, that…threw me for a loop. But I'm willing to do whatever is needed to make this work, because…"

Her face, mostly in shadows now, tipped up and her eyes searched his face. "Because?"

It's the right thing to do seemed like the wrong thing to say. It felt wrong, too. It wasn't what he'd rehearsed, but the truth surged up from his core and he let it out as he leaned closer and brushed her cheek with his free hand. "Because I think we could be really good together. Better than good. Awesome, in fact."

She caught her next breath and held it for a moment before carefully asking, "What are you doing?"

"Asking you to marry me, Evie. I know it's slightly out of order, but I'll make it work."

"Oh, Liam." She slid toward him on the couch, letting his hand drift back into her hair. The silky slide of the blond strands over and around his fingers stirred a physical response that he couldn't wait to act on. At least they wouldn't have to worry about chemistry. That was as good a foundation as any to build a relationship on.

She stopped a few inches away and slid her hands over his shoulders and up his neck to cup his face. Her eyes moved up and down, searching his face before she parted her lips with a sigh.

"Are you insane?"

Uh…his brain actually stuttered for a moment, then blanked completely, like a systems reset. He blinked twice, and when he refocused on her face, the romantic diffuse lighting had faded to a somber dimness. Shit.

"You don't know me. I don't know you. We've had one good chat, one night of good sex, and a bunch of awkwardness in between. That you think we should get married just underlines that you are living in a fantasy world of lunacy." Evie pursed her lips together and took a deep breath. He thought for a moment that she might snap his neck, just to be done with him, but then her grip on his face eased and she dropped her hands back to his shoulders. Her gaze remained firmly on his face, though, a reminder she was in charge of the conversation. "Listen to me carefully, Liam. There is nothing romantic about what's going on. I got knocked up. I'm going to get fat. I'm going to have a baby, *your baby*, and that's going to be difficult and awkward, and eventually expensive and awkward, and one day you'll marry someone else and have other babies of your own, and I'm going to hate you at that point, because you'll start skipping weekends with our kid, and I'll be left explaining why. Between now and then, we'll have some good moments, too, because we're going to share a unique bond, you and I. But don't think for a minute that I'm going to let myself imagine that bond to be anything other than biological."

He was with her until she took a leap into the future and turned him into an asshole. Okay, so proposing had been the wrong idea. He'd known that, and done it anyway. And he noted for the future that romance wasn't the way to win Evie over—check. But he wasn't that guy she already hated a little bit, never mind whatever would come later. "No."

"I'm sorry?"

He reached between them and placed his hand vertically over her lower belly. Hard to imagine a baby growing in such a small space. The heel of his palm rested just above her pelvis, and the flare of anger in her eyes told him he was on thin ice touching her there, or anywhere. His fingertips rested on her sternum, and he pressed gently, a reminder that he wasn't trying to cop a feel. "Our bond isn't *just* biological. You don't know what it is, yet. Neither do I. I know that every time I've seen you since I arrived in town, I've wanted to throttle you one minute, then press you up against the wall and kiss you senseless the next. It's an uncommon feeling for me, and I think I like it. And Evie?" She raised her eyebrow in skeptical, silent response, but her shaky intake of breath gave her away. He leaned closer, sandwiching his hand between their bodies. "I think you like it, too."

He dropped his mouth over hers, mostly because he'd wanted to kiss her for days, but also to ensure she didn't snap back a witty response right away. He didn't normally care about being overtly in control of situations, but with Evie, his inner caveman came roaring to life.

He meant it to be a simple kiss, a promise of future opportunity, and that's how it started. He brushed his lips over hers, then back again, before settling right in the middle, enjoying the plump fullness of her bottom lip between his, then below. The soft cleft that hid secret, warm pleasure. He swelled at the memory of her eager kisses that first night, but tonight wouldn't be a repeat, so he moved to ease away, only Evie's hands tightened around his neck, holding him next to her face.

"Hang on a second," she whispered. "Let me just…"

She licked her lips, their faces so close together he could feel the moist pink tip of her tongue swiping between them, and then it was her turn to close the gap. But her first effort wasn't sweet or promising. It was hungry, and hurried. She laved her tongue across the seam of his mouth, and he opened for her with a groan. This was a terrible idea, but she tasted like heaven and he wanted more. He slid his hands around her waist, pulling her into his lap. Under his fingertips, her dress bunched up, and he knew if he skated his hand south, he'd encounter bare skin. The question of how much bare skin was burning through his mind, and between them, his cock went from alert to ready. Even as Evie ground against him, he knew they needed to stop—that she'd want them to stop, and soon.

But her mouth…

And that was as far as his mind got in the back and forth reasoning, because holy hell, her mouth was joy and angst and the very meaning of passion. So he let her take her fill, and in the process, he got Evie riding his lap, which he certainly hadn't dared hope for. He just waited for the inevitable shove.

When it came, it wasn't as forceful as he expected. *Promising.* She pulled back with a shaky breath, pressing her fingers to her mouth for a moment before speaking. "I didn't know that you wanted to kiss me."

"Did that remind you why I might have been thinking about it?"

She blushed. "This isn't going to be a regular thing, me attacking you."

"That's a shame." He eased her off his lap, ignoring his protesting dick, and lifted her hand to kiss her knuckles. "If you change your mind…"

"I really shouldn't. It'll just complicate things between us." But the glint in her eye told him she was considering it. How long would he have to wait before the hormones kicked in? He feared it was longer than his body would find acceptable.

"Already complicated, sunshine. Might as well make the best of it."

"No." Evie couldn't quite believe what she was about to do. Kissing Liam was like heaven coated in chocolate and peanut butter, and she was about to put a ban on it. "We can't do that again. Not just *not regularly*. Not at all."

"Why not?"

He was still stretched back against the couch, looking hard and sexy, and the woman in her asked the same question. But the mother in her pointed out that they would forever need to be civil, at the least, and hopefully friendly, and a doomed-from-the-start physical relationship would ruin the rest of it. The more important part of it.

When he blandly shrugged at her pronouncement, she jumped up and paced to the kitchen.

He followed. Of course he did.

"Evie, what's wrong?"

She'd opened the tea cupboard, because tea made everything better. After she grabbed the teapot and a box of chamomile, she turned slowly and laid it out, not looking at him because that made thinking difficult. "You. Sitting out there, standing in here, all calm and rational and at peace with the situation—"

"You just said three things that mean the same thing."

"That's..." She jerked her head up. "Is that a West Wing quote?"

He chuckled. "Look at how much we have in common."

"What were you, like, five when it was on the air?"

He squared off his shoulders, successfully projecting look of strength and...damn him, maturity, as if to underline the fact that while he might be a few years younger than her, he didn't have a juvenile bone in his body.

And as he stood in her kitchen, silently chiding her for the unnecessary attack when he was being nothing but mature about this, this... She lay a protective hand over her tummy and his face softened. Damn him for being so nice. "Okay, that was uncalled for, I'm sorry."

"I was a politics nerd in high school and university."

"Oh."

"I'm surprised you recognized the line, it's pretty obscure."

"It's a memorable scene." She muttered the lie under her breath, then sighed and met his unwavering gaze. "That I've seen half a dozen times."

He tilted his head and furrowed his brow.

"You don't have to look so surprised."

"I'm not surprised you liked it. I'm trying to figure out when you had time to watch a seven-year TV series over and over again."

"I was on bedrest a lot during my first pregnancy and spent the first three months with both boys nursing either in bed or on the couch." *Sexy share, Evie.* Although maybe it would help convince Liam to stay hands-off.

From the look on his face, he was definitely concerned at the very least.

"What do you mean, bedrest?"

Oh. Again, with the nice and understanding. "ARGH!"

"Was it something I said?"

"It was everything you said, and everything you didn't. Why aren't you freaking out?"

"I'm sure I'm freaking out. On the inside. Deep down, buried under years of WASPy training by my mother. But my whiplash reaction to becoming a father is secondary to actually becoming a father, right? That's going to happen. So I'd rather not get to that point and be unprepared. Or, god forbid, get to that point before that thing—" he pointed at her stomach "—is ready to come out. So...bedrest?"

"Uhm...I had high blood pressure with my first pregnancy. It's part of what lead me to a healthier lifestyle, and I didn't have any problems with my second pregnancy."

He was nodding, but his attention had shifted to his iPhone. He was alternating between tapping and scrolling with his thumb, and after a minute he glanced up. "Pre-eclampsia?"

"Yes, in the end, but just a mild case."

"Hmmmm."

"What?"

"Are you going to have an OB consult?"

"If my midwife thinks it necessary, yes."

He nodded. "Right."

Right? "Since when do you know so much about...everything?"

"Since you told me you were pregnant." He tucked his phone away. "Evie, I'm an information junkie. There's nothing about your pregnancy that I'm not going to want to research."

"Wait until I start bitching to you about being horny in a few months." The words were out of her mouth before she realized who she was speaking to.

He tucked his thumbs into his pockets and rocked back on his heels, a grin dancing across his face. "The second trimester, right?"

"How do you know that?" She cringed as she heard her voice pitch up at the end. This conversation was not going at all how she'd expected. She was coming off like a nutbar and he was Mr. Know-it-all. She could not take another eight months of this. And then eighteen years after that…

"Have you already researched daycare options as well?"

"No, of course not. I'll do that closer to whenever we need daycare. Do you anticipate that'll be soon after birth?"

She needed him to settle down. Like, completely. She held up one hand and bowed her head.

"Too much?"

"Way too much."

He stepped back and angled his head toward the door. She nodded and followed him out of the kitchen.

At the front door, he started to speak, but cut himself off. She reached out and touched her hand lightly to his chest. Something flashed in his eyes, but she couldn't figure it out before it disappeared again and Mr. Easy returned. She knew it was a mixed signal, but she couldn't help herself.

"Thank you for being patient with me."

He shook his head. "That's not something to thank me for."

"Yeah, well. I appreciate it nonetheless."

Again, he shook his head, but cut himself off from responding further. Instead he reached out and squeezed her hip. The oddly intimate act made her chest squeeze tight, and she pressed her hand more firmly against him. Two points of contact. She'd set the rules, this was all they could have.

It wasn't enough, and they both knew it.

CHAPTER SIX

"Mom. Mom. Mom. Mom." Max took a deep breath. "Mom!"

"Mmmm?"

"She's got stuff on her mind, buddy."

That got her attention. "Connor, I don't have anything on my mind." Lying to her children. Great plan.

"Then are you just ignoring Max?" Ooooh, the cheek. He wasn't wrong, but still. She gave Connor a hairy eyeball, and he turned his attention back to his dinner.

"I'm sorry, Maxster. What did you want to tell me?"

"Ask."

"Ask?"

"I want to *ask* you something, not tell you something."

God, grant me the serenity... "Okay, what did you want to *ask* me?"

"Can we go somewhere fun tomorrow?"

She should have seen that one coming. The boys had enjoyed being home for a day and a half of their summer break, and now they were on hour thirty of a seven-year-old's version of a hunger strike—a whine strike.

"Maybe Kyle could take us to the beach?" Connor muttered his suggestion into his brown rice pilaf, carefully avoiding her gaze, lest it still be hairy.

"I can take you to the beach."

Max took up the cause. "But if you take us, then we'll still have to go to the studio and watch old ladies stretch afterward. Uncle Kyle could take us while you work."

That was probably a good idea, but Laney and Kyle were heading home in a couple of days, and he was babysitting tonight. "I'll ask him. No guarantees. Now eat up."

"Do you think Uncle Kyle wants to play FIFA Soccer?"

Evie bit back a retort that maybe they should play soccer in the backyard, instead. Normally she'd let it fly, but tonight she needed to stay zen, and an argument with her kids about video games wouldn't service that goal.

Tonight, she needed to pretend she wasn't pregnant at a girly drink-fest. And it wasn't optional. Carrie had sent out the batgirl signal in support of their friend Karen Miller, who was currently in the midst of quite the emotional upheaval. Her fledgling relationship was...well, fledgling, with all the ups and downs that would be expected. And her family had just had an unexpected bump in the road as well. Karen needed her tonight. Just her, and not her issues.

Luckily, Laney was happy to come along. Times like this made her extra-sad that her sister was usually on the other side of an international border. Chicago was half a day's drive away, and Laney's job precluded lengthy visits. This week had been lovely, despite being tinged with intrigue and subterfuge, mommy-style.

She stabbed a piece of broccoli off her plate and waved it at Connor. "Remember when you used to call these munchy trees?"

He grinned and rolled his eyes. "Mom, that was forever ago."

"Yeah, only babies say stuff like that." Max piped up, unable to stay out of any conversation, ever. "And we're done with babies in this family." Connor nodded in agreement.

The glib pronouncement stole the air from her lungs. *Oh, boys.* They had no idea what was going to hit them. And they were so close. This baby would be the intruder into their brotherly club.

"You guys know that I love you, right?" She blinked

back tears.

"Are we in trouble?" Connor frowned at her. "Because I don't think that's fair."

She laughed. "No, not in trouble. I just want you to know that even when I'm grumpy or I've got stuff on my mind, you are both the best things in my world."

"Even when we're yelling?" Max's eyes lit up.

"Don't push it, Mr. M, but yes, even when you're yelling."

"Mommy?"

"Yes, bubs?"

"We like you, too."

High praise indeed.

Laney and Kyle arrived while she was washing up after dinner. Laney swept down on the boys, and Kyle came to find her in the kitchen. He wrapped one arm around her shoulders and pulled her in tight for a brotherly hug.

"How you doing, Evie?"

"She told you, huh?"

He kissed the side of her head. "If you need me here…"

"I'll be fine." She returned the hug. "Really, I think I'm over my panic, for now."

"Do you want us to postpone our wedding until you aren't fat?"

She took advantage of their close proximity to lightly punch him in the gut. "Hey!"

"Too soon?"

She laughed. "Always. The boys wanted me to ask you if you'd take them to the beach tomorrow. I know you've got a lot to do—"

"Of course."

"It's okay if—"

"Evie. We're family. It's okay. Are they driving you nuts?"

"Crazy." She sighed. "I should have put them in camp or something, but I wanted to save money."

Kyle frowned. "Shouldn't that be something that Dale helps with?"

"He'd pay half, but it's still a lot of money."

"We could—"

"No. No, no, no, no." She shook her head. "I can stand on my own two feet. I'm not asking my baby sister to help me with this."

"What about an old friend?"

"Didn't you just quit your job?"

"Yeah, but I've got a sugar momma."

Laney poked her head into the kitchen. "Did I hear my name?"

Kyle and Evie shared a private chuckle before Evie brushed past her sister, pausing to squeeze her hand. "In a manner of speaking. Come on, let's go."

They said goodnight to the boys and headed out. It was a short walk to the apartment of Mari Beadie, who was hosting the girls' night.

As they walked down the street, Evie reflected with bittersweet appreciation on how rare this sister time was for them. "Thanks for coming with me tonight. You could have stayed with Kyle and the boys, but I appreciate the company."

Laney shrugged. "It's good practice, being social. I made a promise to myself that I'd do more of that in Chicago, and then I went and fell in love with Kyle, and I've spent the last six months on the road, or on the phone, or working."

"It'll be nice to have him there all the time."

Her sister grinned. "Tell me about it!"

"Hey, no teasing the pregnant lady who's only had sex once in the last two years, and is likely to not have it again for a very long time."

"Maybe, you know, since the barn doors are open and all that…"

"No. Don't go there." Evie fought back a blush. Laney didn't need to suggest it. Liam already had. And visions of the two of them twisted up in her sheets had occupied the three nights since. Three sleepless, erotically-charged nights.

"He's cute."

"He's young."

"So?"

"I'm not interested in giving him an adventure in being a family man. As soon as the caveman delight that he's progenated has passed, he'll remember that he had more fun before his life was tantrums and bedtimes and middle-of-the-night wakeups."

"You know, I've heard a rumour that it's not so horrible when it's your own offspring." Laney wagged a finger in her direction, and she swatted it away.

"I meant that for you." Evie sighed. They both knew it wasn't always true. But Liam... "The truth is, I just don't know him. Outside of confirming he's hot and knows what to do with his mouth, there are still a lot of unknowns."

"So, get to know him."

"Yeah." As they approached the main drag, Evie shifted topics. "Plan for tonight? I'll accept drinks, you'll find a way to guzzle them?"

It worked like a charm, right up until Carrie cornered her in the apartment kitchen. "You aren't drinking."

Evie glanced over her friend's shoulder. They were alone, but for how long? Everyone else was gabbing in the living room, but Mari had a small place.

"I'm not feeling well." She smoothed out her features, projecting a calm, cool—

"It's something you catch from a guy, takes about nine months to resolve?"

Not so cool, now, eh, Calhoun? "How did you know?" Evie screeched as quietly as she could.

"I don't know, it was just a guess. You look different. Good, but different."

"That is such an old wives' tale," she hissed under her breath.

"Don't worry, I won't tell anyone."

"Except Ian."

"He doesn't count. You okay? Anyone else know?"

"Laney knows." Evie puffed out her cheeks. "But my mom doesn't yet, and now I think I'm going to need to hide from her until the end of the summer if it was that obvious to you. Crap. I really don't want anyone to know."

"If you need help, spreading the word would—"

Evie pressed her hand against Carrie's. "I can't handle anyone knowing until…"

Carrie nodded. "You don't want to tell anyone and then lose the pregnancy."

"It would just…"

"No, I get it. Mum's the word." Carrie gave her a quick hug, then twirled past to open the fridge just as Mari walked in. "Oh, look, we need to make more margaritas!"

Evie let out a weak whoop, and stepped out so she wasn't in the way of the blender brigade.

Carrie hadn't asked her about the father. Her friend might be blunt and sometimes bitchy, but she'd really just wanted to know Evie was okay. A tendril of tension uncurled itself from her chest. She wasn't breathing easy, not yet, but at least her panic levels weren't rising. It was something.

As the conversation swirled around her, Evie let her thoughts drift. If Dale wasn't such a judgmental ass, if she lived in a larger, more anonymous community, maybe she wouldn't be so worried about people finding out. Because she wasn't going to mind being a single mom. She wasn't kidding herself—it was going to be hard, being the only adult. Not being able to run out for some precious adult moments without booking a babysitter. But it wouldn't be long before Connor could watch his younger siblings for an hour or two, and if she could organize the kids on the same visitation schedule, she'd have a weekend to herself every two weeks. That's more than a lot of mothers got.

A cackle of laughter snapped her back to the present, and she found herself surrounded by a debate on which West brother might settle down first. Carrie and Stella were laying even money on Evan, but Evie knew that wasn't likely to happen.

Evan West. Another path Evie could have gone down. *Did* go down a few steps, before turning and scurrying home like a scared bunny. Because she'd known they weren't meant for each other. It turned out she wasn't meant for Dale, either, but at the time...Dale was Evan's opposite in almost every way, and that was a big part of his attraction. What a terrible idea that had been.

A niggly little voice in the back of her head pointed out that Liam was a lot like Evan. A rush of heat flooded her chest at the potential. No. She wouldn't just throw herself at him because he made her feel good. She'd done that once, and look where it had gotten her.

And if he was like Evan, making her feel good would be all he was good for. There was no happy ever after in Evan's future.

She didn't realize she was voicing that opinion aloud until everyone turned to look at her.

"Why?" Carrie asked the question everyone else had written on their faces. Evie pressed her lips together and shook her head, but a rousing protest rose around the room. It wasn't like Evan would want her to keep any part of their history a secret—that had always been her issue. No, Dale's issue. She tossed her head back and sighed. Evan proudly wore his sexual identity on his sleeve.

She couldn't help but blush as she searched for the right words. "It's not a secret that Evan's gay, and it's not a secret that we dated for a couple of years. We weren't in love, but we *were* happy, and suffice it to say that being with me wasn't a problem for him." She glanced around the room again. They might all think that Evan would settle down with a guy one day, but Evie was pretty sure she knew why that had never—and would never—happen. "This isn't inside knowledge at all, but my guess is, the type of relationship that would finally hook Evan isn't with one other person."

"What other kind of relationship is there?" Stella

wrinkled her brow, then looked affronted when Laney and Carrie burst into hysterical laughter on either side of her, and that led to a discussion of ménage romances and the hypothetical awesomeness of having two men. *Not so hypothetical for some of us.*

"Threesomes are intense, that's for sure." Evie turned beet red as everyone swiveled their heads back to her again. *Inside voice, Calhoun.* She'd managed to keep this secret for so long, why did it spill out tonight?

Karen blinked hard, processing what she'd just heard. Evie winced, knowing where her friend's thought process would immediately go. "Evie! You and the guy in Toronto?"

Carrie gasped and wagged her finger in the air. Only Laney remained un-phased. This was one secret she'd already shared with her sister.

"No, not the guy in Toronto." She shook her head. Nothing to be embarrassed about. And it was germane to the conversation. "Evan. A long time ago, and it wasn't my scene. But it meant something to him, more than just hot sex."

Everyone processed that for a minute, then the conversation drifted back to Karen's brother. The NHL player was returning to Wardham for rehab, and even the happily married Carrie seemed eager to sign up for nurse duty. Chase was good looking, that was for sure. Lighter colouring than his sister. Evie's thoughts stuttered there, swirling around the fact this kid might not look like her and the boys. Might have Liam's dark hair and eyes. A shiver danced up her spine.

"Evie?" She glanced up at Stella, hovering anxiously beside the couch. "I'm sorry about before, if I seemed...naïve...I didn't mean to suggest that anything...I mean, about what you did. Aw, crap. I'm bungling this."

She reached up and pulled the younger woman down to sit beside her. "Thank you, but really, not necessary. It was a long time ago."

"I hate that I'm so obviously inexperienced."

Oh. Oh! "Nothing wrong with being inexperienced, honey. You know, I've only slept with five men in my entire life. Just so happened, two of them were at the same time. Sex really is..." She'd been about to say that it really is best when it's inside a loving relationship, but that wasn't a truth she could stand behind any more. "It's really something you want to do carefully, with someone who respects you, and what you want."

So she hadn't been careful, but Liam had proven the last two points. And in hindsight, she hadn't loved Evan, not really. It had been far too easy to say goodbye and move on. And she'd loved Dale, but sex between them had been damaging in the end. So love wasn't a prescription for positive intimacy. *But without it, you end up knocked up and alone...*

She blinked and refocused on Stella. "You'll know when it's right. And don't do anything that doesn't feel right." The younger woman nervously licked her lips, a question obviously hovering on the tip of her tongue. Evie leaned closer, like a conspirator. "And even though it wasn't something I'd do again...having two guys paying attention to me, that felt pretty right in the moment."

"Really?" The exclamation was breathy and sweetly innocent, and Evie threw her arms around Stella and laughed.

Evie and Laney headed out before the party ended, but Carrie distracted anyone from asking why. Evie told her sister about the conversation in the kitchen.

"Now that Carrie knows, it's not long before Ian and Kyle take it upon themselves to get in Liam's face, you know."

Evie rolled her eyes. "Do you think it would make a difference if I asked them not to?"

"Nope."

CHAPTER SEVEN

"You were a great help today, boy."

Liam grinned at his uncle over the dinner table. "That's how you're going to play this? I moved the sheep into the back pasture, turned the manure pile, brushed the horses and did a feed run. What did you do, old man?"

Ted chuckled and tapped his plate. "I made dinner."

And it was good. "What did you put on this chicken?"

"Lime juice, cilantro and salt." Ted cocked his head to the side. "You're really sticking around, eh?"

"Yep. I like this place."

"And Evie Calhoun?"

"What about her?"

"Claire says you were talking together at the party."

"Talking's not a crime." Liam learned at an early age not to offer more information than was actually being asked, but he heard the defensive edge creep into his voice anyway, and tamped it down. "Do you want more potatoes?"

Ted nodded and took the dish, but his gaze remained fixed on Liam's face. After a few bites, he set his fork down again. "How's the real estate search going?"

"Nothing new this week, but I'm in no hurry."

"You can stay here as long as you want."

"I'd like to be in town by—" He did a quick mental calculation in his head, figuring out when Evie would hit the third trimester and start needing more help. "November at the very latest, but I'm happy to stay here and give you a break from your chores until then."

"And eat my food. Maybe you could learn to cook, too."

"I know how to cook."

"That right?"

The unspoken question sat between them on the table, and Liam normally would let it lie there, like everything else about his family that he tried to ignore, but Ted and Claire Calhoun were close, and he had something to prove, just no one knew it yet. "I'm not my mother's son."

"Didn't say you were. Wouldn't have you here if I thought you were."

"And I appreciate that."

"But growing up with all that privilege—it's a far cry from what anyone around here knows."

"You introduced me to Ty West the other day. He and his brother were on the cover of the National Post a few weeks ago."

"That's different, they worked hard for that."

"And I'm sure my father would claim he works hard, too, but why are you boxing me into a corner where I need to defend him when you know I don't want to?" Liam pushed hard off the table and grabbed his plate, rattling the fork and knife resting on top of it on his way to the sink.

"You're right." Liam glanced over his shoulder just in time to catch his uncle shrug. The older man was looking tired. "And you worked hard today. For a city boy."

"I'm not going to deny that I'm new to this, but I did okay." Couldn't if he wanted to. He'd had a handful of brief visits to the farm over the years—not long enough to catch a glimpse of the blond girls across the road, or he would have probably angled to spend whole summers here—and while he enjoyed the work, it wasn't what he wanted to do with his life.

"You don't need to convince me. So who are you trying to convince?"

Oh, just wait and see. "Nobody."

They didn't have anything for dessert, so Ted decided to

amble across the road in case Claire still had leftover pie in her fridge. Liam set up his laptop, tethered it to his Blackberry, and by the time Ted returned it was dark and Liam was on his second cup of coffee.

"Whatcha working on now?"

"Renovation budgets." Three of them, actually. Two for rental properties. One for Evie's cottage. It was the project manager in him, he told himself. Just hypothetical workflow. In case Evie decided she wanted a third bedroom. Or a master suite. With a tub big enough for two, and a nook for a crib. A pipe dream, but one of them had to be a dreamer. Evie sure as hell wasn't.

"Well, I'm turning in, I'll leave you to your work." Liam barely noticed as Ted made his way through the kitchen and up the back staircase. Above him, a TV turned on, the steady drone of noise quickly fading into the background as well. At some point, Ted turned it off, but Liam didn't notice until he paused to refill his coffee cup. He was still running numbers and making notes when a quiet thump at the door grabbed his attention.

On the other side, surrounded by the dark of night, were Ian and Kyle Nixon. He didn't have to think hard about why they might be visiting so late, but he wasn't going to give them any more information than they already had, just in case.

He swung the door wide open and gestured for them to come in. Ian, taller, darker and wearing a leather jacket despite the July warmth, stalked in first. Kyle followed, carrying a six pack of beer in a slightly more friendly gesture.

"You guys here to see Ted?"

Two notched brows responded in the negative.

"Well, take a seat." Liam closed his laptop and made room for them at the table, then leaned back against the counter. He wasn't short or small, but his six foot, buck eighty frame needed all the advantage it could get over the farm boys in front of him.

"The girls had a get together tonight." Ian started, but

Kyle shot him a look, as if to say, *back story not necessary*.

"We know about Evie. And we know it's still early."

They were hard to read, but Liam figured this was some sort of test. "Did Evie talk to either of you directly?" They exchanged looks—guilty, Liam hoped. "Look, while I'm happy to make new acquaintances in town, because I'm planning on sticking around for a while, I'm not sure how this is any of your business."

"A while?" Ian pushed away from the table a bit, giving himself space to lean back and plant his feet wide. "Evie's been through a lot, she doesn't need you dicking her around."

"You think that's the danger here? That I'm going to hurt her?" Liam snorted and pressed himself half an inch taller. "She's a big girl, she can take care of herself."

"I'm sure that's true." Kyle lifted a bottle out of the cardboard carrying case and handed it over. "A peace offering."

Liam held the local microbrew for a minute before nodding his thanks. He didn't have a sister, or a sister-in-law, but he had a few close friends from college, and if a stranger got them pregnant, he'd want to clean their clocks.

But it wasn't like that with him and Evie. Or it wouldn't be, eventually. But they couldn't know that. He didn't truly yet himself, it was just a wish and a prayer at this point.

"Listen, I appreciate your concern, but I'm not going to hurt her." If anyone stood to be injured in this adventure, it was him. "But the details are going to stay between us for a while." While he figured out a way to convince Evie to try some more kissing.

"Is this because she's older than you?" Kyle probably meant it in a nice way, but Liam didn't care. He surged forward. Ian's large hand reached up and planted itself in the middle of his chest.

The older man winced at his brother. "Dude, she's the same age as Carrie. And you, for that matter."

"Well, I don't think he's interested in dating me, either,"

muttered Kyle.

Ian snorted. "Evie's hot, what does her age matter?"

Liam twisted to the side, now focusing his distemper on Ian. "Keep your eyes on your wife, *dude*."

Ian chuckled. "Is that how it is, Boy Wonder?"

"Excuse me?"

"That's what he says Evie calls you." Ian nodded at his brother.

"That was supposed to stay between us." Kyle glared at him.

"I'm no good with secrets, man." He helped himself to a beer. "Besides, I don't think she'd give him a nickname if she didn't like him."

Liam had to agree, although he didn't like the specific name she'd chosen. Or that he was the last to hear about it. "Are you guys just about done your hero mission here?"

"You clear on the fact that we'll kick your ass if you hurt her?" Ian tossed the taunt back, and Liam chuckled.

"Crystal clear."

"Good. You play hockey?"

"Nope."

"Shame, thought we might be able to be friends there for a minute." Ian shrugged when his brother slapped his shoulder. "What? We need a forward."

Kyle helped himself to a beer. "How about baseball?"

Liam winced. "I have a kayak, and I used to do judo."

They both groaned.

"How about I buy the beer next time?"

Ian grinned. "That'll do."

CHAPTER EIGHT

In the midst of Evie's life being turned upside down, she'd made an unexpected friend. Karen's neighbour, and new boyfriend, Paul, had been friendly since they met in the spring, but with the arrival of summer, and his ten-year-old daughter Megan spending more time at his house for the holidays, he'd extended a number of invitations to her and the boys to spend time with them. And sometimes, just the boys. Without spilling her secret, it was hard to explain to Paul how much she appreciated his small gestures, but she did. As soon as the morning sickness and food aversions passed, she was going to bake the man cookies.

When she woke up mid-month feeling almost like her old self, she decided to make the most of the probably short-lived energy and take the boys to the beach before work. They were all over the plan, and everyone scarfed a quick breakfast of homemade protein bars and grapes and changed into their swimsuits. Evie squinted at her reflection in her bedroom, looking for some evidence that her black bikini would reveal a bump, but on the outside, she didn't look any different. Ha. What a joke. Her body was rioting to the extreme, nothing felt or tasted right, but she could still rock an itty bitty swim suit. Not that she much appreciated it, but soaking up a bit of sun might help her mood.

"Sunglasses, hats, towels, sunscreen, let's go." She herded the boys out the door. "Do you want to walk, or take the bikes?"

"Bikes!" Connor dashed ahead to the back of the house to pull them out.

Max lingered for a moment, trailing his foot on the ground. Searching for the right words to something.

"Spit it out, Mr. M."

He grinned. "Can we go to Megan's house while you're at work?"

Evie groaned. She didn't know Paul well enough to ask him to babysit. An offer was one thing, a request was another. "You've been having fun with her, eh?"

"Yep."

"Maybe."

"Do you know her phone number?"

"Yes."

"Can you call her now?"

"Well, it would be her dad that I'd call, and I need to think about it."

"Think about what?" Connor wheeled his and Max's bikes up the drive.

"We're going to Megan's house today!"

"Maybe. I don't even know if she's there." Evie pressed a hand to her stomach as the butterflies did their annoying fluttering thing. "Connor, can you get my bike, too? I'm just going to dash back inside and get some more snacks." Ginger root and crackers.

The morning air was still a bit cool when they got to the beach, and they had the place pretty much to themselves, so Evie stretched out on a beach towel instead of joining the boys in the gently lapping waves of Lake Erie.

The municipal beach was small but well maintained by volunteers who picked up garbage and left behind enough smooth rocks and shells to keep things interesting. Evie had done her fair share of shore clean up over the years. Even before people like Evan and Carrie had started revitalizing Wardham's tiny downtown core, their beach had been a draw. Now those visitors finally had other options to keep them, and their money, in town.

She wanted to close her eyes and have a mini-nap. On her towel, out of the wind, the sun was deliciously warm. Tempting. But her mom training ran deep, so she propped herself up on her arms to ward off the nappy feelings, and fixed her gaze on the boys at the water's edge.

In the distance, a small, dark, bobbing figure grabbed her attention. A familiar tingle began to buzz across her skin as he came closer and she recognized the sharp cut of his jaw. The expensive aviator sunglasses and the panty-dropping grin. It didn't take long for the waves to deliver Liam, and a kayak, not ten feet away from where the boys were now building a robot factory out of sand. He deftly unseated himself from his craft, hauled it onto the sand, then sauntered in her direction. He was wearing......not very much. Glistening drops of water covered acres of firm, tan, naked skin, and she wasn't sure where to look first. The last time—the only time—she'd seen this much of him, she'd had beer goggles on. Well, bellini and shots of something purple goggles. In theory, those should have enhanced his attributes.

Nope. If anything, they'd dulled her memory of Liam's perfection. An abdomen carved out of wood, decorated with a touchable layer of warm skin and a focused line of hair that disappeared into his tight spandex swim shorts. On anyone else, they'd look ridiculous. On Liam, they just made sense. Athletic, utilitarian, and drool-inducingly hot. She tore her gaze northward, but got distracted again around the tight brown nipples that she suddenly remembered nibbling on......

"You need to stop looking at me like that," he muttered under his breath.

"Like what?" It was a stupid question. They both knew—

"Pretty much how I'm looking at you, I'm sure." Well, shit. She hadn't noticed, but now that he brought it up, she was suddenly conscious of what her bikini covered...and what it didn't. He puffed out a sigh and nodded toward her towel. "Room for me to sit, too?"

She scrambled up to a sitting position and nodded—then grabbed her t-shirt from the bag and threw it on.

"Your boys are building something impressive over there."

Shit. Her kids. She flushed, and from the embarrassed nod Liam gave her, she was sure her cheeks were a deep scarlet.

"Sorry, maybe I shouldn't have come over."

That would've been easier, since obviously she couldn't control her physical reaction, but they needed to get used to a new normal—one where Liam would be around, maybe a lot, and she didn't treat him like a slice of apple pie with vanilla ice cream. "No, it's okay."

"How are you doing?"

Well, now I'm vaguely turned on and I have to go teach Pilates to a bunch of nosy parkers... "I'm starting to get nauseous. But so far, crackers and an afternoon nap have worked to keep me going."

"I got your email about the midwife's appointment next week, thank you for that. Should we drive together?"

When she hesitated, he lifted his hand as if to wipe away the invitation. But it made sense—there was no reason for them to take two vehicles from Wardham to Essex. And this way, if he had questions afterward, they could deal with them on the drive back. "Yes, let's do that."

From her bag, the alarm sounded on her cell phone. She cupped her hand around her mouth and projected her loudest Mom voice toward the water. "Connor! Max! Time to go in five minutes."

In perfect chorus, they both voiced a loud protest. "We just got here!"

"Leaving so soon? Was it me?" Liam's voice was low and warm, but there was a thread of something uncertain that she wanted to smooth away.

"No, not you. I have a class to teach in thirty minutes." She raised her voice again. "We'll come back later today."

She turned to Liam again. It was hard to look at him and not let herself get carried away with a fantasy of the two of them together. It had been a mistake to kiss him again. The taste of his mouth and the feel of his skin under her fingers, now refreshed in her memory, messed with her focus. But if she could get over that, it was good to see him. Good for the boys to become tangentially aware of Liam as someone in their lives. "Maybe...do you want to come over for dinner after the appointment?"

He lifted his eyebrows, clearly surprised at the invitation. "Yeah, sure. That sounds good." His gaze dropped to her mouth, and she reflexively licked her lips. His growl was so quiet, she almost missed it in the ambient beach sounds. Her pulse picked up. Dinner with Liam sounded good—too good. This was going to be a test of her resolve, and she wasn't confident she'd pass.

She pushed herself up off the towel, kicking up a bit of sand in the process. Liam's hand shot out of nowhere to curve around her calf, brushing up and down twice in an innocent gesture that almost brought her crashing back to the ground. The lick of his fingers against her skin triggered a wave of heat that gathered steam as it surged through her body. She jerked away, much to his amusement, and before she could say anything, he'd jumped up and grabbed the towel, moving a few feet to shake it out. Funny guy. Sexy guy.

Off-limits guy.

As he handed the rolled up towel back to her, she reached out and grabbed his hand. "It's just dinner. So the boys get used to you."

His response was a slow, easy grin that crinkled his eyes and made her stupidly wet. "Sure."

"Liam—"

"Evie, I get it. You don't want life to be any more complicated than it needs to be."

She stammered a few nonsensical noises, then cleared her throat. "Yes, exactly. But it doesn't feel like that's settled." She waved her hand between them. Seriously, he was going to make her spell it out? "It still feels like there's something between us."

His impossibly wide grin widened again. "Oh, yeah. There's something between us. But we're adults, Evie. We might not be able to control our chemistry, but it's entirely up to us if we act on it."

Oh. Exactly the right thing for him to say. So why did it feel like she'd just been dunked in the lake?

"Anyway, you have to get to work. I'm really looking forward to dinner, and meeting the midwives, and…being adults together."

And with a single wicked glance down to her bare legs, he'd restored both her frustration and heated desire.

This would be dangerous territory, spending time with Liam.

She couldn't wait.

The boys were surprisingly cooperative, so they had time to stop at Bun for muffins before she had to be at the studio. They set their bikes in the rack outside the sporting goods store a few doors down, and were in and out of the bakery in record time.

On their way out, they bumped into Megan and Paul, and before she could say anything, Max had invited himself over to their house. Connor waited until Paul acquiesced, but then he crowed right along with his brother.

"You don't need to…" Evie started to apologize to Paul, but he cut her off with a gentle squeeze of his hand on her arm.

"Happy to help out." His smile was understanding and kind, and for a second she wondered if he could know…but how? Carrie hadn't told Karen, she knew that for a fact. And yet there it was again, a glimmer of worry in his eyes that he quickly masked.

"Well, I owe you one. A few, actually. I was just thinking this morning that I should make you cookies or something.

And I'm starting to worry that Max has magical abilities, because it's like he summoned you out of the blue."

"Pretty safe bet that we're here on a day off, Megan's fallen in love with this town. And Carrie's muffins." Paul laughed and nodded to the kids. "I'm glad she's made friends here. There's only so much of her dad she can take."

"Isn't that where Karen comes in?"

"Don't joke, I think everyone likes Karen more than me." He grinned, obviously not minding that fact.

"You guys are good together." Evie smiled. "The whole is greater than the sum of its parts, or something like that."

"Something like that, yeah." There was more there, but it wasn't Evie's place to explore that.

"If you tire of them, bring them to the studio, okay?"

"You got it."

Once at work, Evie checked on the stock of clean towels in the basket along the wall, took a microfibre cloth to the mirrors to make them smudge-free and sparkling, and changed into her own workout wear. Amazing how fifteen kid-free minutes could feel like an hour. Once again she regretted not yet ordering internet service for the studio. She couldn't really afford it, but oh how she'd love to steal a few minutes to check in with her parenting and fitness forums.

But she needed to save all the pennies she could. Maybe next summer.

The door chimed, and she looked up, expecting one of her regulars. Instead, Stella Nixon came in, wearing shorts and a t-shirt. Evie raised a hand in greeting.

"You going to take up Pilates, Stella?"

The younger woman blushed. "Well..."

Evie leaned over the counter. "Are you here for something else? I've got a class starting in five, but if you wanted to talk, I'll have half an hour afterward."

"No, I came..." She reached into her pocket and pulled out a folded piece of newsprint, a coupon Evie had run in the Wardham News for a free class. "I'd like to take one of your classes, but I'm not new to Pilates."

"Oh, yeah? That's cool."

"I've been doing a couple of routines for a while on my own, at home. YouTube videos."

Evie kept her face neutral. It was a reasonable way to get some exercise, although she felt strongly that working with a trained instructor pushed most people to the next level, where they needed to be to see results.

"And the thing is," Stella continued. "I really like it. But I need more. And I can't afford your classes on a regular basis, but I thought maybe…"

Spit it out, honey. But Evie knew from personal experience that asking for favours was hard. Finding the words was the easy part. Admitting you needed something others didn't…that was the killer. "I know all about not being able to afford things. Tell me what you had in mind."

Stella outlined a plan where she helped out in the studio in exchange for a series of free classes, which Evie would have agreed to anyway because she liked the young woman, but then Stella gave her a gift. "If you think I've got potential, I'd like to train as an instructor. And I'd teach classes for you, once I'm ready, as payment for the training."

A freaking gift, because if this worked out, Stella might be able to teach Evie's classes in the immediate post-partum period. She had to restrain herself from leaping over the counter and kissing the shy girl.

"You think you've got what it takes?" Neutral face, neutral face…damnit, the grin was splitting already.

Stella returned the smile. "I've tried a dozen different things at college, one of which was a semester on health and recreation. To be honest, of all the things I've studied, it was the most interesting. But I talked myself out of it and went into the emergency dispatch program."

"You aren't enjoying that?"

"It'll be a good job, and it'll pay the bills." She brightened up. "And if I can get 12 hour shifts, it'll leave more time for this!"

Evie laughed. "Honey, if you pull 12 hour shifts, I doubt

you'll want to do this. When do you graduate?"
"Next June."
"Perfect. Let's give this a shot."

CHAPTER NINE

"You want to see if we can hear a heartbeat?" The midwife, Donna, raised her eyebrows in a teasing offer.

"We might not, right?"

"Wait, why not?" Liam's own heartbeat picked up in a way he really didn't like.

Evie squeezed his hand. "Baby's still pretty low, just might not be able to pick it up yet."

"You've got a real pro on your hands here, Liam." The midwife moved to the sink and washed her hands as Evie jumped up on the exam table. The room was almost like a doctor's office, but all the little details were different. A cotton sheet covered the table instead of a paper roll. Kids' books littered a side table instead of outdated news magazines. The medical practitioner was wearing Birkenstocks and a peasant skirt.

Okay, maybe doctors also wore sandals in the summer. But really, if you drew a cartoon of a hippie midwife, Donna was it. Her confident, quiet voice belied any stereotypes, though, as she deftly answered each of Liam's researched questions. Evie had already answered half of them on the drive to Essex, but she encouraged him to take all the time he needed to get comfortable with Donna and the style of health care Evie had chosen for herself and the baby.

Evie pulled her shirt up, baring her still flat stomach. A mile of pale skin, dotted here and there with freckles. His fingers itched to cover her lower abdomen in a ridiculous show of possession. This was a medical appointment, for Christ's sake. But then she was inching her yoga pants down, first revealing her hip bones, and then lower still, and her abs dipped in the most delicious way into a subtle shadow that couldn't hide her tan lines from that damn bikini, and still she wiggled the fabric southward.

Jesus. He was going to pop a boner in front of the hippie.

He shifted his gaze up to Evie's face. "So this is old hat to you, eh?"

She sucked in a deep breath. "Still a little nerve-wracking. I'm feeling sicker each day, so that's a good sign, right? But it'll be nice to hear that he or she's ticking away."

Donna brought a basket full of supplies over to them. "You're only ten weeks, it's really early, I need to warn you that we might not pick up baby just yet."

Evie waved her hands in the air as the midwife tucked a heavy-duty tissue into the hypnotic yoga pants, protecting the fabric. "I know, but I don't think we're going to do an early ultrasound, so let's give this a shot."

"Okay, this is going to be a bit cool—" Donna squirted some jelly on Evie's belly, then picked up the portable Doppler machine in one hand, the attached wand in the other. "Give me a minute." A loud crackling sound filled the air as she pressed the wand into Evie's skin, and when that faded, Liam found himself leaning forward, craning to hear......something. When the first *whoomp whoomp whoomp* was picked up, his breath caught in his throat, but Evie shook her head, and Donna chuckled. "Smart mama." She looked up at Liam. "That one was Evie. Too slow to be the baby."

The heartbeat disappeared as she pressed harder, tipping the wand in a new direction, and then with unassuming assuredness, a tiny pulse twice as fast as Evie's heartbeat bounced into the air around them. *Whomp whomp whomp* went his kid's tiny heart, and Liam thought his own might just explode.

"Holy shit."

"Pretty cool, eh?"

He swung his gaze to take in Evie's smiling face. "It's incredible."

Another loud crackle filled the air, and the heartbeat disappeared. Donna lifted the Doppler wand and handed Evie a tissue from underneath the table. "Baby's turned, but I think we've heard enough. Good steady rate."

Liam watched as Evie swiped the ultrasound gel from her belly. Her belly, which was growing his baby. He soaked up the unobstructed view of her body with new appreciation. The physical twitch of need was ever present, especially as her fingers dipped beneath her waistband. She had to be brushing the hair on her mound, and the visual made his dick twitch yet again, but on top of his desire for her as a woman was a new layer of gratitude.

She was going to bear his child.

Nothing would be too much for Evie to ask of him. He'd move mountains and slay armies for her. Bring her ice cream and pickles. Or, knowing Evie, maybe cashews and dried seaweed snacks.

On the drive, she'd outlined in general terms her philosophy of diet and exercise, and how it was rooted in her history of getting sick when pregnant with Connor. He didn't quite follow her logic, but when she mentioned it to Donna and the midwife nodded along affirmatively, Liam figured he'd leave it alone.

And after the appointment ended, he saw an opportunity to be supportive. "Do you want to stop at the health food store before we head back?"

"You don't mind?" Evie cocked an eyebrow at him, skepticism written all over her face. So maybe his doubt wasn't as hidden as he'd thought.

"Do you mind if I grab a slice from the pizza shop on the corner while you're in there?"

She laughed, a quiet, rolling wave of comfortable noise. "Not at all."

"You really think this diet will make a difference?"

"You heard Donna. No reason not to be healthy. Might as well try."

"But there's no scientific evidence—" He cut himself off. "I'm not questioning your decision, it's just hard for me to understand how you ended up there."

Frustration flitted across Evie's face. "It just makes sense to me. Part of it is that I had a healthier pregnancy with Max, although I know there could be another explanation." She shrugged. "It just feels right. Don't you ever feel strongly about something that you can't explain, you just know in your gut it feels right? Some decisions are leaps of faith."

"The last time I had a gut instinct about something, I bought a pretty blonde a drink." Her heavy blink told him that wasn't where she expected him to go with his response. Her pink cheeks said she didn't mind. But then she bit her lip, and damned if he could tell what that was supposed to mean.

"And how did that turn out?" She whispered the loaded question, maybe expecting it to be hard for him to answer.

It took him less than a millisecond to respond. "She's sitting in my car, isn't she?"

A soft gasp fluttered out of her mouth, and she stifled it with another adorable bite. He reached across the gear shift and drifted his thumb across that lower lip, pulling the swollen flesh out from between her teeth. Another blink, and he would have sworn he heard her pulse pounding in time with his own.

"I've got another totally illogical idea right now, but I'm pretty sure you won't like it."

"I'm pretty sure I'll like it far too much," she whispered.

He curved his hand around to the back of her neck and tugged, urging her to meet him halfway. They were in a parking lot of a strip mall, this couldn't be anything more than just a kiss, but his brain couldn't figure out a way to convey that message to the rest of his body. Every bit of him was on full alert, aching to pull her into his lap and find a way to get inside her body. The sweet lap of her tongue against his, the hungry pull of her lips and the soft mewling sound she made as he deepened the kiss…it was all going to drive him mad.

She pressed him back into the driver's seat far too quickly. "We need to stop doing that." She smoothed her fingers over her face. "I know, I keep kissing you back, and I'm not going to pretend I don't like it. But I can't do this."

He wanted to curse, to yell at her about mixed messages and making up her mind, but she hadn't actually led him on. She was being as honest as she could be, and whatever she was holding back, it didn't conflict with the obvious fact that she wanted him. She just didn't think she could have him.

He'd have to prove her wrong. Or something that didn't sound quite so adversarial. "Have dinner with me tomorrow night."

"I'm having dinner with you tonight."

"No, I'm coming over tonight, and eating with you and the boys. Let me take you to the city for a nice meal. A secret…" He thought better of admitting he was asking her out on a date. "Outing."

She grinned. "No dates, Liam."

"Why not?"

Her face softened, and she reached across the gear box to momentarily rub his jaw. "Because too much time alone leads to kissing. And that's not fair to you."

"Don't worry about me, I'm a big boy." With a big problem in his pants half the time, but he'd deal.

"Besides, I work tomorrow night."

"Another time, then."

"Ha. No. But you can buy me lunch before next month's appointment."

"It's a date."

"Not even close."

Nope, not even a little bit. And wasn't that a shame.

CHAPTER TEN

Dinner had gone well enough that Evie invited him back the next week, and dropped a casual mention or three to the boys that Liam would probably start visiting every Wednesday night. By his count, that gave him twenty-nine Wednesdays to prove himself worthy before the baby arrived. Worthy of what...he tried not to think too hard about that. But he wanted more, and she'd started at offering less, so a weekly dinner was progress.

By the beginning of August, they'd settled into a pleasant routine. An awful word, *pleasant*. As the calendar pages ripped by in his head, Liam knew he needed to step up his game. Twenty-eight weeks, twenty-seven...

He parked in the now familiar narrow drive, behind Evie's station wagon covered in bumper stickers promoting local food and outdoor living, and gave himself a mental high five. Evie usually started cooking at half past five. He'd purposefully arrived thirty minutes early so she wouldn't need to do that. Beside him, two large pizzas promised to be a big hit. Pepperoni and mushroom for Connor and himself, Hawaiian for Evie and Max. He'd been paying attention.

At the door, whooping and hollering halted his raised hand mid-knock. The heavy thump of music from the other side told him the effort would be futile, so he let himself in.

Inside, a priceless tableau greeted him. Connor and Max, in sunglasses and sideways baseball caps, legs splayed wide and fierce. Connor with his arms crossed, Max playing air guitar like Smash. And Evie.

Jesus Christ.

In the middle of the room, shaking her tight little booty like mad and laughing hysterically, was the woman carrying his child.

And when she twisted to the side, her tank top riding up a bit, he caught his first glimpse of a roundness to her formerly flat belly, a gentle curve between the low waistband of her shorts and the white cotton above.

He wanted to fall on his knees and press that pale flesh with kisses. Stroke it gently and sing his baby a song. Shit he'd have mocked any guy for a few months earlier. But that was before he'd gotten a taste of what could be.

This felt right. Backwards, yes. But still exactly where he should be, bringing dinner home to Evie and her sons. Except he should have brought flowers for her, too. Or a yoga mat. Seaweed.

Whatever her currency was, Liam was going to find out. This little glimpse into what might be was going to fuel a campaign that would convince Evie—

"Hey, Liam's here!" Max yelled over the music. "And he brought pizza!"

"Pizza. You da man, Liam." Connor sauntered over, still being Mr. Chill. "Put it there." He held out a fist. Liam might be an engineer, but he could pound it with the best of them. Or at least, the best of nine-year-olds. He put it there.

All puffed up like a rooster, he carried the pizzas to the table before spinning around to give Evie a big grin. "Surprise!"

She wasn't grinning. Her booty wasn't shaking. He was definitely not da man.

He should have brought a yoga mat. "You don't like pizza?"

"I adore pizza. And I can't eat it right now."

Technically, she *wouldn't* eat it. But pointing out that she was the only one imposing such strict constraints on herself would be stupid.

"You've been here for dinner, you know what I make. Why on earth would you bring pizza?" She stomped into the kitchen.

"Do you want me to take it away?"

"And make me the bad guy with the boys? Mr. Cool brings over pizza, and I shit-can their happiness? No." She tossed open a kitchen cupboard, grabbed three plates, and thrust them into his chest. "You guys eat. I'll have leftover salad from lunch."

"You need more than salad—" He cut himself off when she shot him a withering look.

"My *salad* has more protein and fiber than your slices, I assure you."

She didn't look like she wanted an apology, so he lifted his hands in silent acquiescence and backed out of the room. As the boys dug into the boxes, he could hear the clink of a spoon in a bowl, the fridge opening and closing...and even though he knew he should give her some space, he pushed back from the table.

"You guys get started, I need to talk to your mom."

Since the kitchen was three feet away, she heard him. The spoon clattered in the sink.

This time, he stepped all the way into the kitchen and pressed the door closed behind him. She was studiously inspecting her salad. Even that was cute.

"Evie, I'm going to make a lot of mistakes. This will be easier if you either give me a set of ground rules to follow, or give me a chance to respond to feedback before you fly off the handle."

"Can I blame the hormones?"

"Sure. Is that the real reason you got upset?" They both knew the answer to that.

"Who knows."

"You do."

"Stop being wise, it's annoying." But she offered him a small smile, so he pressed on.

"Is it easier when you just think of me as the Boy

Wonder?"

She grimaced. "Who told you? Oh, shit. Kyle?"

"A while ago. And Ian. They threatened me."

"Wow. I would have—"

"Flown off the handle?" Her eyebrows shot up, two pink spots popping on her cheeks, but she visibly relaxed when she saw his grin.

"You aren't mad about the nickname?"

"No."

She wrinkled her brow. Damn cute. "I don't get it. You don't like the nickname, but you aren't pissed at me?"

"Nope. Don't get me wrong, it's an awful name. And it speaks to an issue between us, where you think I'm too young for this and won't even give me a chance to prove that wrong. But what would getting mad accomplish?"

"Oh." Her lips flushed and softened, and damnit, if she bit her lower lip, he'd be across the room and kissing her before she could squeak a protest. Kids be damned. He waited a beat, but she stood like that, frozen. Crying shame, he really did want to kiss her, but it could wait.

"The only part that I truly mind is that I didn't hear it from you. I can laugh at myself, Evie." He crossed his arms and winked. "Maybe I'll give you a nickname of your own."

She shifted her weight to one hip, trailing her free leg around in front, crossing her ankles. She didn't sway with the motion, almost as if her limbs were independent of her core. It was hypnotic. "Like what?"

"I was thinking…Mrs. Robinson."

She jerked upright, tipping herself to the side in the process. As she stumbled back to lean on the counter, he swore he heard a growl of displeasure quietly aimed in his direction.

He was teasing. His lips quirked as he tried to contain a laugh. Tried. Failed.

She joined him. "Mrs. Robinson, huh?"

Heat flashed in his gaze for a second before he stifled the

reaction, but she recognized it. The chemistry between them was undeniable. If she was someone else, she'd make a joke about teaching him a thing or two. Or step right into the role, and play the seductress. Pretend they'd need to meet at a hotel to avoid her husband.

The stab of guilt through her gut ended that train of thought abruptly. Ugh. She hadn't been married to Dale for over a year, and he still had a hold of her.

Yeah, she wasn't that person. Not even in jest.

As if he sensed her discomfort, Liam nodded toward the closed door, ending the conversation. "Bring your salad, join us. Lecture me on nutrition and how my body is a temple."

Good lord, what a temple. She blushed, and when Liam paused for a second before opening the door, she realized he probably caught the gist of her thoughts. The conversation was only over for now.

He took his seat at the table again, and after she'd composed herself, she grabbed her bowl and joined them.

"Why don't you like pineapple on your pizza?" Max asked Liam between bites. He was eating his pizza in pinched off pieces, tossing them into his mouth from ever-increasing distances. Evie quietly reached out and touched his hand, reminding him not to play with food.

"I don't know. I like it by itself." Liam grinned. "Why don't you like pepperoni on your pizza?"

"Because it's not healthy." Max fixed Liam with a solemn stare. "Garbage in, garbage out."

Liam let out a hoot, then kept chuckling as he looked across the table at Evie. "That's true, I suppose."

"I like pepperoni. Treats are okay," Connor protested.

Evie nodded. "Sure they are. We just need to choose what treats are important to us, and which can be cut out." She narrowed her gaze at Liam, and then swept it to include the boys. "Pizza isn't made healthy by topping it with fruit and veggies, right?"

Max gasped. "Wait, you mean *this* is just as bad as *that?*" He leaned over to Liam and lowered his voice to a stage whisper. "Can I have your pepperoni?"

Now it was Evie's turn to laugh. "Go ahead. I'll outlive you all. Mmm, salad."

After dinner, Connor schooled Liam and Max in something on the Wii while Evie snuck away to her room to update her website, such as it was. She needed to hire someone to revamp it, because she didn't have the skill or time, but she also didn't have the money. It had been on the agenda for the fall, but now... She thunked her head back against the headboard, practiced a few deep breaths, and took another stab at adding a sub-page to the exercises section.

"Frustrated?"

She glanced up and blushed. Liam filled the frame of her bedroom door, his thumbs notched into his standard-issue brown leather belt. The man had better accessories than she did, and looked pulled together even after a day working in the fields.

"You don't look like a farmer, you know that?"

He shrugged. "I'm not."

"You seem to be enjoying it."

"I am, for sure. But it's just temporary." He raised one hand, and she wondered what her face must have looked like just then, because he was obviously warning her not to freak out. She needed to work on her poker face. "I'm still planning on moving into town. But this feels right for now."

"At least you're working off all that pizza," she teased.

"True story. Now, stop changing the subject. What's got you all riled up in here?"

"My website. I can only work on it at night, when I have the least patience."

"No time during the day?"

"No internet at the studio."

"Ahhh." He gestured to her laptop. "Can I?"

"Sure, knock yourself out." She climbed off the bed and passed it over. "I'll get the boys moving toward brushing their teeth, etcetera."

It was forty-five minutes before they were settled in their room. When she came out, she expected to find Liam still on her computer, but her laptop sat on the kitchen table and he was finishing up the dishes.

"You don't have to do those."

"I don't mind."

"If you want to take a look at my website, I can dry—"

"All done."

"What?" She spun around, shocked. There on the screen was the exact page she wanted, looking even better than she imagined, and it was findable on a drop-down menu. "How did you know that was what I was trying to do?"

"You had the content doc file open, and I guessed at the design from the other tab in your browser."

"Sneaky. Thank you, it's perfect!"

"It was nothing. If you need anything else done, just let me know, okay?"

She smiled. "You have no idea how dangerous an offer that is."

He stopped behind her, his hand resting on her shoulder. "I've made worse and survived."

She ignored that and closed her laptop. "What can I do to thank you?" He chuckled, and she groaned. "What friend-level something can I do—That's not better, is it?"

From the silent shaking as the laughter rolled from one end of his body to the other, she gathered the answer was no.

"Come on." He pulled her to a stand and wrapped his arms around her for a minute before sliding his hand down her back, stopping at a reasonable but still tingle-inducing spot mid-spine. "Let's sit on the couch for a minute."

"I need to get to bed soon," she muttered, but sitting seemed like a fair request from someone who'd been nothing but helpful all evening.

"Sunshine, you can sit for a minute."

"Don't call me that." She plunked herself on the couch.

"Why not?"

"Because..." Because a nickname like that meant something. It meant she was his, and there was no way that could be true. Even if he thought it was, at some point he'd wake up and realize he'd stumbled into a life he didn't want. A complicated life with an aging wife and an unexpected kid. Two step-kids and a tiny house in a sleepy town, far from the city and all the opportunities it would provide. And she'd end up with a second ex-husband, and this time, it wouldn't be her that did the leaving. "Because I don't like it."

"I don't believe that for a second."

"Doesn't matter."

"You want to tell me what happened to you? What someone else did to you that means you can't trust me?"

Wow. She'd shifted the conversation away from light and fluffy by being a bit sulky, but he'd just pushed it into the deep-end.

"Nope." She moved to push herself off the couch, but he reached out and snagged her bare foot with one hand, and pressed down on her thigh with the other. She protested for a second, but as his thumb started to move on the ball of her foot, she gave in. How could she not? Liam's hands on her...that was heaven.

A dangerous, stupid, delicious kind of heaven. That she should be strong enough to resist, but oh, oh, oh—her eyes rolled back in her head as he stroked a firm line down her arch—she was weak, and she didn't care.

"Tell me. Give me something. Help me understand why I can rub your feet, but I can't continue stroking my way up your leg."

Sadness twisted around the contentment that had begun to unfurl in her chest. "Because I can see how it will end, and it's not pretty."

He grinned, slow and wicked. "I can assure you, I've been where these legs end, and it's very pretty."

His words had the intended effect of distracting her. How could she not be distracted, when her body practically bloomed every time he looked at her for more than a second? "That's not what I meant."

He watched her for a while, a careful, assessing gaze. No argument, no judgment. Just observation, and the occasional heated spark that he tamped down. What did she look like to him? Could he see the true nature of her personality, and not care yet? No amount of chemistry would make a difference if he stopped liking her after a time.

Evie licked her lips, and Liam could practically see the wheels turning in her head. His first instinct was to soothe her ruffled feathers, try and make everything okay, but he sensed she was finally going to open up, and he suppressed his desire to make everything better. He had to own up to the fact that he didn't know her well enough to do that properly yet.

"The thing is...I'm brittle. Hard and untrusting, and far too cynical to make anything easy and fun."

"Who says I want easy and fun?"

She raised one eyebrow. "Why are you here in Wardham?"

"Because you're having my baby." It wasn't the whole truth, but it was true, and it rolled effortlessly off his tongue.

"No, that's why you're staying. Why did you come in the first place?"

For something different. Something easy and fun.

"I think we both know that the reality of parenthood and small-town living is going to wear off after a while, and you'll tire of this."

That wasn't even a little bit true. But how could he tell her, a woman he'd already casually proposed to for all the wrong reasons, a woman who had his number—or at least, the number of the guy he used to be—that every time she was bitchy and short with him, it just made him love her a little bit more? Because she was a mama bear, backed into a corner, and she wasn't going down without a fight. How to tell her that he was pretty sure she was the best thing that had ever happened to him?

It was time to join her in the corner, in a big way, so she'd never doubt his commitment. And while he had no doubt she could do it all on her own, she didn't need to. But words weren't going to do it. He needed to bide his time, and wait for the opportunity to show her how much she could trust him. Until then… "I don't accept the premise, not exactly, but you're in the driver's seat. What do you want me to do?"

"Back off. Just a bit. We need some boundaries."

He didn't need her to explain why. Even now, in the midst of a tense conversation, sparks arced between them. He had a semi-hard cock, and every time he stroked his thumb up her instep, she flexed her hips. He had no doubt that she was wet and ready for him, and at some point, they'd succumb to their desire and move on from pseudo-innocent touches and the occasional kissing and do more of what they did in Toronto. Maybe try some new positions, to work around a growing belly.

Jesus. Pregnant women had never done anything for him in the past, but the thought of Evie swelling with the proof of his seed growing inside her…yeah, maybe they needed some boundaries. Just until she trusted him.

"No touching." To make her point, she slid away from him and stood up. "No kissing. No more lingering after the boys are in bed."

"They don't know yet…when are we going to talk about baby stuff?"

"They'll know soon enough, and we can talk around appointments."

"Dinners can continue?"

She nodded. "I want the boys to be comfortable with you, so your visits when the baby arrives aren't yet another change in their lives."

He could live with that.

"It's really important to me that we have a positive co-parenting relationship for this baby." She pressed her hands to her belly. "I'll be honest, I'm not sure that would be easy for me if things between us got more complicated."

She might mean to warn him off, but he could read between the lines. If they had a relationship that ended, she'd be jealous. That pleased him to no end. And he felt the same way. So he'd just need to make sure they didn't start anything until they were sure it wasn't going to end.

He was pretty much already there.

CHAPTER ELEVEN

There were only so many maxi-dresses a girl could wear before it became obvious she had something to hide. The summer had slipped by in an easy enough routine of Wednesday night dinners and ginger tea-controlled nausea. Telling her mother had been surprisingly anti-climactic. Claire had asked a few pointed questions about Liam's planned involvement, then offered the unsolicited advice that perhaps they pretend they had dated for a while. Like Evie was going to tell anyone anything about her relationship, or lack thereof, with Liam. Through gritted teeth, she assured Claire that no details would be shared with anyone, present company included, and that was the end of that. Claire hadn't suggested she and the boys move back to the farm, which Evie appreciated. It felt like a tacit acknowledgment that Evie could handle this change in her life plan.

The next step was telling the boys. Connor had heard her retching in the bathroom a few times, and his sideways glances seemed far too knowing for a nine-year-old. She needed to ask Kyle what would have been covered in his health classes the previous year. At any rate, he was worried about his mom, and she needed to reassure him and his little brother that she was fine.

And then...their father.

She shuddered at the thought of that awkward conversation as she shouldered her way into the ironically named Bun In The Oven, Carrie's bakery/coffee shop, her arms laden down with two bags of duplicate household items she was lending to Karen.

Yesterday, Karen's family had hosted a barbeque as a send-off. Tomorrow, her friend would drive up the highway to Toronto, where she was going to spend the next year studying to be a librarian. Today, it was coffee and confession time.

From behind the espresso machine, Carrie lifted a hand in greeting. Karen sat on a stool at the small bar.

Evie smiled at the familiar scene. "I brought you some things from the *items wanted* list you posted on Facebook." She dumped the bags at Karen's feet. "It was an excellent opportunity to empty out my cupboards. Can opener, spatulas, wooden spoons, a saucepan, a Bodum coffee press, pillow cases, a new shower curtain. And a couple of romance novels."

Karen preferred to read fantasy and young adult novels, but Evie thought her friend might enjoy the comfort of a few strong heroes while she was living a few hours away from her own knight in shining armour.

"You don't mind parting with all of that?"

"None of it has been used since I moved into the house. Except the books, but my mom gives me a steady stream of those."

"Well, thanks!"

"No problem. Hey, listen..." Evie took a deep breath and gestured for Carrie to make her a cup of tea. "I need to tell you a secret I've been keeping."

Carrie grinned, and Karen looked between them. "What is it?"

"You remember the guy in Toronto?"

"Uh huh."

"This is going to freak you out, but it was Liam."

"Ted's nephew? How did that happen?"

"Total coincidence. We talked about Wardham that night, but we, uhm, didn't get into details." Evie blushed.

"So, what, are you dating now? I've seen him around town a fair bit. Did you know he'd be moving here?"

"Not exactly. To both questions."

"What does that mean?"

"You know how sex can have unintended side effects?" She winced. That was not the right language, at all. "The thing is...I missed my period in June. So I took a test."

Karen snapped to attention. "You're...pregnant?" She slowly lowered her mug to the counter and started counting on her fingers. "Like, three months pregnant?"

Evie's heart pounded as she nodded a confirmation. Carrie offered a supportive smile, which Karen caught.

"And you, little miss barista, you knew?"

Carrie shrugged. "Wasn't my secret to share."

"She guessed. Other than Liam, my mom and my sister...you're the first person I've told." God, where had her saliva disappeared to? The Sahara had nothing on her mouth right now.

"Holy crap. And Liam's the father? Holy. Crap." Karen stared at her, mouth still slightly agape. "Well. One thing's for sure, that kid is going to be freakin' gorgeous."

Evie wasn't sure she'd heard correctly. "What?"

"You. Him. The resulting DNA mix is going to be pure gold. Except, maybe not literally gold. He's so dark..." Karen shivered and Carrie groaned in agreement.

"Hey!" Evie knew both her friends were happily involved with their own groan and shiver worthy men, but the flare of possessiveness inside her still voiced itself as if she had no control.

Carrie laughed.

"What?" Evie blushed furiously.

"We're not allowed to notice that Liam is more delicious than a box of chocolate truffles?"

"No!"

"Why not?" This time it was Karen who chimed in, her grin way too knowing for Evie's liking.

Absolutely no reason. Evie had no claim on Liam.

Refused to have a claim on him, even though he wouldn't mind. "Because he's too young for either of you."

"Oooooh." Her friends harmonized the stretched out syllable perfectly.

"Oh nothing. And shut up." Evie wanted to go home and crawl into bed. She crossed her arms under her breasts, and the tender ache there and the slight swell beneath her arms were both reminders that she needed to see this through. Needed to put up with the teasing, because her friends were going to be invaluable when everyone else found out, and the way her body was changing every day, it wouldn't be long now.

Carrie came through the gap in the counter, but instead of stopping at her side, went to the door, threw the lock and flipped the Open sign to Closed. "Come on, let's go sit in the back."

Karen pressed gently on Evie's shoulders, and she found herself being ushered back to the kitchen, where Carrie dug out a box of the aforementioned chocolate truffles.

"Dig in, this is the good stuff. Emergency stash."

Evie took one of the dark chocolate bundles and savoured a small nibble.

"So, you think you're too old for him." Karen nodded thoughtfully. "What does he think?"

There was no getting out of this conversation. "He thinks all sorts of impossible things, like having a baby is going to be lovely and sweet, and we should get married because it's the right thing to do."

Carrie pursed her lips, but didn't respond.

"What are you thinking?"

"Well, that's what we did, and it turned out to be pretty wonderful."

"That's different."

"Of course, every situation is different. But it's not the stupidest idea anyone has ever had."

"It's stupid for me." Evie winced again. Seriously, what had happened to her filter? "Ian is rock solid. And he worships you. Liam barely knows me. And I'm not you…I'm not…"

"What?"

"I'm not easy to love."

"Fuck that noise." Karen interjected herself into the conversation again. "Didn't we basically have this conversation in the spring?" Evie didn't bother to point out that at that point, Karen had pretty much the same self-doubt, because she knew that argument would just get turned around against her. "You are adorable. Gorgeous. Can make quinoa and spinach taste super yummy. You are funny, and you have funny kids. So obviously, you're both a good parent and you have great genes that you pass on. I don't know all that Dale did to your head—"

"Hey." There was nothing wrong with her head.

Karen softened her voice. "None of us are perfect. But neither are they. The men, I mean."

"That's the thing…" Damnit. That *was* the thing. "Liam is perfect. Too perfect."

The knock at the door was louder this time. A persistent, happy beat. Her mother had departed with the boys only a few minutes earlier, so it could only be Liam. She rolled her eyes and smiled at the same time. She swung the door open with enough force to cover her breathlessness. It wasn't a secret that he affected her, but she didn't need to be obvious about it when it couldn't lead to anything. But there he was, leaning back against her porch railing, one ankle crossed over the other, sunglasses propped up on his head, and it physically hurt Evie to stay on the threshold instead of sliding across the small landing and folding herself into his hard, lean length.

"I brought you a treat from Bun." He held up a travel mug and a small paper bag.

"I don't do treats."

He chuckled and propelled himself toward her, pausing a foot away to…

"Did you just smell me?"

"Sure did. You smell good."

"You can't do that. It's against the rules."

"Touching you is against the rules. I did not touch." He leaned closer still, until his breath warmed her temple. "I want to, though. Very much. I want to touch you all over, from your pointy little nose to the tips of your toes."

Her nose wasn't pointy. Was it? And did she not put flirting on the no-go list? She really should have.

"Wow, you're easy to rile up." Liam slid past her, bumping his hip gently into her midsection. "That wasn't me touching you, by the way. I was just saying hello to my daughter."

She thunked her head back against the door frame and closed her eyes for a second. "It might be a boy."

"It's going to be a girl, and she's going to be beautiful. She'll have your nose." He turned and gave her a panty-melting smile over his shoulder. "Are you coming? I'm happy to eat the muffin if you don't want it, but it has six different ancient grains and absolutely no sugar."

"Give it." He handed the bag over and took a seat at the kitchen table. Very boundary-respecting.

She eyed him warily. "What are you doing here?"

"I wanted to chat about the next midwife appointment, and I figured it would be best to do that while the boys are at school." Again with the perfect. She sighed audibly, and he raised his eyebrows. "Did I assume incorrectly?"

"No."

"Then what's with the heavy, long-suffering sigh?"

"Don't worry about it. What about the appointment?"

"We have the ultrasound at the end of the month, right? I was hoping you might be willing to find out the gender, but I didn't want to argue about it on the day of the appointment."

She laughed. "Why would it be an argument?"

"I assumed you wouldn't want to find out."

"Why?"

"Your mom said that you didn't know with the boys."

It took a moment for that statement to land. So, that was less than perfect. "Excuse me?"

His eyes shifted from left to right, as if reviewing what he'd just said. It didn't take long for comprehension to dawn and he splayed his hands wide, slowly and carefully, like he was negotiating a hostage situation. "I'm not, generally-speaking, talking to your mom about you."

"So just specifically-speaking, this one time, you discussed my prenatal health care choices with my mother?" Evie knew that wasn't fair, could see on his face that there was an explanation, but over the years it had become second-nature to verbally spar with Dale. Attack, counter-attack. Knowing it wasn't mature wasn't enough to stop her from doing it, even with someone who didn't know that's how the game was played.

But once again, Liam proved more clever than she gave him credit for. "I discussed nothing, of course. I live across the road from her, temporarily, and from time to time she shares things with me. Like your first food was banana, and your first word was run. That's adorable, by the way. I have no idea about my first food or word. I'd have to find a former nanny to find out, I'm sure. So when she comes over and is all proud and concerned grandma, I listen. I don't say anything, but I listen, because it's polite, and it's a way for me to learn about you, someone I've got a vested interest in understanding. Also, because she brings me cookies. I'm not above being bribed for my time."

Damn him. If he kept doing that, she'd have no choice but to like him. And liking him would lead to a gates-wide-open approach to wanting him, and lord help her, he was very wantable.

"Okay. Mom told you that I didn't find out the gender for the boys?"

"Yeah. If it's important to you, then okay, but it's more in my nature to plan ahead."

"So you came here to talk about that in advance."

He shrugged. "Seemed like the decent thing to do."

Damn him. "It wasn't me. The surprise—that was Dale's choice. I'm okay with finding out. Particularly if this one is a girl—"

"I have no doubt it will be."

"You can't possibly know that."

"Whatever." He grinned, she laughed, and her good mood was officially restored. "I won't demand anything of you, Evie."

"Of course not, you're perfect." She said it lightly, but he shook his head. "Don't deny it. You probably also write poetry and donate ten percent of your income to charity."

"What's wrong with that?"

"Nothing. And that's the freaking point, Liam! No one is perfect. And yet you pretend to be, so that scares me."

For the first time since they'd started spending time together, Evie watched Liam turn stone cold. She didn't remember the day she told him about the pregnancy as clearly as she'd like, but she was pretty sure this reaction was worse.

"Pretend?"

"Okay, that was the wrong choice of words." Once again she found herself floundering. What was it about this guy that made her so flustered, so completely incapable of logical thought? *His DNA parasite is doing its best to weaken you.*

"I'm not pretending to be perfect, Evie. I'm trying damn hard to do the right thing, at every turn, because I don't think enough people have done that for you in the past, and right now, while you're carrying my child, that's my job. To be there for you. I'm sure as hell not perfect."

"I guess I just don't know you, and that's a problem, given the circumstances we've found ourselves in. Like, why couldn't you ask your parents what your first word was?"

He shrugged. "They weren't that involved in raising me."

"Wow." She wanted to know more about that, but she didn't want to pry. No, she did. But she wanted even more for him to freely offer the information.

"Yeah. That's not how I plan to parent, you need to know that. It's part of why I left the city, because I could see the future and I didn't like it."

"And then you came here and I dumped all of this on you."

"I like this. I like working with my uncle, and I'm going to like being a landlord when I find the right property. I like..." He trailed off, his eyes raking over her. "I like you, Evie. And I guess I've stumbled along the way. I was just trying to be the best I can be. For you. For our baby."

"You don't need to impress me."

"I want to. I want you to know you can trust me."

So much for hoping he'd magically know what she wanted. Time to be brave and ask for it. "Tell me something about yourself, then. Share something messy and ugly that you aren't proud of."

His eyes twinkled. "You mean other than having a one-night stand with someone who doesn't like me?"

"I like you." She couldn't help but grin for a minute. But that wasn't the whole story. How to convey that without sounding like a bitch? She eased onto a chair at the table and reached across to hold his hand. "I just don't trust you yet. For my own reasons."

"Yeah." He squeezed her hand in his, his thumb lingering to rub against her knuckles. They sat there silently, staring at their connected hands, and when he spoke again, it was barely louder than a whisper. "I'm not a good son."

To the people who weren't involved in raising you? But she didn't voice the skeptical question. He was sharing something painful, and she appreciated it.

"I cause my mother a lot of pain, by fighting with my father. I know that, and I'm not doing a damn thing about it. That's pretty imperfect, I'd say."

"There are reasons?"

"Yeah."

"Then it's human."

He barked a short laugh. "Humanity is not a valued

condition in my family."

"Well, that says more about your family than you." She wiggled her fingers out from his, and patted his hand. "I'd like to hear more about this, but I have to get to work. Do you want to drop me off?" He nodded, and she dashed to her room to grab one of her three empire-waisted dance shirts. As she smoothed the no-longer loose top over her belly, she realized it was probably the last day of this baby being their little secret. She raised her voice. "Liam?"

His footsteps in the small hallway to her bedroom caused her pulse to race, and she rolled her eyes at herself.

He didn't say anything, just leaned in the doorway. She turned around, and the look on his face said it all. Her pulse picked up yet again. *Work*. Right. She pointed to her belly. "I don't think this is going to be a secret much longer."

His lips curled, and so did her toes. "Yeah, you've really popped, eh?"

She nodded.

"So, you tell people." He scanned her face. "You worried about that?"

She didn't want to be, but... "I'm not looking forward to telling my ex."

Liam's brows tugged together, and he chewed on his lower lip. She knew he was thinking about the different options why she might be wary of that conversation, and she wanted to set his mind at ease, but the real reason sounded stupid to her own ears. It was hard to will oneself to knowingly sound stupid out loud.

After a moment, he shrugged, and reached his hand into the space between them. "Come on, I'll take you to work."

As she interlaced her fingers into his, his gaze dropped to the belly between them. "Pretty soon you'll be able to feel the baby kick," she offered.

His face lit up. "Yeah?"

She nodded. "That's definitely an allowable exception to the no-touching rule."

"I can't wait."

When they got to the front door and she had to let go of his hand to lock up, she realized that was a rule she'd have trouble enforcing on every level.

CHAPTER TWELVE

Liam dropped Evie off at the studio, then parked his SUV two blocks down the main drag and stepped into the real estate office he'd first visited at the beginning of the summer. It was time to put down some roots. Thirty minutes later, Willa Stephens was letting him into a large brick house that had been converted into multiple dwellings—more than once.

"Right now, it's a duplex, but in a previous incarnation, it was four small apartments, and it wouldn't take much work to restore it to that, if you wanted to maximize profit." The realtor paused in the foyer and gestured at first the door on the right, then the left. "There are only tenants in one unit. We didn't give them enough notice, but this side is vacant. And if you like what you see, we can come back tomorrow to check out the other side."

Liam had helped his friends move in and out of enough rental units not to be shocked by the state of the empty unit. An abandoned couch, a bag of cat food and more than a few dust bunnies. It could be much worse. From the front room, a narrow hallway wound past a bedroom to a small back kitchen. The cabinets and plumbing were in good shape. The windows were not, but if he squinted, he could see the potential.

"Back here is the internal staircase to the second floor." Willa nodded to a hidden nook that would be easy enough to drywall over.

"And if we split upstairs into its own unit, where would their entrance be?"

"There's a deck out back, off the parking lot."

He followed her to the backyard, which had been covered in gravel to provide parking for four cars. A solid looking deck soared above them. "Can we go in this way?"

"One way to find out." She jogged to the door and tried the key, which worked.

Inside, he was in what had probably been a bedroom, but was big enough to be retrofitted as a kitchen. Or re-retrofitted, he supposed, peering closely at the wall. A dry wall patch at sink height made him think that the plumbing might already be in the right spots, and in the corner was an electrical socket appropriate for a stove. Yes, this place had potential.

"There are two other rooms like this, and a bathroom, on this level."

He barely heard Willa's rehearsed patter as he turned slowly in the space. "Okay. Let the tenants know I want to see the other side tomorrow."

The last few years, Evie had had mixed feelings about September and the return to school. She'd really enjoyed having summers with the boys. But between an increased schedule at the studio and the craptastic feelings of a secret first trimester, there had barely been enough trips to the beach to justify the whining about being bored. Having to get everyone up and out of the house early was a small price to pay for five kid-free days in a row. Bring on autumn.

Ha, enjoy it while you can.

So she would. Between her lunchtime class and her only private client for the afternoon, she had time to grab a tea, so off she ran to Bun. Where Carrie made no attempt to hide a double take at the visibility of her belly.

"I know, eh?" Evie rubbed the ever-growing home for her little bean. "I swear, it's doubled in size over the course of the day."

"Holy crap, Evie. There's no hiding that thing."

"Yeah." It wasn't really that big, but given that only a handful of people knew she was pregnant before this morning, the news was sure to spread like wildfire. "I got a few lingering looks in my ten-thirty class. By the end of my one o'clock class, people were just saying congratulations."

"Not the nightmare you expected?"

"I haven't seen Dale yet."

Carrie didn't bother to suppress a snort. "Who cares what he says?"

"He's the father of my children." Evie looked down. "Well, some of them, anyway." She sank onto one of the stools with a groan. "Shit, I really hate that."

"It's not that big a deal."

"It's still not how I saw my life working out."

Carrie knew better than to argue, which Evie appreciated, so she changed the subject. "How's everything going with Liam?"

"Good, actually." Evie smiled. "He stopped by this morning to ask me if I minded finding out the gender at the ultrasound, if we can. He's...very considerate."

Her friend nodded. "Do you want your tea to stay, or do you need to get back?"

"I've got half an hour." She watched as Carrie poured hot water over a tea bag in a china mug. "You know what he told me this morning? He doesn't think his parents would know what his first word was. He'd have to ask a nanny. Isn't that strange?"

"Is he rich?"

"No, I don't think so. He's Ted's nephew, for heaven's sake."

Carrie rolled her eyes. "Evie, how is it that you're having this man's baby and you haven't demanded his last five tax returns? What about child support?"

"He just graduated from school! He worked for a bit between degrees, and I know he has some money that he's going to reinvest in property here, but really...I don't need anything from him for the first while. Once this kid has daycare and soccer registration to worry about, that'll be a different story. But then he'll be more settled."

She hoped. God, she hated how much she wanted Liam to settle in Wardham. How much her heart would ache if he decided to head back to the city, and not just for her baby's sake.

Carrie moved to the nook in the corner where she kept her laptop.

"What are you doing?"

"Googling him."

"Carrie, no! You can't do that."

"Actually, I'm pretty sure that I can."

"Well, I don't want you to." Evie knew it was a futile argument. "Besides, he friended me on Facebook last month. He's not hiding anything from me."

Carrie made some non-committal noises as she first searched his name, then went to the social network site and clicked through Evie's profile to see Liam's picture. Evie couldn't help but be fascinated as she watched Carrie click on Liam's picture and drag it into another browser tab. The computer worked for a minute, then the screen was filled with a dozen Liams. And as Carrie scrolled down the page, Evie realized there were actually an endless stream of pictures of this man on the internet. Not a huge variety, many different shots of the same moments, but there was Liam, in the society pages of the National Post, and on the red carpet at the Toronto International Film Festival. At the re-opening gala for the Royal Ontario Museum. Liam in a tuxedo. Liam with a beautiful brunette, then a different one, and another still. *Her* Liam.

"Holy shit." She whispered the words as she pressed closer to screen, crowding Carrie.

"Evie, is it possible that your baby daddy might be rich? And possibly famous?"

"But you Googled him. He's not famous." But he was something. Something that she had no clue about.

"Are we sure that's his real name?" Carrie clicked on one of the photos and shrugged as she read the caption. *"Annabeth Scott and her date, Liam McIntosh.* Huh. Okay, that's his real name."

Evie backed up, shaking her head. "No. Close the window. Let's pretend we didn't do that. He'll tell me what that's all about when it matters." Carrie raised her eyebrows. Yeah, that sounded like a terrible idea to Evie's ears as well. "Damn it. Damn it! How do I ask him about this without sounding like a stalker?"

"You just finished telling me he's considerate. Blame me. He'll understand."

"Damn damn damn."

"On the other hand, you can probably feel better about asking him for child support now."

Evie shot her friend a dirty look before turning back to her tea. This was not a good turn to the day.

Liam arrived at the studio at half past two, but he didn't head inside. Through the plate glass window, he could see Evie coaching someone through exercises. There was a bench a few yards away, so he made himself comfortable and pulled out his phone to check if he'd gotten any emails back yet. A lot of puzzle pieces had to come together in order for him to put in a clean offer on the potential fourplex. Willa's preferred home inspector was available to come to the viewing tomorrow, thankfully, which would be the only thing he'd hold out for. But the money? He'd walk away from the deal before he asked for help on that front. He needed to be able to do this on his own. Not having a job would make qualifying for a mortgage difficult, so he needed to liquidate what he had access to.

As he plotted and planned, a half hour passed. Evie's client left the studio, and Liam stood to head inside when a shiny, dark blue Ford Explorer pulled up to the curb. They hadn't yet been formally introduced, but Liam had seen Evie's ex-husband around town enough to instantly recognize him. He climbed out at the same moment that Evie stepped onto the sidewalk. Liam stood there, waiting to see what would happen. Waiting to see what Evie would do when she saw him. When she saw Dale. *Awww, shit*. This wouldn't be good.

Liam was torn between knowing he should let Evie fight her own battles—and win, because she deserved that—and wanting to get between his woman and an obvious threat.

Not that Dale posed any physical threat to his ex-wife. His hands were stuffed in his pockets and his body language clearly spelled out that his attack was going to be more pointed. More vicious. He was going to strike with words and history and feelings, and Liam would give anything to deflect all of that shit from Evie.

But as she glanced toward him, as much as it killed him, he slowed to a stop, and damned if her eyes didn't soften. The desperate plea and silent thanks…why did she need to do this? Their baby wasn't any of this asshole's business.

"Damn, Evie, I thought it was a rumour." Dale's shoulders sagged and he tipped his head to one side. "You got yourself in a spot of trouble, eh?"

She bristled. "That's not how I'd describe it."

"Have you told the boys yet?"

"No. I thought I had more time, but this belly literally popped overnight." She squared off her posture, as if daring him to call her a liar. He didn't. "I'll tell them tonight when you drop them off, and I'd appreciate you not saying anything before that point."

"They're gonna have a lot of questions."

"Not as many as you, I'm sure. Difference is, they have a right to ask me."

"Hey, now, that's not fair. We're *co-parents*, as you keep calling it, and this thing is going to disrupt our sons' lives. That affects me."

"My *baby* isn't going to change a thing about how we co-parent the boys. And mind your tone about how you refer to *their sibling*. He or she is not a thing."

From the way Dale's back stiffened instantly, Liam could tell this was a sore point between them. Was it the judgment on word choice, or the sniped correction? Both? Resentment that this was all they had left between them? He already knew that co-parenting was hard shit, and so far, he and Evie still liked each other. *Screw that.* She would always be a partner in his life, and he would always like her, no matter what happened between them personally.

"Why you gotta harp at me, Evie? I came here to show you some support."

She snorted. "Yeah? Doing a real good job of that, Dale."

"Well, what am I supposed to think? I hear someone saying that you're knocked up, and you're not in a solid relationship. How could you be so irresponsible? I mean, do you even know who the father is?" Liam was on his feet as soon as Dale's tone turned mean and ugly, and at Evie's side before he finished speaking. Dale took one look at the hand Evie pressed to Liam's side—as if that would hold him back—and cracked his jaw from side to side. His eyelids dropped, hooding his gaze, and he rocked back on his heels. Well, at least the man wasn't stupid. Just mean.

"Dale, right? Liam McIntosh, I believe we've met a few times around town." It was stretching the definition of their passing acquaintance, but Liam had learned a thing or two about handling bullies over the years, and it started with disarming them with the unexpected. Change the terms of the game they think they're going to win. "You're out at the Ford dealership, right? Heard great things."

Dale huffed a quiet breath. "Can't say that I've heard much about you, though. You're working with your uncle on his farm, right?"

Liam turned to Evie and smiled. "For now. It's giving me the time I need to watch my baby grow, get used to the idea of being a parent."

"Well, once you *get used* to the idea, you'll realize it's a lot of hard work. Not just with the kids, I mean, but at a job. A real job, that earns money."

Beside him, Evie couldn't contain a semi-hysterical giggle, and he wished they'd had more conversations about how that wouldn't be an issue for them. He hadn't come out and told her all the details of his plans, yet, and she still seemed to harbour some concerns that he might be an impoverished student. He needed to set that record straight, but not here, not in front of Dale.

"Much obliged for the tip, then. Can I give one back in return?" He gave Evie what he hoped would be received as a reassuring squeeze before stepping forward, closing the gap between him and his predecessor. Evie's first husband. Connor and Max's dad. He needed to remember that last piece before he did something stupid. "This is a private conversation, and Evie won't be the only one discussed in the rumour mill if you carry it out on the sidewalk. I'd suggest we move inside, but I understand you're on your way to the school, is that right?"

"This is none of your business, McIntosh."

"That's where you're wrong, Simmons. Everything related to Evie and our baby is my business."

"That's what you think." Dale's lips pulled together so hard they turned white, and his next words were spit out with more venom than Liam had ever heard before from one spouse about another. "She's a dirty slut, man. Don't waste your time."

It wasn't Liam's way to use violence. He wasn't big, he wasn't a fighter. But he fisted his hand in the front of Dale's shirt and shoved the larger man back a giant step, following with lightning speed to maintain the advantage, and grabbed at the other man again, every bit of him shaking with barely restrained hatred. "Out of respect for your children, I'm not going to punch you. Not now. Not here, on the main street of their tiny little town. But at some point, you and I are going to find ourselves alone somewhere, and I'm going to make you eat those fucking words, asshole. She's the mother of *your children*. That better be your first and last thought about Evie Calhoun, you hear me?"

"Get your hands off of me," Dale muttered, and Liam eased back. Dale flexed his shoulders for a moment, but kept his distance.

"They're off, dude. Nothing happened here, right? I just saw a bee or something. Thought you might be allergic. I hear that's common among assholes, didn't want you to get stung." So much for dealing well with the situation. He was breathing hard, his hands balled into fists at his side. He dipped his head to the side, glancing back at Evie. Damn. Her face, white and drawn, told him everything he needed to know. He'd stepped way over the line.

"Evie, I'm going to get the kids. Maybe I'll drop them at your mom's tonight after dinner?"

"Sure thing, Dale." Her words were barely above a whisper.

Liam stepped back and they watched Dale get back into his vehicle before she whirled around and ran back into the studio. He took a deep breath before following.

He expected her to yell, to lecture him on the delicate balance of co-parenting. And she wouldn't be wrong to do so. Man, had he let that situation get way out of hand. But instead, as soon as he was inside, she threw herself into his arms and the dam burst.

Well, then… "You okay, sunshine?"

Inside his arms, Evie trembled like a leaf.

"You mad I got involved there?"

"Yeah, probably…" She sniffed. "But not as mad—" she hiccuped "—as I am at Dale."

"That was pretty shitty of him."

"It's been a while since he's hurled words like that at me."

He couldn't help but tense at the realization that Evie had been married to a class-A jerk. And Liam had let the opportunity to smash his face in slip away. "Hang on. He's said that to you before?"

She sighed into his chest and nodded reluctantly.

"Evie...Awww, Evie, that sucks."

She sniffed hard, and twisted away, probably looking for a tissue. He released her, but followed. He wanted to stay close.

"Do you want me to make you dinner?" *Do you want to tell me more about what that was all about?* They were having a baby together, and Evie would barely let him kiss her. Dale couldn't be more wrong about his ex-wife, but there was a story there, and Liam wanted to hear it. Not for curiosity's sake, but because he wanted to know what to expect next. Be able to anticipate future clashes and prevent them from happening at all.

Not that he'd done a very good job of preventing jack shit today.

"No, that's okay." She let out another sigh, this one stronger, steadying. "What are you doing here, anyway?"

"I was going to ask you if you are free tomorrow at nine-thirty to see a property with me."

She wrinkled her brow, wary suspicion all over her face. "Why?"

He chuckled, and moved closer. "If I said it was a giant house I wanted to move you and the boys into, what would you say?"

"That you're crazy and clearly haven't heard anything I've said." She grinned. "But that's not it, is it?"

"Nope. It's a rental property. I need something to do once we finish with the harvest." *Besides, I've got plans for your little cottage...* Yeah, he wasn't telling her that. Not yet. Maybe after a few more kisses.

"Why do you want me to look at it?"

"You know the town, you're my target demographic for tenants, and..." He left the most important point unspoken.

She understood, and the warm little smile she offered in return made him hope for a hell of a lot more than kisses.

It wasn't until later that Liam realized how many times that afternoon he thought of Evie as *his*. His woman. His partner. His life.

He wasn't sure when that happened, but he liked it. Now he just needed to get her on board. And after seeing Dale in action, he was starting to understand what he was up against.

CHAPTER THIRTEEN

After sleeping on it, Evie decided she needed to let Liam's wealth, or apparent wealth, come up on its own. He probably wouldn't mind if she told him what happened at Carrie's shop, but the more she thought about it, she had a hard time figuring out how it changed anything. Except the strong likelihood that Liam would tire of Wardham, and her. She pushed that fear away. She was doing all she could on that front. Protecting her heart, and maintaining a safe distance.

To that end, she was pleasant but decidedly un-flirty when he came over for dinner the next Wednesday, and gave him absolutely no wiggle room on staying after the boys went to bed. Connor was cool towards him anyway, and she had a fine line to walk there: disrespect wouldn't be tolerated, but the boys were allowed to have an emotional response to news that had rocked their word.

She'd told them the night before, after they'd played soccer for a bit in the backyard. Connor immediately put two and two together, and shut down. Max said he hoped the baby was a boy, so they could go camping together at the Pinery.

"That's something we do with Dad," Connor muttered.

"So?" Max looked at her in total confusion and her heart cracked in two.

"This baby has a different daddy, sweetheart." She swallowed hard against the tears rising fast.

"It's not really my brother?"

"This baby will be your brother or sister, of course. And when you guys do stuff with your daddy, this baby will be with Liam."

Connor crossed his arms and scowled. "Why does Liam get to come over for dinner once a week, but Dad doesn't?"

Ugh. "Because you guys are growing up, and you don't need to be with me all the time. When this baby is born, Liam won't be able to take him or her for overnight visits until he or she is old enough be away from me."

A thought which gutted her, but that was the bed she'd made.

"I like Liam," Max said in a quiet voice, looking at his older brother for guidance.

Connor sighed. "I like him too. But he's not my dad."

Evie gasped. "No, honey, of course not. Liam's just like Grandma or Megan's dad—a grown-up you can trust. Nothing more, okay?"

"Is he your boyfriend?"

She took a deep breath and looked her first born in the eye. "My relationship with Liam is hard to describe, Connor, but I promise, if he was my boyfriend you'd be the first person I told. Right now, he's just this baby's father."

It was probably too much, but she didn't want to baby him, either. Max had tuned out already, turning his sweet potato chunks into turrets for salmon cannons, and when Connor tossed a pea bomb onto his brother's plate, she accepted the conversation as over. For the moment.

So the next night, as she said goodnight to Liam at the door, she was relieved that the short visit had gone without incident.

"Listen," he said, turning back to look at her from halfway down the front steps. "I have some video games that I'm not using right now since my system isn't set up. Could I bring them over for the boys? I thought I should check with you first."

"Sure. Thanks for asking."

"No problem. You're the mom, I'm just the interloper." He winked.

"You picked up on that, eh?"

"Little bit. It's okay, I was expecting way worse. So, I could drop them off on Saturday?"

"Yep. We'll be home all afternoon."

"Great. I'll bring stuff for dinner, too."

"Hey!" She groaned as he chuckled and jogged to his vehicle. She wasn't sure that was a good idea at all.

So when Karen called and said she'd be in town for the weekend, and they were going to take Megan to Danny's for wings Saturday night, Evie saw an out. As she called Liam, she tamped down the pang of disappointment at the lost opportunity to spend time with him.

"You're taking the boys to a bar for dinner?" It wasn't the first thing he said, but it was uncharacteristically brusque for Liam.

"It's a pretty kid-friendly bar, particularly across the dinner hour."

"I had chicken breasts, broccoli and butternut squash to make for dinner tonight. I wasn't going to bring over pizza. And now you're going out for wings."

"Liam, are you pouting?" She couldn't keep the teasing out of her voice. So much for not flirting. "I'm sure it'll save for another day. We don't have any plans tomorrow."

"Excellent, it's a date."

"Stop it."

"What time are going to Danny's?"

Oh, no. "You can't come with us."

"It's a public place."

"That's weird!"

"Drinking beer in a bar is weird?"

"Liam!"

There was a long pause before he responded. "I can't promise that I won't show up. What if I get thirsty?"

"Drive into Essex and buy a two-four."

"I don't want a full case, I just want a pint. Maybe served

by the pretty brunette who works there."

Evie saw that coming a mile away, and still felt a stab of jealousy. Like Mari would even look at Liam twice now that the entire town probably knew he was the cause of Evie's bump. *The entire town knows...* "Liam, are you trying to protect me, somehow?"

"If you get any more flack—well, if there is any flack, we should wear it equally."

"There shouldn't be. This is none of anyone's business."

He laughed. "Sunshine, I've only been here a few months, and I already understand that's not how this town operates."

"Fine." She sighed. "We'll be there from five to seven."

"I'm looking forward to it."

"That makes one of us."

If he hadn't said he'd be there, she wouldn't have changed. Three times. She would have worn her now standard uniform of yoga pants and flowy top or a maxi dress. Just looking at her limited selection of other options made Evie wince. It wouldn't be long before she'd have to shell out for maternity clothes. She made a mental note to post a wanted ad on craigslist, and drive into Essex to visit the used clothing stores. And not the fancy consignment shop, either. She was only going to be wearing these things for five months. Her budget was strictly Goodwill.

In the end, she pulled on a pair of jeans, looping an elastic band through the button hole and over the button—a brilliant idea she read on her Mommy board—and tugged a fitted black t-shirt over top. She looked at herself critically in the mirror.

"You look fine, let's go!" Connor piped up from the doorway.

"Looking forward to seeing Megan?"

He shrugged. "Looking forward to eating wings." At her askance look, he sheepishly added, "and seeing Megan."

"That's better. Also, eating out is a big treat, right?

Watch your tone, and be appreciative."

"I am!" He swallowed his protest when she frowned, instead opting to turn on the charm. "You look nice."

"Thank you. Liam's going to be there, too." She said it casually, to test the waters, and was relieved when he shrugged.

"You should put a scarf around your neck. Or your waist! And maybe some earrings." He leaned into the hallway. "Max! Do you have your socks on yet?"

Evie did a double-take at her mini clone. Only nine, and oh so grown up. But he was right. She grabbed a pair of sparkly chandelier earrings and a matching purple scarf. She'd decide how to wear it on the way. She followed him into the living room, where Max was sitting on the couch, playing with Lego. His socks were sitting on the throw pillow next to him.

He felt her as much as saw her, a wrap of positive energy that enveloped him as he stepped into Danny's. He'd been to the bar a couple of times before, once with Ted, once for a lunch meeting with Ty West. Somehow Evie, her family and friends had transformed the bar into a family eatery with their simple presence. They were holding court at a few tables pushed together in the front window. Liam had to turn around to see them from the recessed entrance, and when he did, she was watching him. They held each other's gaze for a moment, then she quietly gestured for an empty chair on the far side of Connor. It was hard not to slip past her first, press his hands onto her shoulders and a kiss to her head. Instead, he lifted his brows in acknowledgment, then shifted his attention to her friends. He'd been at Karen's going away party, but so had a hundred other people. He imagined they knew all about him. That could go either way. But looking back at him were two friendly, open faces—Karen and Paul weren't hostile, at any rate.

Before long, they were caught up in a conversation about Toronto and Wardham, big city versus sleepy village. Karen was studying in the city for a year, and Paul was almost as new to their little town as Liam. Every so often, he caught Evie watching him with a strange look on her face, and when Max tipped over his water and Evie headed to the bar for a replacement, he seized the opportunity to join her.

"You okay?" He murmured the question under his breath as they waited for Mari to make her way down to their end of the bar.

"Mmm-hmmm. It's nice to have another adult around the table."

"Glad I'm of some use." He chuckled. "You had a funny look on your face back there at the table, when I was saying how much I like Wardham."

She sighed. "Sorry. It's just..." She waved around the simple establishment. "This is a completely different world for you. You don't miss your former life?"

"Working like crazy and paying a ridiculous mortgage on a condo I barely saw? Nope, not even a little bit."

She flushed. "I meant the rest of your life."

"Evie, I didn't have anything else in my life. The last two years have been non-stop school work. Before that, it was working like a loon to save up for school."

The pink spots on her cheeks got darker as a frown gathered between her eyes and around her mouth. "Really?"

"I dated a bit. Very sporadically."

"Annabeth Scott?" She asked the name quickly, then pinched her lips shut. "Nevermind."

"Hey, where did you...yes, sometimes with Annabeth. She's a family friend." Who he'd seen three times in the last five years, and had never been intimate with. "Just a friend, if that."

"I don't think I understand your world, Liam."

"I didn't realize my world was different than your world, Evie." The pissy response was out before he could reign it in. Before he could think about how long she'd been stewing on whatever it was she thought she knew about him.

"Then you haven't thought about it enough. Maybe I'm

right to be worried that you're just playing at all of this."

Before he could respond, Mari popped up in front of them. "What can I get you guys?"

Evie pushed Max's empty glass across the bar. "Lemon water for Max, please, and I'll take an iced green tea."

Liam leaned over and brushed his mouth against Evie's ear, ignoring how she tensed at his approach. "That's a pretty big city drink there, Evie."

She glanced up at him with a glare. "Don't make light of this."

"I'm honestly not. I just don't know what this is."

"This," she hissed. "Is me being blasted in the face with the reality that I don't know shit fuck all about you." And she spun around, heading back to her table without her drinks. Liam waited until Mari returned, then he asked for another pint of beer.

So much for not caring about Liam's life in Toronto. Damnit. Evie puffed out her cheeks in a pathetic attempt to relax, then pasted on a smile as she returned to the group.

"Mommy, you forgot my water."

"Liam'll bring it, honey," she murmured. And he would. It was her style to yell and grump and storm away. Liam would batten down the hatches and ride it out, but he wouldn't have a tantrum of his own. Good grief. She was the immature one. The realization pained her.

She listened with half an ear as Karen, Megan and Connor talked about a movie adaptation of a book they'd all enjoyed. Paul tilted his head at her in a silent question, but she shook her head. It was nothing. Just a hormonal overreaction.

Liam soon rejoined them, carrying three glasses with ease.

"You've got that trick down pat, man," Paul said as Liam sat down.

He glanced over at Evie, holding her gaze as he answered. "I bartended my way through school."

"I thought I'd heard you can't work while doing an MBA?" Paul leaned forward, bracing his forearms on the table. Evie watched as Karen lazily reached out and stroked her boyfriend's arm, dancing her fingers through the light brown hair there. As they shared a private look. If they hadn't had such a long journey to happiness, it would be sickeningly sweet. Instead, it was just…sweet. Achingly so, and Evie pushed away the pang of envy.

"You can't work full-time, that's true. And if my former company found out that I was working Saturday nights, they might have grumbled because I took a leave of absence, but you gotta do what you gotta do." He nodded to Karen. "It's a big commitment, right?"

"Totally. If I wasn't renting out my house, and mooching off this guy here on the weekends, this year would be really expensive."

"You can mooch off me anytime, baby." They kissed, and Megan and Connor made matching grossed out noises before dissolving into giggles. Max joined in belatedly, which led to another round of laughs, this time including the grownups.

The conversation faded as the wings arrived, but Evie could feel Liam's attention pinned on her as they ate, but soon there was a temporary distraction. Karen's brother Chase came in, an unwelcome arrival if her friend's low groan was any indication.

Evie glanced between brother and sister as Chase took a seat at the bar without a glance in their direction. "What's that all about?"

Paul held up his hand. "Don't get her started."

Too late. "That is my spoiled thirty-two year old brother acting like a toddler."

"Are you guys fighting?"

"Sort of." Karen lifted her shoulders defensively. "He's absolutely no fun to be around right now, and I may have told him as much. Multiple times."

Paul sighed and rubbed the back of his girlfriend's neck.

"His life has been tipped sidewise, with a heap of pain piled on top. Give him a break."

"The rest of the world is giving him all the breaks he needs. Big sister calls it like she sees it." Karen winced. "Okay, that's a bit mean. But he's just so..."

Evie didn't need Karen to finish the sentence. Her brother had been in a career-ending car accident in the summer, and from the cane he was heavily leaning on, Evie could tell he still had a long rehabilitation journey ahead of him. From an NHL All-Star to professional patient. It was quite the left turn in his life plan. Evie knew all about how that could throw someone for a loop, and she wasn't in constant agony. Didn't have metal rods in her legs or screws in her elbow.

And here she was pissed that Liam had a life before her. *Huh.*

She normally loved the lemon pepper wings at Danny's, a wonderful healthy find in the midst of a bunch of breaded and deep fried options, but tonight she wasn't tasting much. She reached for a celery stick and munched on that instead. When Max started yawning, she took the opportunity to beg off.

She hugged Paul first, then Karen. Her friend squeezed her tight, then whispered in her ear, "You giving him hell?"

Evie laughed weakly. "Maybe. It wasn't a plan or anything."

"Does he deserve it?"

"Probably not."

"Will he take it anyway?"

"Yeah." She sighed. He would. Even if he fought back, it wouldn't escalate. That wasn't his way. "It's all just...so much, you know?"

"I can imagine." Karen gave her one more tight squeeze. "Hey, a couple more months and I'm going to do my best to give your little one a playmate."

Evie sucked in a happy gasp. "Seriously? What about school?"

Karen shrugged. "One of my classmates is more pregnant than you. It'll work out. And we're not getting any younger."

Tell me about it, Evie thought. "Are you guys going to get married first?" *Do you judge me for not marrying Liam?*

"All in good time. I'm not sure how I feel about a big wedding that my mother would just take over, anyway."

"You can't go to Vegas, honey, there's no way I can leave this one, or afford to take all three of them!"

Karen laughed. "We're not going to Vegas. Although, yeah, that sounds more our style. But I wouldn't do that. It'll be here, just...I'm not sure when. Or how."

"You should have a surprise wedding." Evie said. "We should have a code word so I don't skip it in favour of a nap."

They both giggled, then Karen rubbed her chin thoughtfully. "Okay, it's a plan."

"What is?" Paul leaned in, interrupting their private conversation.

"I'll tell you later." Karen moved toward Liam and waved off his hand when he offered it, instead wrapping her arms around him. "In Wardham, friends hug goodbye."

Evie couldn't tell what Liam said in return, but it made Karen laugh. That made her smile.

There was still a lot to know about Liam, but one thing was for sure. Her friends liked him a lot more than Dale.

Liam pulled out his phone for the umpteenth time. No response from Evie. He'd texted her that night, offering to talk more if she wanted. *I'm an open book, Evie, I promise.*

Now it was Monday morning, and he wasn't sure if he would still be invited to dinner on Wednesday. He was almost desperate enough to head across the road and plead his case to her mother, even knowing that would piss off Evie.

Jeez, that would be counter-productive.

"Hey, there, boy."

Liam rolled his eyes and smothered a grin before he turned around to greet his uncle.

"Take the truck across the road and grab the fertilizer I've got stored in Claire's barn. We'll need it later this week." Ted jerked his head in the direction of Evening Lane Farm.

"How about I go muck out some stalls or something, and you do that?" He'd thought about going to see Claire. He wasn't insane enough to actually do it.

"How about you man up and go see your future mother-in-law about whatever has you looking at your phone every five minutes?"

"If she was actually my future mother-in-law, I'd have no problem manning up." Liam scrubbed his face with one hand. "Evie's not talking to me. We sort of had a fight."

"Sort of? Had?" Ted laughed. "Boy, if your woman is mad at you, you're definitely having a fight. Present tense."

"She thinks I'm going to tire of Wardham, of her, and be lured back to the big city by the fancy galas and buckets of money."

"Won't you?"

Liam jerked back, as if his uncle had punched him. "No. Hell, no. My baby's here, I'm here."

"Babies turn into kids, and kids can be annoying."

"I'm never leaving her."

"You having a baby girl?"

"What?"

"You just said you're never leaving *her*." Ted leaned back against the tractor and crossed his arms, a lazy grin crawling across his face. "That's a hell of a trick, eh?"

"Shut up, old man." But Liam grinned right back. "You want me to take the truck across the road?"

He should have known Claire would be waiting. He parked in front of her house and hopped out.

"Liam, nice of you to stop by."

"Mrs. Calhoun." He dipped his head. "Is there any fertilizer to pick up, or has my uncle sent me here strictly for a talking to?"

She laughed. "Come inside. Coffee?"

He puffed out his cheeks and followed her in to the large farmhouse kitchen. He accepted a steaming mug from her, and waited until she sat before he took his own seat at the table.

"So, Ted says you've been miserable for a couple days."

He furrowed his brow. "I wouldn't say that."

"No, you wouldn't complain." She pursed her lips. "I'm not sure that's as noble a trait as you think it is."

"I really haven't been—"

"Something you should know about my daughter," Claire continued blithely, as if he hadn't responded. "Is that she's got her own set of ignoble traits. She's quick-tempered and tends toward self-doubt."

"I don't care about the former, and I'm working on the latter." Liam set his mug down and leaned forward. "We've gone about this in a strange way, Evie and I, but you need to know that I have no reservations about her. I'm in, all the way. She just doesn't believe it yet."

"I know. But you're going about it the wrong way." She smiled a secret smile as Liam blinked at her, processing what she'd just said.

"You know?"

"Oh, honey, it's all over your face. If you were teenagers, I'd be afraid you were going to do something stupid and knock her up, but since that's already happened, I think it's safe to say that's not just lust." He winced, unable to help his childish reaction to Claire talking about him and Evie and sex, and she laughed. "I'm sorry. That's Laney's influence on me. My younger daughter has been burning up the phone lines, filling me in on everything that Evie's trying to keep to herself."

He cleared his throat. "With all due respect, and I promise you I know it's a lot...have you considered letting her have her privacy through this?"

Claire made a humming noise in the back of her throat as she looked him up and down. "You might care greatly for

Evie, but you still don't know her as well as I do. I made a mistake with her last relationship, letting her suffer in silence for far too long. And she will, you know. She'll suffer."

The thought of Evie struggling on her own pained him more than he realized was possible. He clenched his fist and rocked his knuckles back and forth slowly on the tabletop. "So what do I do?"

"Be there for her. Go to her. Let her push you away, but always go back. Become a constant she can depend on."

He looked up and held the gaze of his future mother-in-law with firm conviction. "I am, you know."

"I know." She smiled. "Give her some space, but not too much. It's a tough balance, but I have no doubt you'll find it."

He had enough doubt for both of them.

CHAPTER FOURTEEN

Another week went by. Another Wednesday dinner, but this time, Liam didn't stay long. His offer on the fourplex had been accepted, and he was working around the clock to have reno plans in place for when he took possession. Evie couldn't decide how she felt about that. Of course, it was a good thing that Liam was making noises about ties to the community, and the property had so much potential. But renovating it was going to be a ton of work. And Liam thought he could do a lot of it himself.

Earlier in the summer, she would have worried about him getting in over his head. Now that she knew—or thought she knew, she corrected herself—that he had substantial means. Well, if he decided he didn't like playing Bob the Builder, he could always hire a contractor. But what if he didn't like being a landlord? What if this all proved less fun and more work than he expected?

They hadn't had a chance to talk further. She'd had the boys all weekend, and Ted had him busy at the farm whenever he was available. Maybe this coming weekend, if he could get away. Or on the drive to the ultrasound week after next. She curved her hand over her belly as the baby fluttered around inside. No, she should invite him over sooner than that. To feel the miracle inside her, if nothing else. Baby hadn't been active at all when he'd been over for dinner, but started a marching band impersonation as soon as Liam left.

"Making life difficult for your daddy already, eh?" she whispered, but not quietly enough that Max didn't hear. He looked up from his video game and rolled his eyes at her, as only a seven-year-old can. "Mom, I don't think the baby can hear you."

She grinned at him. "Oh yeah, smarty pants? How do you know?"

"Because he's floating around in a lot of liquid, right? And when I'm in the bath, and you yell at me to get out, I can't hear you."

She rolled to her side, reaching down off the couch to tickle his side. "Then how do you know that I'm yelling at you, huh?"

He laughed, gently at first, then more hysterically as her fingers found the right spot on his ribs and wiggled back and forth. "Your face and the sound of your voice, Mommy. No! Don't! Ahhhh! Connor, help me! HELP ME!"

Connor came running, about to take a flying leap onto Evie, but then froze just before he would have launched himself into the air. She took a deep breath and pushed herself back up to a seated position. "It's okay, Con. You can play wrestle with me still."

He looked uncomfortable. "I don't want to hurt the baby."

They'd been so good after she told them. Hard to believe they shared the same DNA as Dale, except that they looked just like him. Big, strong, blond. Connor had her more delicate features, but Max was a clone of his father. Neither, though, had inherited or learned his brusque behaviour. They were silly and boisterous, but also thoughtful and considerate beyond their young years. They'd continued to have questions, Connor more than his younger brother, and they had a new suspicion of Liam which she hoped wouldn't linger. But their new normal was better than she had expected.

"How about I make us some popcorn and we watch part of a movie before bedtime?" She pushed to a stand, pausing to give her first born a quick hug on her way to the kitchen. The sounds of tussling resumed as she found a bowl and set the air popper up on the counter. Before long, both boys had joined her in the kitchen, Connor helping himself to a handful of still hot popcorn, Max carefully getting a glass from the cupboard and pouring himself a glass of water.

"You thirsty, kiddo?" He'd had a big glass of water before sitting down to play his video game.

"Mmm-hmmm. Wrestling is hard work." She watched as he chugged the refreshing liquid. He was tall and sturdy, not as lean as his brother, but no longer a little kid, either. All muscle. God, they were both going to be heartbreakers in a few short years.

They piled onto the couch, Evie in the middle. She'd like to think it was because they both wanted to cuddle with her, but she was more of a Swiss neutral ground in their constant good-natured battling. If she didn't sit between them, they wouldn't watch much of the movie, because one poke would be responded to with another, then a smelly foot would get shoved in someone's face, followed by a few well-aimed punches before it devolved into a brawl that would most definitely result in popcorn flying all over her living room. As they were both trying hard to be nice to her, they took up positions on either side of their mother.

Whatever, she'd take what she could get. She wound her arms around her boys, her baby bopping away inside her, and gave a silent word of thanks for the little moments.

The next morning, Max was hard to wake up. He stood at the toilet for a while, still half asleep, before Connor jostled him and he pulled down his pajama pants and took the world's longest pee.

"Come on, boys," she gently encouraged them from the doorway. "Remember, your dad is picking you up from school today, it's his weekend."

A chorus of affirmative noises echoed off the tiles, and she scurried off to make them breakfast.

"Mom, can I have some juice with my oatmeal?" Max propped one elbow on the table and started playing with the autumnal bowl of decorations her mom had brought over a few days earlier. He had faint dark circles under his eyes, and normally she'd say no, but maybe he was coming down with something.

"Sure, honey." She poured him a glass of mango juice and slid it across to him. Again, she watched him down it in unusual speed. "Max, are you feeling okay? Do you have a sore throat?"

"Nope. Just thirsty." He yawned.

"Okay."

Backpacks, light fall jackets, and a bottle of water for Max, by request, and they were ready to head out the door. She had an appointment at the bank before her first class, so she was heading out for the day as well, instead of coming home after school drop off. All of it made her glad that at least they wouldn't have much winter left when the baby arrived. An infant car seat would add yet another layer to the juggling act, that was for sure.

Before she forgot, she pulled out her phone and sent Dale a brief text message letting him know Max might be coming down with something.

Laney had made her promise to call after the meeting at the bank, so she did.

"They'll give me a small line of credit, so I can pay off my credit card balance, and have some wiggle room for bills if I need to cut back on classes for a while."

"I could have done the same thing for you, you know." She did, and she appreciated the offer, but… "You really want to do this on your own terms?"

"I do. Is that stupid?"

"No. A bit more expensive, maybe. Did they give you a good interest rate?"

"Yep."

"Okay, then. How's the baby? How are my nephews?"

Evie grinned. "Baby's good. Moving around more. The boys are...well, you know. They're amazing. I think Max is coming down with something, though."

"'Tis the season for colds, etc. Back to school, back to sharing germs."

"Hmmm, maybe. He says he doesn't feel sick, but he's drinking a crap ton of water, and he's been really tired lately."

"Yeah? What do you mean by lately?"

Evie barely heard the shift in tone, might not have noticed it if they weren't sisters. But Laney had just put on her doctor voice. "Uhm, I'm not sure. Why? What are you thinking?"

"Might be nothing. Remember that I'm a surgeon, and it's been seven years since I spent any time on a medicine rotation, but I think you should take him to see a doctor."

"Okay, I'll make an appointment with the clinic for early next week."

Laney hesitated for a beat. "Look, I don't want to alarm you, but I think you should see if you could get him in this afternoon. Or take him to urgent care tonight."

Evie's heartrate picked up. "Stop beating around the bush, Laney. What could this be?"

"Increased thirst and fatigue are two signs of juvenile diabetes, honey."

Heat flooded Evie's arms and legs, and she sank to the floor. "Seriously?"

"It's something that needs to be ruled out, yeah."

"Dale has them this weekend. He's going to think I'm overreacting if I ask him to take Max to urgent care." She swallowed hard. Oh god. Why couldn't she remember when he'd started sleeping more? He'd always been a tired kid, not a morning person like his brother. Hot tears slipped down her cheeks. She hadn't been paying close attention. Wouldn't have thought anything about it at all if Laney hadn't picked up on a careless, off-hand comment. Her poor baby.

"It might be nothing. Could be a growth spurt." Laney's

voice droned on in her ear, debating the merits of taking him straight into Windsor, or going to see the doctor in Wardham instead, if she could squeeze into their afternoon schedule.

"Laney? I'll call you back, okay?" She hung up without waiting for a response, and dialed Dale.

He picked up on the third ring. "Yes?"

"I'm calling about Max."

"Yeah, Evie, I got your text message."

"Well, the thing is..." *Be brave. Be strong. Be a mama bear.* "I've decided to take him to a doctor this afternoon, so you'll just be picking up Connor, most likely."

"Do you really think you should pull him out of school?"

"Yes."

His silence spoke volumes.

"I'm not asking you..."

"Yeah, I know, you don't need to do that. My weekend with them doesn't start until the end of the school day."

"I didn't mean it like that."

"Whatever. You'll keep me posted?" He didn't wait for an answer. Apparently that was catching.

Her next call was to the Wardham medical building, to see if the family medicine clinic there could fit him in. They couldn't, and after she explained her reason for calling, the receptionist put her on hold, and after a minute, Dr. Wickens came on the line. "Evie, I'm sorry we can't fit Max in, but honestly, urgent care in the city might be your best bet anyway. Take him in before the evening rush, okay?"

A quick call back to Laney reassured her she didn't need to cancel her morning classes, but she did prepare a sign that she would be closed for the afternoon. One of the many nice things about living and working in a small town—no one was coming very far for her classes, and there wasn't any competition. No one would be upset about not getting sweaty this Friday afternoon. The only damage was to her pocketbook, but there were more important things to worry about right now.

After she half-assed her way through her second lunch-hour group class, she closed up and swung past the school, stopping in at the office to sign Max out. As he wasn't expecting her, she walked down to his classroom, and took a minute to watch him through the small glass window. He sat at a desk on the far side of the room, close to the teacher's desk. *Oh, Max.* He looked tired, and she wasn't sure if it was whatever was ravaging his body right now, or the tiresome nature of sitting at a desk for most of the day.

His teacher glanced up when Evie tapped tentatively on the glass. She waved the dismissal slip in her hand, and the teacher nodded and gestured for Max's attention. He grinned, and waved goodbye to his classmates, but he didn't run to the door, just walked somewhat carefully.

"Mom!" Not Mommy, not at school. Her heart ached just a little bit at the bittersweet realization. "What are you doing here?"

She waved goodbye to his teacher and directed him to his cubby to collect his backpack. "I spoke with your aunt Laney after dropping you off this morning, and she thinks you need to see a doctor."

"Why?"

"Well, we're a bit worried that you're not well and maybe don't realize it."

"I told you, I don't have a sore throat."

"I know, sweetie." They navigated their way around a few errant rain boots that had tumbled into the center of the corridor, and out the main doors. "But I don't think you have as much energy as you usually do, either."

"Do I have to go back to school later?"

"Nope." She winked.

"Okay, then we can go to the doctor."

She laughed. As long as he thought he was in control of the decision, it was all good.

"Can we get a snack on the way?"

"Didn't you just have lunch?"

Max shrugged. "I'm still hungry."

"I probably have a Larabar in my bag, I'll look once we get in the car, okay?"

Even though he'd asked for it, Max hadn't opened the wrapper on the nut and fruit bar by the time they hit the highway, and a pang of worry shot through Evie's gut. She asked him if he needed help, and he shook his head. At some point before they arrived at the hospital, he'd quietly scarfed it down.

After navigating the parking garage, they found their way to the urgent care centre and announced themselves at the triage desk. Luck was upon them, because they weren't in the waiting room for more than a few minutes before the receptionist quietly called out Max's name and they were ushered into a nook where a nurse took his vitals and pricked his finger for a rapid blood sugar reading. Evie didn't see the number, not that it would have meant much to her, but after entering some information in the computer, the nurse turned and told them to follow her. An itch of panic crawled up the back of her neck. They'd only been to emergency a few times, but each time they'd had to wait again after being triaged. The swell of fear rose inside her again. So this was what it was like to be triaged as more urgent than others. It didn't feel great.

Through a swinging door, they were directed to a private room. Max climbed onto the gurney, then started fiddling with the opthalmoscope on the wall. Evie quietly climbed up next to him and stilled his hand, eager for the sweet contact with her little boy. He snuggled against her, and she swallowed hard to keep the worry at bay.

It didn't take long for a quick knock to come at the door and a young resident joined them. "I'm Dr. Gupta. Let me just wash my hands, then you can tell me what brings you in today…"

Evie explained her conversation with Laney, and flushed as she admitted that she really hadn't noticed anything out of the ordinary, but in hindsight, there had been some recent changes, but she couldn't pinpoint when they started. "I've been distracted lately, and Max doesn't feel sick..."

The young doctor smiled. "Okay, let's just take a quick look at you, and I'll ask some questions as we go. You mentioned increased thirst. How about your appetite, bubs?"

Max wrinkled his brow. "It's okay?"

"Mom? What do you think...has Max changed how much he's been eating lately?"

"Maybe...he asked for a snack on the way here. I thought he was maybe having a growth spurt." Evie thought back over the last few weeks. "Actually, he's been eating a fair bit more at every meal."

"And what was it that he ate on the way here?"

"A fruit and nut bar."

Dr. Gupta nodded. "Has he put on any weight with this increased consumption?"

Evie's heart pounded in her chest. "No. If anything, I was just noticing that he's losing that baby fat—"

"Mommy, I'm not a baby!"

"Nope, you're growing up fast." Evie turned to the doctor. "He's still really healthy looking, it didn't occur to me..."

"He does look healthy." The other woman pressed her hand to Evie's arm. "And we're going to do our best to keep him that way."

Evie nodded.

"I need to talk to the consultant on call, but I think we're going to admit Max for at least the night, it'll be more comfortable for him to be on the paediatric floor than here while we run some tests." Her eyes dropped to Evie's belly. "Will you be staying with him, or is there someone else that you want to call?"

Evie's breath caught in her throat. "The night?"

"Depending on what the test results are, it might be longer than that, but let's take it one day at a time."

"So you're thinking..."

"I think your sister is smart, and so are you."

They turned together to look at Max. With his big, scared eyes and brave firm chin, he looked extra little. Evie wrapped her arms around him and squeezed. "Wow, honey, I wasn't expecting that we'd have to stay in the hospital tonight, I'm sorry."

"It's okay, Mommy." One little arm wrapped around her waist from behind, gripping her hip hard enough to bely his brave words. But the other patted her belly in a sweet gesture that made her heart trip a beat.

Dr. Gupta excused herself for a moment, then returned with an older doctor, who repeated in a rapid fire instruction what the resident had already told her. Evie didn't catch his name. She knew from Laney's training that Dr. Gupta was more than capable, and really, what more was there to say? They'd tumbled down the rabbit hole. This was just the first bump.

Liam unhitched the fertilizer spreader from the back of the tractor and took a minute to stretch his aching muscles before parking the large farm vehicle in the implement shed. He chuckled as he thought of what his mother would say if she could see him covered in field dust, wearing a baseball cap. He wondered if his hair was starting to curl around the edges. Probably not. You can take the man out of the city, but it was harder to take the city routines out of the man. He wasn't really a farmer, and he'd be glad when this season was over, but man...this was honest work. Good, hard work, and he was happy to be doing it.

He'd be happier to be in town, though. Even though it was a short two minute drive in, there was something about being a long sprint from Evie that made him more comfortable. He'd like to be in the same house even more, but there was time still for that.

Glancing at his watch, he was relieved to see there was time for a shower. She hadn't invited him over, not exactly, but she texted him the night before, letting him know that the boys would be with their dad this weekend. So he'd drop by. See what might happen. Hopefully some talking, they had a lot of that still to do. Maybe some kissing. *Wishful thinking.*

But as he trotted toward the house, Claire Calhoun stepped out onto the porch, Ted's arm around her. A friendly, comforting gesture. Her face was pale, and Liam's stomach turned over.

"Claire!" He shouted her name and dashed the last few yards.

She shook her head. "Evie's fine, Liam, but she's at the hospital in Windsor. It's Max...he's being admitted for testing."

"What's wrong?"

"Evie said that they suspect juvenile diabetes."

Liam cast his mind back to grade one, when his friend Sarah was away from school for a week, and came back with a special kit she pulled out a few times a day. "He hasn't been sick?"

"Evie said if this is diabetes, they've caught it early. I asked her about symptoms and in hindsight there were some clues, but how were we to know? He wet the bed here a few weeks ago, but at home he's been waking up and going to the bathroom in the middle of the night. Evie didn't know. She feels terrible." Claire glanced up at him, and Liam felt it, too. The guilt of how distracted they'd both been. Can't be helped, but there'd be no telling Evie that.

"What do you need?"

"She needs an overnight bag packed for Max. Dale's going to meet me at her house after he picks up Connor, and take it with him to the city. I'll bring Connor back to my place for the night."

"Do you want me to stay with him so you can go to the hospital?"

She shook her head. "I heard about your run-in with Dale last week. You can't do that again, but...I need you to go to her. Dale's a good father, and this is about Max, but he's not good to her, and someone needs to protect her and the baby right now."

"She might not want me there."

Claire lifted her brow in reflection. "Maybe not, but she needs you."

CHAPTER FIFTEEN

By Sunday, Max had settled into a decent routine in the hospital. As his mood improved, that of the three adults around him grew more tense. Evie and Dale were taking turns being with their son, but Liam made sure he was there, silent and polite, but always keeping watch as the two ships passed in the night. And Dale didn't like that, it was clear.

Liam didn't care. The man had crossed a line, and Liam wasn't sure he wouldn't do it again. Wasn't going to give him a chance to test that theory, though.

Evie didn't argue his presence, but she didn't say much either. It wasn't that she was upset, just...she didn't have any time for him. She was pulling away from whatever they had been flirting around the edges of. This week wouldn't be the time to argue with her on that point, but he didn't like it. So he did what he could—he went back to Wardham to pick up Connor for a shorter visit, he found a vegan restaurant that made a variation of Evie's beloved protein bowl, and he fetched umpteen cups of tea and water for both mother and son.

Sunday night, Max told his parents he didn't need one of them to sleep with him. As they were both coming in the next day for their diabetes education session, they reluctantly agreed to leave, but not before Dale tucked a new Power Rangers action figure into bed with him and Evie peppered him with a dozen kisses. Liam stepped into the hall, letting them have their moment together. One of the paediatric ward nurses stopped and asked him if he needed anything.

"Just waiting, thanks." He flashed her a quick smile.

"Your nephew is a great little guy, he's being very brave about all the needles."

"He's not..." Wow, that was a hard one to explain. *My future child's brother? My I-wish-she-was-my-woman's son?* "I'm just a family friend, but thanks."

She smiled back, and then it hit him. She was flirting. Oh boy, was she barking up the wrong tree.

Right on cue, Evie joined him. Her eyes flashed at the cozy conversation she'd interrupted. He took a chance and reached out to rub her arm. "Ready to go?"

"Sure." She drifted past him, and he waved goodbye to the nurse.

At the elevator, Evie crossed her arms. "Sorry to drag you away."

He grinned. "You didn't."

"Is something funny?"

"Hell, no."

She let out a long sigh and jabbed her finger at the elevator button. He was glad he'd driven today, otherwise he might have found himself abandoned in the city. He wondered how this grump was going to play out. "You don't need to come in with me tomorrow."

"Sure I do."

"Dale's been well-behaved."

"Barely."

"Your presence probably isn't helping that."

The elevator car arrived. "I could care less about helping him act like a human being. That's on him. I care about you, and keeping that little bit of stress away from you and my baby if I can."

The doors closed, the car jerked, and they began their slow descent. She chewed on her lower lip, her gaze flicking up to the numbers above the door every few seconds.

"Evie, I don't want to be any kind of problem for you. But I can't sit by and not do anything when you're shouldering so much."

"The thing is, I can't repay any of that kindness, Liam."

"It's not kindness!" He didn't mean for it to sound like a shout, but it kind of did. He was getting frustrated and needed to reel it in. "It's just what I need to do."

"Why?" She spun and looked at him, a clear challenge in her eye.

"Because..." *Because you're mine.*

As if he'd said the words out loud, although he was certain he hadn't, she shook her head. "You're acting like a spouse, Liam, and we're not that."

He clenched his jaw together. He wouldn't agree, and couldn't disagree. They reached the ground floor, and walked across the lobby and out to the parking lot in silence.

She didn't speak again until he'd navigated his way onto the highway. "I can't. You understand that, right? I thought I had everything together, thought I was balancing my kids and work and life and the baby and you, but I didn't notice Max was getting sick."

He shook his head. "That's not what I've heard this weekend. I've heard doctors and nurses telling you over and over again that you caught this really early."

"It wasn't me, it was Laney. From six hundred kilometers away, over the phone, she instantly knew something was wrong."

"She's a doctor." That old feeling, like he wanted to throttle her, surged through him. It was followed immediately by its twin, the overwhelming desire to kiss her. And not just to shut her up. It had been too long since he'd tasted Evie, and it had felt like they were heading in that direction again when all of this blew up.

Evie turned and looked out the window at the dark nothing of night. After a time, she finally admitted what Liam knew had been on her mind. What he didn't want to hear her say. "He's not wrong, you know."

He twisted his fist around the steering wheel, his knuckles white, his fingers shaking. Instead of responding right away, he took a deep breath and counted backwards from ten. "Let's not have this conversation while I'm driving, okay?"

Fifteen minutes later, he pulled into her driveway, turned the car off, and hopped out, going around to her side. She started to say goodnight, but he wasn't having any of that. He held up one hand to silence her, and used the other to guide her up the stairs. Even as pissed off as he was, knowing the bullshit self-hate he was about to hear, he loved the momentary contact, the small curve of her back under his palm.

Inside, she turned on a lamp and busied herself with folding a blanket.

"You want to say that again?"

"You heard me the first time."

"You've put me in a tough spot here, Evie. I can't yell at you for being stupid when you're carrying my baby."

"So you'll wait until after I'm tied to you permanently to put me down?"

"You're already tied to me, woman!" He threw his hands up in the air. "And damn it, you're smarter than that. Don't let him get in your head."

"I'm selfish. This week proves that."

"You're owed some selfishness. The way I hear it, you've spent more than a decade giving to everyone around you."

"I let my wants interfere with my parenting."

"I don't see how." A guilty stain spread across her cheeks. "You don't have anything to be sorry about. I know that what we did had an unexpected consequence, but that was one night, four months ago. And it was the first time in a long time before that, right?"

"And since then, I've let you into our lives, gotten distracted with…with…with…" She flailed her hands between them.

"With us? The PG-13 pace at which I've been distracting you is nothing to be embarrassed about. Hell, if I knew you were feeling guilty, I'd have given you something more substantial to twirl your mind around."

She gasped and her pupils dilated.

"Is that what you want, Evie?" She set her jaw and shook her head. "Okay, but the offer is a standing one, just so you know."

"I won't take you up on it."

"I wish you would. I'll be back in the morning to take you into the city."

"You don't need to—"

"Yes, I do." He moved closer to her, and while the temptation to haul her into his arms was almost too much to bear, their next kiss had to be fully on her terms. Instead, he reached out and pressed two fingers lightly to her belly. "For better or worse, Evie Calhoun, I'm tied to you. Up to you what you do with that. But I'm here, no matter what."

The next morning, Liam knocked on the door thirty seconds after Evie turned on the living room light.

"What time did you get here?" She tossed the question over her shoulder after swinging the door open and walking away.

He followed her inside. "I thought I'd better get here early, in case you decided to head to the city without me."

"It occurred to me, yes." She narrowed her gaze. "You get that would be my right?"

"Sure."

"Liam..."

"Evie..." He echoed her exasperated tone. "I just want to be a friend." She arched one eyebrow. "Okay, that's a lie. But at the very least, I offer friendship. No matter what."

It was a quiet drive into the city. Evie couldn't think about Liam, or their relationship, and his easy calm seemed to promise that was okay.

After a quick hug and check in with Max's nurse, Evie and Dale went to the Endocrinology Clinic to meet with the diabetes care team. She asked Liam if he wanted to come along, but he waved her off, pointing to the backpack he'd brought with them that morning. "We've got boy stuff to do, don't worry about us."

Evie had been expecting a large group of specialists. She'd read about the multidisciplinary team approach to managing diabetes, but waiting for them were just two people—a medicine resident and a certified diabetes educator, who explained she was also a registered nurse. It was less of an education session and more of an exhaustive exploration of all the facets of Max's life, and where each of those points intersected with his health. Evie's apprehension was high as the topic of living in two homes came up, but Dale was well behaved and the professionals used exactly the right words to keep the conversation positive.

Afterward, Dale said he'd meet her back at the room. He wanted to swing past the cafeteria.

"Do you want something?" It was the closest he'd come to saying anything nice in months, although he'd done a good job of not saying anything at all, which for Dale was pretty kind.

"No, thanks, I'll head up to Max's room. Do you need to get back to work this afternoon?"

"Naw, I took the whole day off." He looked tired. She felt tired, to the bone, so they probably made a pretty sorry looking pair.

"We can go, let you have the afternoon with Mr. M, and then come back? I can get Connor from school and bring him in for dinner."

"Sure." He went to move away, then stopped. "Evie?"

"Yeah?"

"You serious about this guy?"

She did a double take, then paused before answering. "That's not where my head is at right now, Dale."

"He seems serious about you."

"He's a serious guy. I don't think it's me." *It's the baby*, she thought, but she wasn't going to share that with her volatile ex.

He worked his jaw back and forth for a minute, like maybe he was going to say something nice, a peace-offering, but Evie knew better. This was as much peace as they'd ever have between them.

"I'm going to head up, then." She turned and left him standing in the hall, or maybe he turned just as quickly—she didn't look back to find out.

She could hear silly laughter as she approached Max's room—a shared room, actually, but the other bed had been empty all weekend. She would have entered, but Liam's voice carried to the hall just as she reached the doorway.

"I'll ask your mom and dad."

"I'd be really careful with it," Max pleaded.

"I'm sure you would. But I don't have a six year old, so I'm not sure what's appropriate."

"I'm almost seven."

"Dude, when I first met you, I thought you were eight."

Max giggled. "No you didn't."

"Seriously. I thought, that kid has to be in grade three or four."

"If I was in grade three, you'd let me keep your iPad."

"Nope. I'd still ask your mom."

"She'll say no."

"Then the answer will be no."

"Did your mom say no a lot to you when you were growing up?" Liam didn't answer, and Evie pressed against the door frame, wondering if she'd just missed a quiet answer. After a beat, Max continued. "When I'm a grown up, I'm going to let my kids do whatever they want."

This time it was Liam that laughed. "Good luck with that."

"Grandma says technology rots the brain."

"It's a bit more complicated than that, but your Grandma is a smart lady. Too much noise in our lives is not a good thing."

"I like noise."

"I bet." Evie heard the squeak of plastic and metal as

Liam joined Max on the hospital bed. "Want to see something cool?"

Soon, a soft musical beat filled the air, and a delicate voice started reading words out loud. Evie stepped into the room and peeked around the curtain. Max was poking at a storybook on Liam's tablet, getting it to read him a book. Liam kept his eyes on Max for another moment. "After she reads it to you, you can read it back to her, and it'll record your voice."

"Cool…" Max hunkered down and propped the iPad on his legs.

Only once Max was fully settled did Liam turn and smile at Evie. "How did it go?"

She nodded. "Good. We'll meet with more of the team again tomorrow, learn how to do injections, get some nutrition counseling."

"Gotcha. Hey, can I talk to you in the hall?"

Max looked up from his story. "Mommy, he's going to ask you if I can borrow his iPad. You should say yes."

Liam held up his hands as Evie laughed. "Your call, I didn't make any promises."

"Well, how about we leave it with you for the afternoon, and I think about it?" She turned to Liam. "Dale's going to hang out here until dinner time. We can head home until then, and Connor and I will come back for the evening. I can bring it home with me if I decide that's for the best."

He arched one brow, but didn't directly answer, instead looking at Max. "See? Your mom's in charge, and she's going to be fair, right?"

"Right." Max's agreement was an afterthought as he drifted back into the game in front of him.

Liam tugged Evie out into the hall and down a ways to ensure her son wouldn't overhear, which she appreciated. "You want to come back without me tonight?"

She nodded.

"Okay. You're the boss. But if he pulls anything, says anything…will you tell me?"

Yes, she probably would. The answer surprised her, and she felt a stab of guilt at that fact. "If you want to know."

He picked up her hands and wove his fingers into hers. "You've got a problem, Evie, I'm going to want to fix it. Nothing is going to change that."

"Not even me being a bitch?" She offered a rueful smile, and he grinned in return.

"You're hardly a bitch, but yeah, not even that."

Right on cue, Dale sauntered down the hall, interrupting their moment, but he didn't say anything. Evie took a minute to follow him and say goodbye to Max, then she rejoined Liam and they headed home.

Periodically, Liam looked over, as if he wanted to start a conversation, but if he wasn't going to do it, she wasn't either. She didn't want another blow up like the night before. But there was something…reasonable about talking in the middle of the day. So when he finally talked, she listened, and shared a lot more than she meant to.

"So it really went well today? With Dale and you, in a room together?"

She laughed. "Yep. He didn't talk to me, but he wasn't rude."

"That's a pretty low standard." She could see the concern on his face. A low standard that Dale didn't always meet.

"I hurt him in the divorce, or at least, that's how he'd spin it."

"What really happened?"

She took a deep breath. "Some of that is private."

"You don't need to tell me anything you don't want to." Again, his unspoken addendum was all over his face. He wanted to be a part of her private life.

Well, this would be a good test if he could handle it. "Our sex life was…dysfunctional. And there were jealousy issues. Eventually, I got tired of being a wife in name only."

"He cheated on you?"

She blinked in surprise. "Actually, no, I really doubt that he did. If he had, it would have been easier."

"So what were you jealous about?"

"Ha. No, it wasn't me that was jealous. It was Dale, which was ironic, because he didn't really want to have sex with me, but he was convinced other people did. One particular person." Liam notched an eyebrow in silent question. Evie ripped off the bandaid. "My first really serious boyfriend, Evan. Evan West. You'll probably meet him at some point."

"Ty's brother and business partner?" Liam made an appraising face. "Yeah, I could see how Dale would be jealous of him."

"We're still friends. Not super close, but there's a bond there…" She didn't look over at Liam, didn't want to see how he was reacting. Didn't want to chicken out. This had been a crack in the foundation of her marriage, and she wouldn't let it be an issue in a relationship again. Wouldn't have a relationship where it would be an issue. "I made the mistake of telling Dale some details of our relationship that he couldn't get over. Things we'd done together." Her voice wavered, but she kept going. "Sexual things. And even though it's been a lifetime since, and Evan's come out of the closet—"

"Evan's gay?"

"Yes."

Liam slowed the car down and pulled off to the shoulder. He pressed a hand to her arm and Evie turned, looking first at his hand, then slowly lifted her gaze to meet his. "Your ex was jealous of someone you had sex with in the past, who now only has sex with men?"

She winced. "I may have told Dale that I suspected Evan still had the occasional fling with women."

"Oh." At least he didn't look disgusted. "Why did you tell him that?"

"Because he was my husband? And I thought I could safely tell him anything. Besides, they were just off-the-cuff comments. But he hung on to them, stewed over them for years, and his doubt festered between us until there was nothing else left."

"Has Evan ever hinted at still being interested in you?"

She shook her head fiercely. "No. He's definitely not. For one thing, he knows I'm a relationship type of woman, and he's pretty allergic to that variety of estrogen. For another, we've been there, and got the t-shirt. There's nothing left but platonic affection between us. He's more like a brother than anything else to me now."

"Evie, I haven't known you that long, and you don't owe me any reassurances in that area, but your ex is an idiot if he didn't trust you." Liam reached up and stroked her cheek. "I'd be jealous of him, too—Evan's far too good looking for his own good—but I'd never in million years doubt your word." He cleared his throat and turned his attention back to the road.

A few kilometers down the highway, he glanced over slyly. "I gotta admit, I'm curious about what you did with him."

She could feel herself blushing. "What if I told you he was into the whole adult baby thing, and I changed his diaper?"

He laughed. "A threesome would be hotter."

"Well, then, I guess what we did was hotter." Her cheeks flamed as she stared straight out the front window.

"Yeah?" She didn't dare turn and look at him, but the warm curiosity in his voice gave her hope. "That your idea or his?"

"Definitely his." She bit her lip. "I don't like to share."

"Dale know that?"

She nodded.

"That man is a fucking idiot."

CHAPTER SIXTEEN

Liam had been rolling the conversation with Evie around in his head for weeks. She'd been mortified to share her history with Evan. Liam had wanted to ask more about her threesome, because damn, that was hot, but he didn't want to scare her off. Evie had many sides, and only a few were anything less than pure and clean. Not that he was overly kinky or anything, but he liked sex, a lot, and appreciated women who did as well. The Evie he'd met in Toronto was totally comfortable with her wants and desires. He was starting to understand that healthy sexuality had the limit of only outside Wardham.

A ridiculous limit that Liam would do his best to show her was unnecessary. In a strange, backwards way, they were building something between them, something permanent and special. But it couldn't be hurried. He might strangle his dick before Evie came around, but he'd wait.

Wait, and think about Evie, plastered between two sweaty bodies. Two men? A man and a woman? Either image made him hard as rocks. He couldn't deny that there was a tinge of jealousy in there, but neither of them were coming into this relationship as virgins. And she'd had one wicked experience, more than a decade ago, and spent the intervening years feeling guilty for something that probably blew her mind at the time. At least, he hoped it did. God, if it didn't, he'd have to kill Evan.

Liam did some math, then chuckled to himself. When

Evie was dating Evan, he would've been too young to even be on her radar. Yeah, jealousy would be misplaced.

Now he just needed to keep some perspective. Just because she'd shared a private piece of herself didn't mean they'd made much progress. And now wasn't the time to put the pressure on. With all that was going on with Max, he needed to step back. Let Evie have some breathing room, to process everything. To see he wasn't going anywhere, but he wasn't going to push, either. Because she'd made it crystal clear that there wasn't going to be a relationship between them for a while. Not formally. Not intimately. In a different place and time, their connection would lead to something deeper, and they'd create a few fantasy memories of their own.

Jesus, they'd already done that in a single night.

But Evie's life, right here and now, couldn't accommodate Liam as anything other than father-to-be. He should be grateful she was as open as she could be on that front. *Was* grateful. Really.

He'd been playing it cool for three weeks, while she got settled in a new routine with Max at home, school and at Dale's house. That last point was especially tough for Evie, trusting her ex-husband to monitor Max's blood sugar levels as closely as she did. The first night the boys spent at their dad's, Liam had almost gotten in his car three times to go to her.

But that wasn't what she wanted. She could ask. He'd made it clear he'd be whatever she needed, whenever she needed it. And she wanted him to be a friend, a co-parent, and nothing more.

The *nothing more* was going to be a challenge today.

He pulled up in front of her house, not bothering to turn into the drive because she was already trotting down the steps. They were both excited. It was time for the twenty-week anatomy scan ultrasound, and Evie had it on good authority that the clinic they were going to would show them the goods, so to speak.

"You ready to meet your baby?" Evie hopped into his SUV, grinning from ear to ear.

He laughed and resisted the urge to reach across the center console and pat her belly. "You betcha."

At the clinic in Essex, Evie was escorted back to an exam room first. She'd warned him about this, how the tech would take all the pictures first before inviting any support people back to have a look. Forty minutes slowly twisted past, his nervous energy ramping up with each passing tick of the clock. There were a few other people in the waiting room, but no one made eye contact. He pulled out his cell phone for a bit, but he couldn't concentrate on his stock reports or any emails he was drafting. He picked up a prenatal magazine, but nothing in it was new information.

By the time the technician popped her out into the waiting room and called his name, he was a ball of tension. Good, excited tension. Stressed, worried tension. A small taste of parenthood, probably.

Inside the room, Evie was all smiles. *All good?* He mouthed the question at her, and she nodded. The tech pointed to a chair next to Evie's head. "Dad, you can have a seat there." She swiveled a screen in their direction, immune to the impact her casual use of the title had on him. *Holy shit.* "Okay, Mom here says you would like to know the gender, is that right?"

He bobbed his head. Words were impossible right now, as the grey blur on the screen shifted and re-focused on a face.

A face. With a delicate nose, and a round forehead, a wiggling chin and moving lips.

He leaned in, only vaguely aware that he was crowding Evie. From the slight tilt of her forehead, pressing into his cheek, she didn't mind.

"Here's the profile, and if we wait just a minute...yes, there we go. That's your baby, sucking on its thumb."

Evie's hand found his and squeezed. "Wonderful, isn't it?" she whispered.

He nodded, and didn't give a damn that his eyes felt suspiciously wet.

The tech showed them the major organs, and helped them count ten toes. They tried to count fingers, but that tiny little fist next to the even tinier little mouth wouldn't budge.

And then it was time for the big reveal. "Here are the legs," the tech said. "And if baby shifts just a little, there we go…"

"What are we looking for?" Evie asked.

"Well, with this one, it's what we're looking for and not seeing." The tech smiled. "Remember that this isn't one hundred percent, but this baby looks like a girl."

A girl. Damn, now those wet eyes were leaking. Liam cleared his throat. "We're having a daughter?"

"Looks like it. The radiologist will have a look at the pictures I took earlier and confirm with your doctor or midwife."

"Can we have a picture to take home? Of her face, maybe?"

"Of course. I'll print you a couple." She flipped to a different screen of saved images and selected a few, which scrolled out of a small printer in short order. "We also have a DVD available for fifteen dollars, if you are interested."

He already had his credit card out of his wallet. The tech laughed and told him he could pay at the reception.

A girl. Evie couldn't quite believe it. She rubbed her tummy as Liam collected their DVD, then leaned against his shoulder as he guided her back out into the bright October afternoon. The leaves, in full autumnal splendour, provided a colourful backdrop that echoed the joy in her heart quite perfectly.

"Oh, Liam, that was amazing!" she said, twirling twice on the sidewalk as they headed back to his car. "And the boys are going to have a little sister!"

He grinned. "You wanna talk about names?"

"Mmmm, maybe." She threw her hands into the air and hooted. "I'm having a girl!"

She would have been happy either way. Boys were what she knew, and another brother would have been fun, especially for Max. But there was something about a little girl, the future promise of mother/daughter outings and secret sharing. Evie had a wonderful relationship with her own mother and sister, and she looked forward to building that female bond with this little one. "You, sir, are brilliant." She was being silly and giddy, and didn't care. "A DVD! I never would have shelled out the money for it, but now we can watch it over and over again."

His grin softened to an indulgent smile, and her heart ached for how complicated she'd made everything. "That's the plan, sunshine."

"Liam..." She stepped closer, and his smile dropped, but the warmth in his eyes didn't budge. She licked her lips. "We made a little girl."

"We did." His voice, rough and raw, tore the last shred of her self-consciousness to bits, and she pressed her body into his. He wrapped his arms around her waist, tipping her back slightly to make room for her belly against his lean, strong middle.

"Your life has changed so much," she whispered, afraid her voice might crack if she spoke any louder.

"You think today isn't worth all of that?" He shook his head, his face solemn. He didn't look like a Boy Wonder any more. Hadn't for a while, she realized. When did that happen? How did she miss it?

"I don't know." She didn't know what was in his past, actually. That hopping thought led her into a warren of worries, though, and today wasn't the day for worries. She stretched onto the tips of her toes, and though he froze for a second, Liam let her brush her lips across his.

What was it about this baby that made her want to kiss him? What was it about herself that drew the line there? She was an idiot. The arms that held her shook with restraint.

The lips that kissed her promised the world. And she'd pushed him away. No more of that. She slid the tip of her tongue across his lower lip, and with a groan, he let her in. She poured everything she wanted to say into an eager kiss, long and sweet and deep, and it wasn't long before those strong arms had twisted up and down her back, one tangled in her hair, the other curved dangerously low on her hip.

Another groan, this one a bittersweet acknowledgment that they should stop while they were still decent. Liam eased her away from his body, but not too far. He tightened his grip on the back of her neck for just a moment, then pulled her face into his chest.

"I didn't need to see her to know that this is worth the world, Evie." He kissed her hair. "There's nothing I wouldn't give for her. And she's not even born yet."

She breathed him in. His shirts smelled different of late, like laundry soap instead of…"Liam, can I ask you a stupid question?"

His chest vibrated against her cheek. "Sure."

"Did you used to get all of your clothes laundered at the dry cleaners?"

"Why?"

"Just a guess."

"You're a smart girl." He cleared his throat. "I don't anymore."

"I know. You smell like Tide."

"Ted buys it."

"I like it."

"I'll never use anything else."

She curled a secret smile into his newly plebian garment. "Do you want to come over for dinner tonight?"

"Why?"

"It's Wednesday? We missed you last week."

He rubbed his thumb lightly along her cheekbone, then up her temple. With a groan, he wove his entire hand into her hair and tipped her head back, kissing her brow. "I can't, Evie. It's best if we stick to baby appointments for a while."

She couldn't read the expression on his face, but it wasn't good. "What's going on?"

He frowned, lips drawn tight together, holding back words he didn't want to let spill out. Words she probably didn't want to hear, but he'd never held back before.

"The boys miss you." She was grasping at straws. "I miss you, too. And today was so wonderful."

His lips softened, and then the sweetness returned to his eyes. "It really was. Don't worry about me, I'm not going anywhere."

"But—"

"No buts, Evie. I've got some stuff I've gotta take care of, and you need time and space to figure out what you want. When you're ready, I'm here."

What if she was ready now?

If you have to ask... Damn him for being smart. And she couldn't argue. He was giving her what she wanted, a respectful co-parenting relationship without any complications. But she couldn't help but feel like she'd lost something important.

CHAPTER SEVENTEEN

He'd put off this phone call long enough. Liam looked at the ultrasound image he'd tucked into the inside cover of his project binder and took a deep breath. He could do this.

His mother answered on the second ring. "William, I was starting to think you'd lost your phone."

"Mother." They both hated those names. But as long as she insisted on calling him by his father's name, she wasn't getting the warm and fuzzy back.

"How is your little adventure going?"

"I've sold my condo, and bought an investment property here."

She sighed. He knew what she was going to say next. McIntoshes didn't sell property that would increase in value, that was foolish. "It was such a good investment. You should have asked your father—"

"That's not going to happen."

"I don't understand this feud, William. He's a very generous man."

"That's not why I called, Mother. I have some other news that I'd like to share with you."

"Do tell."

"I'm going to be a father. In February."

Over the telephone line, he could hear a tick of a grandfather clock. She was sitting in her favourite chair in the library. A slight rustle of silky fabric. And then she sighed. "There are some questions I have, of course, but I wouldn't want to be indelicate..."

"Oh, go ahead. Be indelicate." He huffed a humourless laugh. "You want to know if I'm sure it's mine? How much this will cost the family?"

"I was thinking more along the lines of when did you find out and when will the wedding be, but yes, those are good questions as well." She sighed again. She was an expert at that. "Maybe you should connect with a lawyer?"

"I don't need a lawyer."

"Don't be foolish, William. There's nothing romantic about—"

"About what? Being saddled with the responsibility of a child for eighteen years?" He snorted. "Just what would you know about that?"

"There's no call to be rude."

She was right. Not to her, at least. His father had some decidedly evil tendencies, but Amelia McIntosh had never done anything worse than care too much about what certain segments of society thought. "My apologies. Truly, I'm sorry. I didn't call to get into a quarrel, Mother. I just wanted to inform you of my news. Happy news, I assure you."

"Well, thank you. Will you and the mother-to-be come for Thanksgiving or Christmas?"

"Probably not, no." There was no chance he was exposing Evie to his father. She'd run screaming in the other direction.

"Can I tell your father that you called?"

"Knock yourself out. I mean, yes, please do."

"Are you keeping yourself busy there?"

"I'm helping Ted on the farm. Renovating this property I bought. Spending time with..."

"Yes, what is this young woman's name?" Liam didn't answer, and his mother sighed. "Is she from Wardham?"

"She is." He deliberately only answered the second question. He wouldn't be surprised if his father already knew all about Evie. It would be just like him to hire a private investigator to keep tabs on Liam. If he hadn't already, he definitely would after this call, but he wasn't making it easy for the old man.

"Well, if you're happy..." She trailed off, like there was still significant doubt in her mind that was possible in what she would surely think of as a godforsaken little backwater.

"I am." He cleared his throat. "I didn't just find out, Mother. It's taken some time to make this call."

"I probably owe you some sort of apology for that?"

"We're past apologies."

She laughed softly, a sad sound. "So like your father."

Liam closed his eyes. That was a direct hit. "I have to go."

"I understand. Please keep me up-to-date. I do check my email, you know."

After hanging up, Liam picked up the ultrasound picture. The soft paper curled in his hand. They should sell hard plastic sleeves to protect the delicate images from freaked-out first time parents, Liam thought, then laughed. Hell, they should sell the same thing for newborns. *Holy fuck.* He was going to have a baby. Soon. Evie would know what to do, but when she was tired? He'd watched some YouTube videos, a series of soothing strategies that ironically all started with s. But those dads were *there*. All the time. Not across town in a half-renovated house. And he couldn't bring the baby here, anyway. Evie wanted to breastfeed. She'd stressed how important it was that visits work around that.

Hands shaking, Liam set the ultrasound image down. Damn. They were still stuck in that co-parenting nonsense that wasn't nonsense, but it wasn't right for *them*. Nineteen weeks to go.

Time to get serious. On multiple tracks. His unit was almost ready to move into. He'd call the moving company and arrange for his belongings to be delivered. He'd set up a home here, even if he knew in his heart it was a sham apartment he had no intention of living in for very long. He had his eyes on a tiny cottage a few blocks away.

With that vision warming his heart, he pulled out his phone and snapped a picture of the ultrasound image, careful to cut Evie's name out of the shot at the top. Before he could second guess the charitable gesture, he sent in attached to a brief email to his mother. **Meet your granddaughter. She'll be accepting visitors in March**.

When Evie arrived at work the Thursday before Thanksgiving, there was an Essex Telecom van sitting at the curb. As she unlocked, a man climbed out carrying a toolbox.

"You work at the Pilates studio?" he asked.

"Yes, it's my business. Is there a problem with the phone line?"

"No, ma'am. I'm here to upgrade your service."

"I didn't order anything?"

He handed over a work order sheet. "Internet installation."

"I really didn't…" Liam. She sighed. "Can you hang on a second?"

She left the confused man outside and called her apparent benefactor. He picked up on the first ring. "Evie!"

"Don't 'Evie' me, you know why I'm calling."

"I really don't, sunshine, but it's nice to hear your voice."

"Did you order internet for my studio?"

"Oh, that. I thought the install was next week, I was going to tell you…"

"Liam! I can't afford that."

"It's a gift."

"You can't gift my business anything, it's…"

He laughed. "Did you send the man away? I bet that's going to cost double to get him to come back."

"No, he's waiting outside."

"Let him in. This is a little thing I can do for you."

"The dishes is a little thing."

"I'll do those, too." He sighed. "Think about it as something for the baby. In case you need to look up something for her while at work."

That was a stretch. She glanced out the window. It would be nice... "Fine. But I owe you one. Many, actually."

"I love the sound of that."

The installation took an hour, and afterward she called and invited him to Thanksgiving at her mom's. She told him he could bring Ted, but she stressed that she wanted him to come.

Liam slid the bottles of wine and the jar of spiced pumpkin seeds into his backpack, next to the book of Thanksgiving Mad Libs for the boys. He should be nervous, but instead a quiet optimism filled his being. She wanted him there, as part of her family.

Claire was bustling around the kitchen when he arrived, thirty seconds after his uncle. She pointed to the living room, where he could hear the boys arguing over the rules to something. He left Ted and the wine with their hostess, and headed in the direction of his woman.

They were crowded around the coffee table, working on a puzzle. Evie was rubbing Max's back, maybe keeping him focused on the task, or soothing him after whatever altercation Liam had just missed. Connor was examining the loose pieces with a fierce focus.

Underneath Liam's foot, the floor creaked, and Evie glanced up. Her lips curled and her eyes crinkled as a smile spread across her face, and he thought his heart might just explode.

Dude, you've turned into a sap was warring with *dude, look at her*. Sexy, caring, sweet.

"Liam!" Max abandoned the puzzle and jumped up. "Want to see my new alert bracelet?"

"Heck ya."

"It's orange!" Max shook his wrist back and forth rapidly in front of Liam's face.

"What happened to the camo one?"

"Grandma didn't like it, so she got me this one for

Thanksgiving. It matches my winter coat, so it's cool."

"Awesome. Now you've got two."

"Three. Remember? That ugly metal one, too?" The seven-year-old looked askance at the idea that Liam had dropped such an important detail from his memory.

"But you haven't worn it since you got the other one...is it still in rotation?"

"Only for e-merg-en-cies." Max used his hands in the air to help drag out the word.

"Ah. Hey, how's the puzzle going?"

"Puzzles are stup—"

"Max!" Evie frowned, and Liam had to fight to keep a neutral expression on his face.

"Oh, right. Bad word. I mean, puzzles are not my kind of thing."

"I like puzzles, but you know what I like even more?"

"What?"

"Mad Libs." Liam pulled the book out of his bag and before long Connor had joined them on the couch. Once they got settled and Connor had taken over filling in the words, he left them to their silly giggles and moved over to help Evie with the puzzle.

She watched him place up a few pieces, then reached out and tapped his hand. "Come on." She led him up the stairs to a bedroom. "That was nice, with the boys."

"I didn't do it to be nice. I saw it and thought it would be fun." He pressed the door shut. "Also fun, by the way, is being alone with you in a room with a bed."

She laughed, and pulled him in for a hug.

"Sorry, I couldn't resist." He pressed a kiss to the top of her head. "Happy Thanksgiving."

"You, too." She found his hand and pressed it to the side of her belly, where a hard, pointy ball was wriggling around. "Your daughter wanted to say hi."

He tugged up Evie's shirt, keeping his eyes on hers to make sure she was okay with the contact, and slowly smoothed his hand over the growing bump. She softened against him, and he was hard-pressed not to keep touching, higher and lower, until she melted.

"Evie..." he muttered her name, his face pressed into her hair, and as she shifted, her thigh found contact with his hard-on.

"Oh!"

"Yeah." He cleared his throat. "Sorry."

She tipped her head up to look at him, lips parted, eyes hooded, and he knew he could kiss her. Maybe even do more, but their family was downstairs and until she asked for it, he wasn't going to press his luck.

"Don't be sorry," she whispered. "I'm the one who should be sorry."

"You don't have anything to apologize for, Evie. We're getting there, don't you think?"

She nodded, and he brushed his mouth against hers as he gave their baby one last pat.

"Come on. I can't wait to discover what combination of seeds and beans you've convinced your mother to serve instead of stuffing and gravy."

"Hey!" She playfully shoved him out the door. "I'll have you know, we're having seeds, beans, stuffing *and* gravy. It's a veritable feast!"

"Can't wait."

While Evie and Max did his pre-meal blood sugar check and insulin shot, Liam helped Claire carry dishes to the table. And it was a feast, with a large turkey, mashed potatoes, sweet potato casserole, wild rice with cashews, apricots and cranberries, green beans, stuffing, squash and gravy. Even though none of them overindulged, they all felt decidedly nappy afterward. Evie cuddled with the boys for a bit on the couch, watching football and making up answers to their questions about the rules, but when Liam joined them, with answers that sounded real, she took her leave.

"I'm going to go help my mom with the last of the dishes, okay?" she asked Liam. He waved her off, and resumed his explanation of a fair catch kick to Connor.

In the kitchen, she put the last slice of pumpkin pie into a small container, stuck it in the fridge, then picked up a dish towel and started drying the plates. At the sink, her mother was humming quietly.

"You really don't mind not having a dishwasher?" Evie shook her head. "I can't wait until I have one again."

Claire smiled. "There were some lean years when you girls were young, years during which we didn't run the furnace very often, and the hot dishwater was something I looked forward to at the end of the day."

"Mom?" Evie couldn't believe what she'd just heard. She'd always thought of her parents' farm as very successful.

"Mmm?"

"Mom. You just told me you couldn't afford heating oil when I was little."

"So?"

"So…. I'm not sure. That feels significant."

"I haven't thought about it in a long time." Claire paused and looked at Evie. "I guess I'm grateful for that period of struggle. I give thanks for it."

"Are you trying to teach me something through this story?" Evie opened the cupboard to her right and placed the stack of dried plates in their spot.

"I think I'm losing my touch in my old age."

"Hardly. Are you trying to give me hope that things will get easier, or reprimand me for wearing some sort of hair shirt?"

Claire chuckled. "Probably the latter, but I wouldn't use the word reprimand. Struggling is one thing, sweetheart. Refusing opportunity is another."

"I don't think—"

"Of course not."

Evie thumped her tea towel on the counter and glowered at her mother. "Don't interrupt me like I'm a mindless teenager!"

"You weren't mindless then, and you aren't now. But

you've got a good thing in there, Evie. What's stopping you?"

She didn't have an answer for that, not right away, and as they tidied up, the thoughts that came to her weren't ones she could share with her mother.

Liam helped her carry a bag of leftovers to the car, and while the boys buckled up, she turned and pressed her hand against his chest. It was cold, but he wasn't wearing a coat, and through his dress shirt, she could feel the flex of his muscles.

"Thank you," she whispered.

"Sleep tight tonight, sunshine." He pressed a quick kiss to her temple and opened her door for her.

But once the boys were asleep, and after she'd spent a few hours reading and online, she gave up on rest and reached for her phone. It only took three false starts before she completely dialed his number.

He picked up right away, but his voice was thick with sleep. "Evie, is everything okay?"

"Yes. I just wanted to hear your voice."

"Yeah?" She could hear rustling as he sat up in bed. "That all?"

"Is that okay?"

"Absolutely." The affirmation rolled over her, low, warm and sexy, and she wasn't sure if she wanted to laugh or cry, but all of a sudden she was overwhelmed with feelings.

"Today was nice." It was an inane conversation starter at one in the morning, but she didn't actually have anything to say. She just wanted...

"Mmm-hmm." He waited for her to say something else, but that was all she had. She was an idiot. After a long silence, he cleared his throat. "Hey, do you...do you want me to come over for a bit? I could be gone before the boys wake up."

Yes! "No, not tonight."

"Maybe sometime soon?"

Hell, yes. "I think so, yeah."

"Okay, we can work with that. Are you having trouble sleeping?"

For so many reasons. "Uh-huh."

"Tuck into bed, I'll tell you a bedtime story." And from across town, his voice seeped under her skin and wrapped itself around her heart. His words themselves were dry. He told her about an engineering project he worked on with a mildly entertaining group of co-workers, but it was just what she needed, and she slowly unwound. When she yawned, he promised he didn't take offense, and told her to close her eyes and count sheep.

"I will. Thanks for this."

"Sunshine, I wish you'd call me more often." As it so often did, his voice held an edge to it, one sharpened by something that felt suspiciously like love held at bay. "And Evie…"

She didn't know if she wanted him to finish that sentence. *Yes, you do.* It was time to stop lying to herself.

"The next time you call me in the middle of the night, your voice full of longing and ache…I'm not going to ask if you want me to come over. I'll just come over. Because I hate this, being away from you. Knowing there's a side of your bed that could have my name on it, if you'd stop worrying about what anyone would think. The next time you call me in the middle of the night, I'm not going to worry about your rules, because I know that deep down, you think they suck too."

"I'm getting there. I miss you." It was ridiculous to realize that now, on a day when they'd spent hours together.

"I miss you, too. How about I bring muffins over for the boys tomorrow and have a brief visit after school?"

He meant it in the nicest of ways, but his constant giving and her not being able to reciprocate in the way he deserved…it wasn't fair. She needed to get her act together.

CHAPTER EIGHTEEN

He thought they'd turned a corner at Thanksgiving, but the next two weeks went by with no more late night phone calls and very little flirting. They had another midwife's appointment, and held hands on the drive there and back, talked a bit about names, but nothing more than a chaste kiss passed between them. Well, not *nothing*. He was pretty sure the currents were live and arcing with overloaded x-rated thoughts on both sides. Evie kept blushing when she thought he couldn't see her. After dinner with the boys one night, he was helping Connor with his science homework, and he noticed Evie's reflection in the large mirror on the wall beside the table. She was standing in the archway between the living room and the small hallway to the two bedrooms, watching them, want all over her face. He almost excused himself, ready to push her into her bedroom and kiss her senseless, when Max needed help reaching his toothpaste and the moment was gone.

But Evie wasn't wasting his time, or her own. She was thinking, trying to get her head clear, and he liked wherever her thoughts were heading. And in the interim, they were doing things together, without limit or restraint. Not the clothing-optional things he really wanted to do, but regular almost-coupley things. Good in a different way things. The weekend before Halloween, she asked him to provide his geeky expertise in helping her build a clone trooper costume for Max, and after he spent the morning painting the downstairs unit, now fully separated from his own apartment, he headed to her place, armed with his iPad and two Star Wars reference books. He had five others, but he didn't need her to know that until they were living together.

She answered the door in a cut-off pair of jean shorts and a plaid shirt over a tank top. He allowed himself an internal groan as his cock came to life. Damn, why did she have to be so hot all the time?

"Hey!" She was out of breath, which he stupidly also found sexy, even though it probably meant she was working too hard. "You've arrived just in time to save the storm trooper from my destructive fingers."

"Storm trooper or clone trooper?" He lifted the reference books and grinned. "It's an important distinction."

"Oh, crap! I don't know. I'll call Max and find out."

"He's not here?"

"No, they're at Dale's for the night." She glanced back over her shoulder. "Did I not tell you this was just going to be the two of us?"

Just the two of us. Blood pulsed south at those magic words. "You failed to mention that. Good thing I like you." He winked, slid past her, put his stuff on the table, and took off his jacket. Then he took his time rolling up his cuffs, enjoying the way Evie watched with hunger as he revealed his forearms.

Why wouldn't she just kiss him?

Because she doesn't think she should. Something was still holding her back. He nodded for her to lead the way, and followed her to the boys' bedroom, where she had white cardboard, duct tape, markers and a glue gun set out. He passed her his cell phone and she called Dale's house. Max confirmed it was in fact a clone trooper that he wanted to be, and Liam set about cutting and curving and shaping cardboard pieces until they had a helmet and a breastplate to wear over white sweats Evie had already sourced.

She clapped and cheered when he finished, which made

him feel like Superman, and he didn't even blink when she offered him one of her protein bowls for dinner.

She dished out the colourful spoonfuls of lentils mixed with couscous, spinach, red pepper, tomato, garlic, onion and a creamy dressing that he suspected was made of lemons and ground up seeds, but he didn't care because it was freaking delicious.

"I'm surprised you didn't push for pizza after working so hard this afternoon," she said.

"Maybe I want to be on your good side tonight." He shot her a heated glance. He wasn't going to push her. He didn't think. But damn, he wanted to. He wanted to slide that plaid shirt slowly off her body, and cover the revealed bare skin with his hands and mouth and body.

She blushed. "Would it shock you if I said I thought we should slow things down?"

His mind screeched to a halt. *Oh, for fuck's sake.* Slow down from their already glacial pace? "Maybe, yeah. Why?"

"There's still a lot I want to know about you."

"Okay." It really wasn't, but she had him over a barrel.

"And I think...maybe it's my pregnancy hormones, or something, but you've got the wrong idea about me."

His jaw twitched. "Evie, don't do this."

She swallowed hard. "I know I'm sending mixed messages, and I don't mean to."

"You're not sending them to me, sweetheart. You're sending them to yourself."

"What do you think is going to happen between us?"

"Clearly nothing. But a guy's gotta have an impossible fantasy."

"I'm no fantasy."

"You keep telling yourself that, sunshine." Damn. He didn't want to be mad. He didn't want to be chippy and bitter, but enough was enough.

Evie tried not to think about what that fantasy might be. She chewed the last few bites of her dinner carefully, then carried her bowl to the kitchen sink and washed it out. She returned to the table, grabbed her glass, and repeated the action.

Liam smirked as she returned once again, and when she silently gestured at his bowl, he held up his hands in surrender. She grabbed both his bowl and his glass, to avoid being laughed at *again*, and after cleaning and drying all of the dishes, she paced back and forth in the kitchen. Inside her tummy, Liam's daughter took great delight at her mother's activity and started doing her own acrobatics.

She was playing with fire, but hell, she'd already been burnt. And it was Liam. If she could trust anyone, it was him, even if she'd pushed and pulled and pushed more than was fair. Her pulse picked up. Could she? She took a deep breath and turned around, only to find him standing in the doorway. Liam in her kitchen was becoming a regular occurrence.

"Okay, tell me."

He narrowed his gaze, like he wasn't expecting that to be her tack. "Tell you what?"

"What's your impossible fantasy?"

"Evie, you don't want to do this."

"Don't tell me what I want." Even as the words were spilling out of her mouth, she knew they were the wrong choice.

His lips twitched, and he shifted his shoulders back and forth. "Then how can I tell you my fantasy?"

This was a dangerous game. And she didn't care. She leveled him with an even glare and adopted her best couldn't-care-less attitude. "We need to get this out into the open and deal with it. Tell me what you want, I'll tell you how it won't happen, and we can move on."

His jaw twitched. "And what, just be friends?"

She nodded, then shook her head. "No. Not just friends...but for the next while. Until..." She puffed out her cheeks. "Damnit, Liam, I don't know, but you make me want things that I know will just break my heart in the end."

"You want *me* to tell *you* that I want you underneath me, naked in my bed." He stood up straighter and crossed his arms. "That I want you to give me control for a night, let me lick, suck, fuck you into oblivion." His bicep flexed under his tight t-shirt and she shivered. "That I want you wet and ready for me to make you come, over and over again, all night long. That's what you want to hear?"

Every part of her was wound tight. Most of it was anxiety, but at her very core, she knew she was aroused. She closed her eyes and took a deep breath. "Right. See, that's my point. Liam, I'm not that kind of woman." It sounded thin even to her own ears. She flushed. "I'm not interested in meaningless sex."

He fisted his hands in front of his face and groaned. Evie swallowed hard and stood firm, even as he advanced toward her. His face was unreadable. "Sunshine, when you spit out a lie and a truth at the same time, it makes this very complicated."

She shook her head. "I'm not lying."

He stopped a foot away. She could feel tension rolling off his body in hot waves. "Yes, you are. But I'll ignore that, because I lied too."

She huffed a burst of air instead of asking. He was going to tell her anyway.

"That's a pretty awesome fantasy, and yes, I want all of that. Particularly the part about you being naked. That features front and center in all of my fantasies right now. But my impossible fantasy? The one that tortures me? That's where you finally admit that I'm your man. Where I'm sleeping in your bed, not one night, but every night. Where you don't give up any control, where you tell me exactly what you want, where you want it and how many times."

It took Evie a few seconds to absorb it, and then she backed up a step, hitting the wall. "Oh."

Liam closed the gap between them, pressing his thighs hard against hers, but being as careful as always around her belly. "So. That was my honesty. Now let's deal with yours."

She closed her eyes. One word, and this could end. All she had to do was tell him no, and he'd back off. She rolled the word over in her head, willing it to spill out of her mouth. It didn't.

"Truth. You're not interested in meaningless sex. Lie. You're not that kind of woman. You absolutely are. You are hot, inside and out. You are made brick by brick of passion and desire, and you long for a safe partner with whom you can share a really—" he slid his hands down her thighs, to where her shorts met soft, warm skin, and curved his hands around to cup her legs just beneath her bottom "—hard—" with a jerk, he lifted her up and ground his erection into her core "—fuck."

An unholy noise, halfway between a moan and a sob, ripped forth from her chest. "Oh, Liam," she whispered, her body in a desperate race against her mind.

He buried his face in her neck. "I want all of you, Evie. Your passion. Your faith that I'll always be there for you. Your softness and your fire."

"What if I'm never able to trust you with my heart?" She wrapped her arms around his head, running her hands through his short hair, breathing in the scent of his unmistakably expensive shampoo. Traced her fingers along the fine cotton of his tailored shirt. Pressed a hand to one side of his face, then eased her feet to the ground and reached up with the other hand, holding his gaze. "We come from two impossibly different worlds. What if I never believe that this could be all that you want?"

"I'm here, aren't I?" He looked down at her, desire still rolling off of him.

"I know I'm being awful to you. I do. I'm sorry." Her voice petered into a pathetic whisper.

He groaned and dropped his head gently onto hers for a minute. "You're not. It's okay."

"You're not the only one who's frustrated right now, I promise."

"I get that, sweetheart." He dipped his head lower still

and brushed his mouth against her ear. "I can smell how frustrated you are."

She gasped and jerked backward, thumping into the wall, but that just gave his mouth a bit of room to play against her jaw. He kissed her slowly and with deliberate intent, raining a slowing patter of affection across her face, finishing at her lips.

"Lest you get all weird about that, I promise, it's a good thing."

"God, Liam, what are you doing?" She gripped his head in her hands and mock shook it from side to side.

"I'm trying to show you what you mean to me. What you *are* to me." He exhaled heavily. "My life was nothing before you, Evie Calhoun."

"It was something. That's what's holding me back. You seem too good to be true, maybe because you don't share anything. Good or bad, I want to know about it."

"My old life…it was empty steps in a sad direction."

"I don't know what that means," she whispered, pulling his face back to her neck. She stroked her fingers through his hair, the spiky ends of the short crop at the base of his skull teasing her nerve endings.

"I don't want you to know. I don't want any part of that world bothering you."

"God, you make it sound like you were in the mob." She froze. "You weren't, were you?"

He laughed without humour. "God, that would be easy. I told you once, I'm an open book. But it's not a story I like."

"You're running away."

"No, I'm running toward you, Evie. From the very first taste, I've wanted more of you. I came here because of you."

"Tell me what you've given up."

"Nothing."

"A career."

"I'm building a new one here, with my bare hands." He pulled away, replacing the physical presence of his body with a fierce gaze.

She licked her lips, ignoring the flare of heat in response, and steeled herself to continue. "Events with red carpets."

"Never my scene." He laced his fingers into hers and tugged, stepping backwards into the living room.

"Google says otherwise."

He laughed. "Don't believe everything you read on the internet."

"Pictures, Liam!"

"Fine." He pulled her onto the couch, settling her between his legs. She resisted for a second, but his chest was warm and inviting, and he *was* opening up. Sort of. "You want more?"

She nodded.

He took a deep breath, and told her about the unexpected dinner guests and awkward introductions at parties. From the moment he started working, his mother had wanted him married to someone she approved of. Someone just like herself. Liam couldn't imagine a more awful future, a life built around china patterns and political fundraisers. Enter Annabeth, and her unexpectedly honest appraisal of the matchmaking.

"My mother introduced us at a meet and greet with the local member of parliament, and the first moment we were alone, she leaned over and whispered, 'Do you think your mother has any idea that I'm a giant lesbian?'" He chuckled at the memory.

"What?" Evie pressed herself upright, needing to see his face. "Seriously? That beautiful woman in the pictures?"

"Beautiful women are allowed to love women. In fact, I think it should be encouraged." He winked, and she groaned.

"I didn't mean that! Of course she can love whomever she wants. But you really weren't a couple? You look so...intimate."

"Evie." His voice was stern, but his eyes were warm. "Sunshine, this is intimate. You and me, right here. That was just play acting. I was probably quoting The Simpsons in her ear."

"So you were her cover, and she was yours?"

"Nothing that formal, but yes. I let my mother think we were dating. Annabeth was dating a woman who couldn't come out...I don't know the details. I wasn't lying when I said we weren't close. It turned out that her cousin and I went to school together, and our parents know each other, but other than those few times I accompanied her to events, we never spent any time together."

"Okay, so I was wrong about the red carpet." She took a deep breath. "Your Wikipedia page says that you walked away from a trust fund."

He didn't move a muscle, just looked at her for a few long moments. She thought it was possible that her heart might just pound its way out of her chest.

"Don't believe everything I read?"

"No." He slowly sounded it out, dragging out the *oh*. "That part is sort of true. I have a Wikipedia page?"

"Don't you ever Google yourself? It's all Carrie's fault, she started it." Evie knew she was beet red and stammering.

"No, I don't."

"But you have all the gadgets and what not!"

"And I'm not a megalomaniac! I barely visit Facebook. I use the internet for trading stocks and playing Settlers of Catan, not preening over myself like a peacock on steroids."

She couldn't help herself from laughing at the subtle admission of geekiness in the middle of his self-righteous response. "Seriously, Settlers?"

"Seriously. Evie, what else does my Wiki page say?"

"That you attended Upper Canada College, then the University of Toronto, and Rotman School of Business. You chose not to participate in the family business, and rumour has it, you recently walked away from a trust fund that was tied to a condition of employment."

"All true."

"You quit your job to come to Wardham."

He shrugged. "Something like that."

"You came here because of me."

"Finally, you believe me."

"You quit your job for a second date."

"And a third and fourth." He kissed the top of her head. "I also quit my job because I didn't like it. I had other options and I exercised them."

"Liam..." She twisted around on the couch, perching on her hands and knees over his body. She glared at him. "Just how much money did you give up for me?"

"That's a terribly personal question, don't you—"

"Argh! Liam!" She glared at him and he laughed.

"Okay, settle down." He tried to tug her into a hug, but her belly got in the way. "Woman, turn around again, please." He manhandled her back into his preferred position, where he could hold her with one arm and touch the baby with the other. "I don't know exactly how much money. A lot. But I don't need it, and I don't want it. It comes with strings a mile long."

"You have a Wikipedia page." She closed her eyes and sighed. "That's just so far out of my realm of comprehension."

"It's probably just a stub."

"I don't have a stub, Liam! No one in Wardham has a stub."

He snorted. "I'm pretty sure Evan has a full page, and you had no problem falling in love with him."

Evan wasn't rich when they dated, but that wasn't the point. "I didn't love him, not like..."

He waited for her to finish the sentence, but when she didn't, he pressed on. "So that's a requirement of love, that your man be a nobody?"

"No." She pressed her hand to his chest. He needed to slow down, so she could think. "Stop pushing me."

"But you loved Dale." The humour had disappeared from his voice, and there was a hard edge she didn't like.

With some effort, she pushed herself up and stood. "Stop it."

"We can talk about me, but not you?" He stood too, and crossed his arms.

"What? No, of course we can talk about me. That's what started this whole conversation, wasn't it?" She shook her head. "I married Dale, yes, and I divorced him, too. But he's the father of my—"

"So am I, Evie!" Liam's raised voice stopped her dead in her tracks. She stared at him. "And I'm not going anywhere. I didn't pause my life in Toronto, I left it behind. Completely. I don't live in another world, I share this one with you. So if one of these days you want to admit you love me, that would be grand."

Of course she loved him. How could he not know that? "Liam—"

But he was too far gone, too worked up to notice she was trying to placate him. Or maybe she wasn't very good at projecting a calm, rational vibe.

Liam stalked past her to the door. With his hand on the doorknob, he paused and shook his head, then looked at her. The hurt on his face cut her to her core. "Evan was a selfish bastard who hung on to you for too long and used you to figure himself out. Dale broke your faith in yourself. Sunshine, you've got terrible taste in men."

If this was a fight with Dale, she'd have snapped out a pithy response, something like *tell me about it* or *present company included*, but Liam didn't deserve that. And it wasn't true. He was mad, but he was still so good it made her heart ache.

So instead, she offered a simple plea. "Please don't go."

"I'm not going far, Evie. You let me know when you want me to come back."

CHAPTER NINETEEN

It took her two days to call, even though she wanted him to come back that night. First she called her mother, and asked Claire to pick the boys up from school. She didn't have any evening classes on Monday, because it was usually one of her nights with the boys, so she was home by three in the afternoon. She'd been thinking about it all day. Days, really. And still her hands shook.

When he answered, his voice made her knees wobble. Time to get real. She was loony for him.

"I vaguely remember being a reasonable, rational person."

He laughed. "Hi, Evie."

"I'm calling you."

"I see that."

"Want to come over?"

"For dinner?"

"Sure. The boys are at my mom's for the evening."

He didn't say anything, just hung up the phone, and seven minutes later, he walked in her front door.

"I'm a pain in the ass," she said as he stalked towards her.

"Shut up. You're gorgeous."

"That's about to change. The last few months of pregnancy aren't glamorous, you know. And then there's the postpartum period..."

"I know, I've done the reading." He pulled her into his arms, and it took all of her effort to not moan.

"It'll probably be next summer before I'm feeling like myself again. And even then, I'll still be nursing."

Liam's eyes lit up. "So the boobs will stick around for a while?"

"Hey!" She wiggled her arms free and crossed them over her chest, a much more challenging task than it would have been a few months earlier. Truth was, she liked her pregnancy and nursing breasts better, too, but she wasn't one for surgery, so the regular, little—

"Hey, yourself, sunshine. I was just teasing you." He dropped his gaze to her chest for a moment, and when it returned to her face, it was full of naked heat. "I loved your breasts when we were first together. I like them now, even though they're terribly off-limits to me. And I'm sure I'd be all over them next year if you ever wanted to…"

Heat pulsed between her legs and tickled up her chest. Her already heavy breasts throbbed at the thought of his nimble fingers stroking and plucking, teasing her with more than just his words. "Wanted to what?" she whispered.

He just stared at her for a minute, then cleared his throat twice. *Hell*, she realized. *He's turned on, too.* The thought of Liam's growing erection pushed her over the edge. "Like I said, it's going to be a long time until I'm back to my old self. And as you have tried to convince me, more than once……"

"Evie, are you giving me a green light here?"

She swallowed hard. "Yes?"

"You need to be sure. Any more concerns about me?"

"I don't think—"

"Yep, let's stick with that. No more thinking for today, okay?" He wove one hand into her hair, cupping the back of her neck, tilting her head just right so he could press a searing kiss to her mouth. The other hand stroked down her side, skating along the edge of her belly, then her hip, before curving around to her ever-expanding ass.

She closed her eyes. She'd been thinking about the wrong things. What she'd say, how he'd react. She hadn't considered the logistics of actually getting naked together. She didn't look anything like the woman Liam slept with in May. She hadn't shaved in a few days, and if he got under her clothes, he'd discover the most unattractive maternity bra and panties possible. She pulled her lips free, gasping. "Maybe I should hop in the shower quickly."

"No more thinking." He nibbled his way down her throat. "We're about to get really sweaty, we can shower together after."

"I'm not prepared…"

"We don't need a condom, do we?"

"Not that kind of—" She groaned as his tongue swirled at the base of her neck.

"Evie?" He growled her name into her throat at the same time as he pressed his erection into the swell of her belly. "Stop. Thinking. I want you so much it physically hurts. I don't care if you need a shower. I've only had one night of you, and it's not enough. You're giving me this, please believe me when I tell you it's what I want. All of it. You, pregnant, unexpected afternoon sex."

"My underwear is hideous."

"Let's take it off."

"Underneath it…I haven't shaved or anything…"

He stopped and pulled back, breathing hard. Between them, she could still feel the hard length of his cock. "Are you uncomfortable with this?"

She winced. "A little."

"Because of me?"

She shook her head. "Of course not."

"Do you believe that I want you?" As if to underline the point, his cock twitched, and she laughed. He smiled and dipped his head to kiss her gently. As his lips teased hers, soft and sweet and nothing like the devouring he'd just promised, she wanted to cry out. Beg for the passion. But she didn't need to, because he quickly deepened the kiss, his hunger equaling hers. He wound her up good and tight before groaning into her mouth and breaking it off again.

"God, Evie, tell me this is going to happen."

"Can we turn out the lights?"

"Not a chance in hell." He pulled back, laced his fingers into hers, and pulled her through the living room and into her bedroom. He shucked off his t-shirt, loosened his belt, and pushed his jeans to the floor.

She watched him for a moment, then moved to the window, closing the blinds halfway. "A compromise," she whispered as he joined her, touching her gently along her collarbone and around the back of her neck.

"Genius." His voice hitched a little, and she reminded herself that he'd given her no reason to be self-conscious. And before they started stripping, she'd really wanted to do this. Now that he'd removed most of his clothes, she really wanted to do *him*. Maybe she could find a way to have sex with most of her clothes on.

But this was Liam. *Liam*. With his magic fingers and *trust-me* eyes. And Lord help her, but she did. Furry bikini-line and all. And she knew what would make it all okay. "Kiss me, okay? Just kiss me, and keep kissing me until I pass out."

"I thought you'd never ask." He cupped her face in his hands and brought them together, noses brushing gently as lips touched and tongues teased, more his than hers at first, but as his desire wore down her defenses, she surged into the kiss and gave as good as she got.

As she wound her arms around his neck, Liam pushed her pants off and guided them to the bed, where they lay side by side, legs entwined, and kissed some more. Evie couldn't think straight, let alone keep track of Liam's hands, so she didn't register that he had rucked up her shirt until his thumb dusted over her nipple and made her gasp.

"Is this okay?" His question was muffled against her mouth, because he'd honoured her request and was still keeping her dizzy with kisses. Her answer was a groan as she fumbled to yank off her t-shirt, getting it caught up between their faces.

A laugh vibrated through his chest, but it wrapped her in warmth. Oh how she'd missed this, the press of his hard body against hers. Their night together had fueled many fantasies over the past six months, but they all paled in comparison to the real thing. She whipped her maternity bra across the room—even if Liam wasn't offended by it, she wanted to be naked with him.

"Can I look at you?" His determination to stay within her comfort zones completely undid her, and her eyes filled with tears. "Oh, holy shit, Evie, don't cry!" He pressed his forehead against hers, their entire world reduced to the faint space between their faces. "Hey, what is it?"

She wiggled her head from side to side. "Just…you. I've been so hard on you, and you've been nothing but good to me."

His lips quirked. "I have an idea of how you can make it up to me."

She sucked in a breath. "Name your price."

"Let me look at you." This time, it wasn't a request. It was a suggestion, a dare, a taunt full of love. *Take a leap, Evie*, he said with his eyes.

Good lord, she thought. *How do I do this?* All of her seductive abilities were rooted in dance, in being slim and lithe and impressively flexible. Su*ck it up, buttercup. What do you have going for you right now?* Between them, Liam's hand still cupped her breast, and that gave her an idea. She pressed her hand against his chest, pressing him back against the bed. His gaze immediately filled the space between them, hungrily taking in her temporary breasts and below them, the ever-increasing curve of their baby.

He looked back up at her, his eyelids heavy and his pupils dark. "I should spank you for withholding all of this from me."

He'd done that in his shower, that night, and the memory of how much it had turned her on made her squirm next to him. "Maybe you should."

"Maybe we should work on you trusting me with your

body first," he whispered, reaching up to stroke her bare skin. "You've changed so much. It's amazing."

"It doesn't feel amazing, it feels big and swollen and uncomfortable."

"Then let me tell you what I see." Evie watched in amazement as the perfect male specimen beside her started listing all the parts of her pregnant body that she hated, in the most beautiful of terms. "Your breasts are gorgeous, like a marble bust." He traced one finger over the blue veins highlighting her pale skin there. "A road map to heaven, right here." With a twist, he had her on her back, and he hovered above her, his lips dancing over first one nipple, than the other. "These are fucking gorgeous, too. Dark and big and delicious." She shivered. "Are they more sensitive?"

He gently pulled one into his mouth and they both moaned. He nudged her legs open with one knee, and she ground herself against his thigh. "I'll take as a yes. So, where was I…"

"I get the idea." Evie writhed under the cage of Liam's taut body, searching for more definitive contact with the erection she could feel nudging her inner thigh.

He chuckled and shifted his stance to use both of his knees to press her legs further apart. "I'm just getting started." He sat back on his heels, running his hands down her torso. "Although having you wiggle like that…it's almost as good as begging."

"I'm pretty horny, Liam, I'm not above begging." His lips curled in a knowing smile. "What?"

"I love you like this, all feisty and turned on. Much better than uncertain and doubtful." He rested his hands on her hips, as if he hadn't just used the l-word so casually, and squeezed the soft flesh there. "You're lush and glowing, Evie. You're beautiful when you aren't pregnant, strong and fit, but your body was built to make babies, too." His fingers looped into the waistband of her underwear, already low on her hips, and tugged. She tilted her hips to help, and as he stripped the last barriers between them, she left her legs spread wide. He didn't disappoint, running his hands up from her ankles, all the way to the juncture of her thighs. He cupped her sex in his palm as he climbed back up her body, rocking gently over her clitoris. "You're making my baby, Evie. That's amazing."

"Who would've thought that the last time we did this, that would've happened, huh?"

He stilled for a second, holding her gaze, then slowly dropped to his side, pulling her on top of him. This she could still do, Evie thought with confidence. She took his cock in hand, enjoying the shudder that wracked Liam's body as she stroked him a few times. He stroked his hands up and down her thighs, then reached around her busy hands to get closer to her sex. "Do we need a condom today?"

She shook her head. They'd both been tested in the first trimester, and she trusted Liam. He hadn't been with anyone else since then.

She rose off the cradle of his hips enough to give him access to line them up, sex to sex. A sensation of completion rocked over her as the hard, smooth head of Liam's cock glided through her wet folds. She pressed down, inviting him into her body. Into her soul.

"This is how it should have been, that night." Liam's grip on her hips tightened as she rolled them back and forth, relishing the edge between pleasure and pain as her body stretched to accommodate Liam's girth. He gritted his teeth and made a barely restrained noise as she slowly rose up on her thighs again, beginning to ride him.

"Just you and me, no condom?" Evie shivered. "Yeah, I like that." She licked her lips and looked down at Liam. He was watching her with the same heat she'd seen that first night.

"Not just that. It shouldn't have been a single night." *This won't be a single afternoon.* Evie couldn't disagree with either sentiment.

"It was all I had room in my life for," she whispered, the

conversation fading as the feelings—gorgeous, carnal, uninhibited feelings—took over. She started to moan, quietly at first and then louder, as with each rise and fall, Liam nudged against that spot inside her that made her want to do this all the time.

"That's it, sunshine. Come on me." Liam's thumb found the side of her clitoris, and gently started rolling up and over and back again, tweaking her approach to her orgasm like an air-traffic controller. Calm, cool, collected.

"Come with me, Liam. I want you to come inside me." The words spilled out in a breathless squeak as she rode him faster and faster, chasing nirvana.

"I will. Next one. I need to see this first. You're so fucking beautiful. Come on, sunshine. That's it. God, you're such a good girl, so fucking sexy. You make me so hard, do you feel that? Come for me, then I'm going to flip you over and fuck you so hard you'll—" Liam's chain of dirty talk pushed her over the edge. Heat and hormones flooded her body, sending little twitches skittering down her extremities and making it impossible to think, or speak, or probably see, although she wasn't going to open her eyes just yet to test that theory.

She sucked in a breath, then another, her whole body desperate for new oxygen. She'd probably held her breath for the last minute of that...that...

"That was awesome." Liam's arms wrapped around her as he rolled her somewhat awkwardly to her side. She had a vague thought about him still needing to come, but it drifted away as he stroked her arms and legs, entwining them once again. They weren't done, just taking a break.

"You feel incredible, inside and out," he murmured.

"And you know all the words to make me melt." She fluttered her eyes open for a moment, long enough to see a reassuring grin on his face.

"And make you come."

"And that." A soft smile played across her face, and she gave in to the joy. "I liked it all."

"I'm glad. I remembered that working for you the first time, but I wasn't sure…" He drifted off, leaving the question hanging. Up to her to pick it up or not.

"Before you, it would have only been a drunken thing for me."

"That's too bad."

She couldn't agree more. "You really don't think it's…slutty?"

He started laughing, gently at first, then harder, until he was shaking against her. "You ask that like it's a bad thing, Evie!" He sighed deeply and pulled her face into his chest. "I hate to bring him into this moment, but when you ask questions like that, I want to punch Dale in the face. And anyone else who gave you the impression that you shouldn't get off however you want to."

"You like it?"

"I love it. Bring on slutty Evie."

"Even with a baby on the way?"

"You know, I never thought I'd have a pregnancy fetish, but this works for me." He rocked against her.

"What else works for you?" She took a deep breath. "You said some things the other night, but I wasn't sure how much was the truth and how much you were just trying to get a rise out of me." She'd been afraid to think too much about it, if she was being honest. "I wouldn't want to do anything to freak you out."

"Evie, if you do something that freaks me out, I'll just tell you that doesn't work for me. And I hope you do the same. But if you want, we can talk about what we do like, sure. That sounds kinda hot."

She nodded, too embarrassed to respond out loud.

"Okay. I like the idea of sex outside." He glanced at the window. "In the summer, so you're safe today."

"Have you ever done that before?"

"Had balcony sex once, that was fun. But never truly in nature. Some things work just as a fantasy, you know."

"Yeah?"

"Yeah. The thought of you and me, sneaking onto the beach in the middle of the night. Rolling around on the sand, kissing, touching, grinding against each other..." As he started telling her about his fantasy, he kissed his way down her neck to her collarbone. "And then I'd pick you up and toss you into the water. You'd stand up, all righteous and proud, pissed off that I got your dress wet—"

"I'm wearing a dress?"

"Not for long. But then you surprise me, and instead of storming out of the water, you pull your dress over your head and toss it back onto the beach. Then you turn around, your body outlined in the moon light, your breasts bouncing and swaying like a hypnotist's watch, and you dive in, swimming out to deeper waters."

"And what do you do?" Evie was breathless and aching between her legs again.

"I pull my clothes off and follow you. Do I look like an idiot? And when I catch you, you wrap your legs around me and I push inside you." Liam shifted his body, aligning his hips, and entered her in a quick, smooth thrust. "Fuck, Evie..."

"Yes, fuck Evie," she whispered, and he groaned. "You like the dirty talk, too."

"Coming from your mouth, you bet I do."

"My mouth does other things, too." She pushed herself up on her elbows. The belly between them changed the missionary position into a bit of a challenge, but she still wanted to kiss him. Needed his mouth, and his breath. His eyes, hovering close enough to reassure her that this wasn't a dream.

"This is how it should have been," he muttered, snaking one hand behind her neck, using the other to brace himself as he surged into her. "When I made you pregnant, this is how it should have been. I should have known I was giving you my seed."

And with that unexpected pronouncement, Liam exploded, and Evie went with him.

CHAPTER TWENTY

They'd had a brief nap together that afternoon, then separate showers, and he'd sent her a sweet dreams text that night, but Evie hadn't spoken to him since.

Of course, it had only been thirty-six hours, but Liam was pretty sure he'd fucked something up. So he was working up the courage to call her, and using hanging drywall as an excuse to put it off for another hour, when his doorbell rang. He wasn't in his own unit, but next door, so by the time he'd finished securing the sheet he was holding to the wall and set down the screw gun, Evie was standing in the doorway.

"Hey." He wanted to grab her up in his arms, kiss her hard enough to make her dizzy and forget any concerns she might have. But he held himself back, at least physically. He couldn't help but let his gaze rake over her body, dressed in snug black yoga wear.

"Hey. I'm sorry I didn't call yesterday, Max had a little episode and we had to go to Windsor."

"You should have called me. About that, I mean, not about us. I could have—"

She shook her head. "No, really, it was fine. And you're way behind schedule here."

"He's okay?"

"He's fine. They warned us that we'd end up at Emerg sometimes, and really, if he was older, we probably could have dealt with it at home. His blood sugar levels came back up and we were home in time for bedtime."

"Where was he when it happened?"

"At school."

He crossed the room and pulled her into his arms. "Fuck, that's scary, eh?"

"Yeah." She wrapped her arms around his waist. "Maybe I should have called you yesterday. I needed a hug."

He tightened his grip. He never wanted to let her go. This was agony, because after they'd made love again, he thought that's where they were, but if she didn't think of him when she needed support...

"Liam..." If she told him to back off, he was going to have a tantrum, he didn't care how immature she thought that might be.

"Yeah?"

"You're not wearing a shirt."

That was true. He'd gotten warm while working. Hope, and something else, stirred inside him. "I took it off."

"And you've got quite a nice toolbelt..."

He glanced down, taking in her bright eyes. How she was nibbling on her lower lip. Fuck him. "Evie, do you have a construction worker fantasy, by any chance?"

"Little bit."

"How much time do you have?"

"Not much."

He could do a lot of things in not much time. If he put his mind to it.

"But that's not...That's not why I came here." She reached up and pulled his head down to hers, giving him a lingering, promising kiss. "And it's not going to happen. Not today, although..."

"Yeah." He was going to wear the toolbelt every day until she jumped him. "Okay, we'll save that for another afternoon."

She rubbed her hand across his chest, leaving a trail of goosebumps in her wake. "Soon, I promise. Before I get too uncomfortable to care."

"I like the sound of soon."

Evie took a step back before she molested him, and got back to the point of her visit. "I've got an hour break before my next class, thought you might want to go for a walk, grab a coffee."

"Be seen with you in public?"

She offered a sweet smile. "Sure, why not?"

"People might get the wrong idea about us."

"I don't care what people think, Liam. I truly don't. I may have in the past, or maybe that was just my heart being silly, but I'm just…it's *me* that's complicated, okay?"

"I don't think you are, not really." He slung his toolbelt over a nearby ladder, grabbed his jacket and put it on before pulling her close for a hug. "No more than me, anyway."

She didn't get a chance to think about that before he was herding her out the door. The air had a decided nip to it, and when Liam wove his fingers through hers, she didn't resist. Warm and strong, with rough callouses that reminded her of his gentle touches, his hand felt exactly right wrapped around hers. Her resistance had melted, and it didn't flood her with panic. She nudged her shoulder into Liam's arm, and he flashed her a smile. "This is nice. Rustling leaves, cool breeze, going for a walk together." Not wanting to be left out, the baby jabbed her in the cervix, and Evie winced.

Liam immediately stopped and took her in his arms. "You okay?"

"Mmm." She half-groaned, half-nodded. "Just some baby movements hurt more than others."

"Anything I can do?"

She shook her head, and they resumed walking. "Want to talk about names?"

"I was thinking Claire would be a good middle name."

"My mom would like that." Evie stumbled to a stop again. "Oh god, Liam. I don't know what your mother's name is!"

He shrugged. "Amelia, but we won't be using it."

The disquiet any mention of his parents caused was something that Evie would have a hard time getting used to. She believed him that there was nothing to talk about there, but it was so far from her realm of understanding that she literally tripped up on it from time to time. But as long as she refused to talk about their relationship, she could hardly press him to talk about his family. "Okay, what about first names?"

"I have some thoughts, but do you have any names you wanted to use with either of the boys?"

"Maya was my girl name for Connor, and Anna for Max, but I'd feel funny *re-using* one of those, if that makes sense." Evie smiled. "I have tossed up Lexi and Becca, what do you think?"

He winced. "I like Anna better than either of those. I want my daughter to have a name that she could be Prime Minister with."

"Hey! I can see a Prime Minister Lexi McIntosh!" He didn't say anything for a minute, and when she glanced over, he was wearing the biggest shit-eating grin she'd ever seen, bigger than at the ultrasound. "You like the sound of that, eh?"

He laughed, a big sound from the depths of his belly. "All but the Lexi part, yeah. You don't want to give her your last name?"

She nodded. "I will, as a middle name."

"You didn't change your name when you got married?"

"No, not really. I answered to Mrs. Simmons at the school and church picnics, but my driver's license stayed Evie Calhoun the whole time." She glanced over to gauge his reaction, but he wasn't looking at her, he was staring straight ahead.

They were almost to the main street when he quietly said under his breath, "Would you ever change your name?"

She didn't answer right away, although it wasn't because she needed time to consider her response. She didn't, but she didn't want to hurt his feelings, either. "No…it's just not who I am, ya know? Why...would you want me to?"

"Careful there, Evie. That's getting dangerously close to a serious talk." He tugged her close and wrapped his arm around her shoulders. "I'd like to dress you head to toe in McIntosh plaid and slap a Property of Liam bumper sticker on your gorgeous ass. Yeah, I'd *want* you to change your name if we got married. I'd also want to keep you naked and in my bed, making more babies. But that's just the product of our culture. You can tell me to cram it and that won't change how I feel about you."

"You're something else, you know that, Liam? I..." The main intersection of Wardham wasn't the place to have this conversation, but it needed to happen soon. "Let's go grab a hot chocolate and argue some more about names."

He squeezed her hand. "You sure? Nothing more that needed to be said there?"

"It's just that I appreciate you, more than you know." She swallowed hard. What she wanted to tell him deserved to be front and center, a main stage production. Followed by a very private celebration.

He shot her a quizzical look, then nodded. "Okay. Off we go."

There was a line inside Bun, but Liam pushed Evie toward one of the bar stools. "Save us a spot, I'll get us drinks."

"I said hot chocolate but I really want—"

"Carrie's *Mother's Tea* blend." It smelled like moldy hay, how could he forget it? But it made her happy, and if she wanted him to, Liam would drink it himself. Maybe with a heaping spoonful of honey. "How about an oat bar with it?"

"Wow, you've been paying attention." She smiled up at him. If only that smile meant more than appreciation. He tamped down that bitterness. The rest would come in time. For now, he needed to appreciate a bit more himself. That they were finally dating, or whatever this was. *Exactly what you asked of her.* And now that he had it, he wanted more. He wanted her heart, and not at some point in the future. Now. Ungrateful bastard.

He paid the part-timer at the counter for their drinks, then turned to join Evie, but she wasn't alone anymore. She had her arms wrapped around a man who was whispering something in her ear. Were all the men of Wardham giants? Liam had never felt small before he moved to the sleepy village. He stretched to the full extent of his six feet and took a deep breath. He didn't have any right to get upset about her hugging a friend, not even one with whom she had an intimate history. Because that's all that it was—history.

"Liam!" She turned toward him, flushed and glowing. "Look who I found. This is Evan. Ev, this is Liam."

The other man extended his hand. Liam recognized his grip as practiced, professional. Smooth, like his smile. But his eyes crinkled as he looked back at Evie, and there was no challenge in his posture. "Nice to meet you. Evie's told me…well, not a lot, but what she's said has been good."

"Same. Except she's told me a lot."

Evan lifted his eyebrows in surprise. *That's right, dude. I know all about you and I'm not threatened, either.* Liam could lie with the best of them. At the moment, he was feeling a bit threatened, but not really by Evan. By the weeks ticking by, the impending arrival of their baby, and the fact they were just starting to date now. "Good, then. And you've met with Ty a few times."

Liam slid a glance in Evie's direction before responding. "Hopefully I can help you guys out with your expansion next year."

"That would be great. And you guys will come out to the winery for New Year's Eve?"

Evie shook her head. "Probably not this year, Ev." She tugged Liam closer and leaned her head against his chest, and he fought back a stupid grin. "I think we might stay in."

Evan pulled out his phone and shot off a quick text message before nodding. "Well, hopefully we'll catch up again real soon. Nice to meet you, Liam."

As her ex-boyfriend dodged his way through the line of customers, Evie snaked her arms around Liam's waist. "You're going to help them out, eh?"

"I might be useful to them."

"You're useful to me."

"That so?"

"Mmm-hmmm. Want to come over tonight and we can talk more about that?"

"Hell, yes."

From the other side of the raised bar, Carrie cleared her throat. He looked up, expecting a chastisement, but she was beaming at them. "I'd ask if you two need a room, but I'm seven months too late, aren't I?"

Evie screeched her friend's name, and Liam hooted with laughter. God, he loved this town. Had it really been seven months since he caught sight of Evie on that barstool and lost his mind? Or found it, maybe? She'd changed his life so much, and she had no idea.

He didn't want to rush into the next proposal, but it was time to go ring shopping. So he'd be prepared, when the time was right.

CHAPTER TWENTY-ONE

"What are you doing here?" Evie looked at Karen with suspicion.

Her friend shrugged out of her winter coat, still coated with fat, fluffy flakes. "I come to classes from time to time."

"Only when you want to gossip."

"So sue me, I don't have the grocery store mainline option anymore. Anyway, today I'm really here for Stella."

Evie grinned. Her unexpected disciple was teaching her first set of classes today, and as an early Christmas present, they'd made them free to the community. "She's going to rock this. She might look meek and mild, but underneath that innocent farm girl exterior is the spirit of a jailhouse guard."

Karen glanced to the door. "Too late for me to leave?"

"Don't even think about it."

They laid out their mats at the back of the room. Evie wanted to stay out of Stella's way as much as possible. Eighteen other people joined them, including Carrie and Mari, Eleanor Nixon, and Beth Stewart, the marketing manager at Go West Winery, who waved at Karen.

"Is Beth a friend of Stella's?" Evie asked.

"I don't think so," said Karen. "She's closer to our age."

"She's never come out before. That's awesome, I'm going to say hi." Evie did a loop of the room to greet people, ending at Beth's mat. "Welcome to our studio, Beth!"

"Thank you. Karen was raving about the classes, and I've been doing a ton of overtime lately, so I thought I'd reward myself with an extra-long lunch hour."

"Good, you should do that more often. I can hook you up with a multi-class pass at a great discount."

Beth smiled. "No wonder this place is such a success, you really know what you're doing."

"That's high praise, coming from you. I hope you enjoy Stella's class."

Evie padded back to her mat as Stella clapped twice and introduced herself. She outlined what the goals were for the session, reminded everyone that it wasn't a competition with anyone but themselves, and promised to get them all sweaty. Everyone smiled at that except Karen.

"You could sneak out, you know." Evie whispered. "I'd judge you, but no one else would."

Karen laughed as they rolled backwards onto their mats. "I've got my reasons for being here."

Evie bit back a retort about exercise needing to be a constant part of one's daily life. She was just a student today, time to turn it off. "That was nice, my little chat with Beth just then."

"Mmmm?" Karen pulled one knee against her chest and stretched, then the other, half listening to Evie as they followed Stella's directions.

"She didn't comment on the giant belly or talk about the pregnancy at all. It was just business. I'm not getting a lot of that lately."

"That's because business talk is boring."

"Says the woman who is dying to get knocked up."

Karen grinned. "It's so much fun trying."

"This is a place of business, let's keep it clean, okay?" Evie stuck her tongue out at her friend. "So how do you know Beth?"

"Oh, you know, the winery."

They moved into leg lifts, and Evie reached for a pillow she used to alter some of the conditioning exercises to be more pregnancy-friendly.

Karen dropped her legs to the mat. "I was out there yesterday, talking to her about New Year's Eve."

"Bah. New Year's Eve. Who in their right mind wants to stay up until midnight?"

A stricken look dropped onto Karen's face. "Not you?"

"Not any pregnant woman, honey. Bed time is nine thirty, if I'm lucky."

"Even with Liam, you know…?"

She laughed. "Poor guy. We finally start dating, and it turns out that his girlfriend isn't up for much after the kids go to bed." She lowered her voice. "The afternoon sex makes up for that, though."

"So even though you're getting bigger, it's still…good?"

Evie nodded. "It's different, but still good. Great, actually." She breathed through the next set of exercises. "The way Paul looks at you, I'm sure you'll be boinking like bunnies right up until your due date."

"Well, I'm not pregnant yet. And actually…you're serious about not coming out on New Year's Eve?"

"Yes. Why?"

Karen muttered something between heavy breaths, but Evie didn't catch it.

"What?" She pressed the stretch a little deeper.

"Vegas."

Evie let out a wheezing laugh. "No, if I'm not willing to drive the ten minutes to the winery, I'm definitely not going to Vegas. I don't even think I can fly right now."

"No, not Vegas. *Vegas*."

Evie looked at her friend like she was insane. "What are you talking about?" Vegas. When was the last time they'd talked about that? A flashback to a wing night at Danny's in September brought a dawning realization. She whipped her head around to her friend. "Really?"

"It's a secret."

"We didn't even make a code word!"

"I didn't know I'd need one, this just sort of happened."

"You excited?"

Karen grinned. "Uh huh."

"Does Carrie know?" Evie glanced at their friend on the other side of the room.

"I told her this morning, I need her to bake a cake."

"So this secret…"

"Probably won't last long, but I hope it does. I had to tell Chase, because otherwise there would be no way he'd show up, and Audrey because if I didn't let her help me pick out my dress, she'd probably disown me." Karen laughed. "My mom guilted Davis into coming once she heard that the rest of us were going together. That was handy."

"Well, I'll be there." Evie winced. "Although I don't have anything to wear."

"You've got two weeks to find something. And schedule a nap for that afternoon."

It only took six days. On Christmas Eve, Laney and Kyle arrived with their dog Buddy, bearing presents for the boys and three dry-cleaner bags full of dresses that Laney thought might fit her sister.

"I tried these on with a pillow underneath," she told Evie in a conspiratorial whisper when they were alone. "I think one of them should work for you."

Evie hadn't told her sister why she was getting dressed to the nines for New Year's. Laney probably assumed it was a hot date, and maybe it would be. She hadn't spoiled herself with any pampering since she found out she was pregnant, but at the beginning of December, Liam had presented her with a basic child support agreement and a stack of post-dated cheques, plus one that covered to the beginning of her pregnancy. She'd tried to refuse it, but he'd kissed the arguments right out of her. And she'd let him, because she was done making life harder than it needed to be.

Liam showed up while Laney and Kyle took a quick visit out to the Nixon farm, where they'd leave Buddy to have a holiday meal with Kyle's parents' dogs, and where they'd return later to spend the night.

Liam had gone into Windsor on a secret mission, and from the giant toy store bag he immediately stashed in the basement, she knew what it had been. "Honey, they're going to be spoiled by Dale's family tonight. I don't want to get caught up in that cycle."

"Don't worry about," he said, pressing her against the kitchen counter, and that's where Laney and Kyle found them, tangled up and a little breathless. The men shook hands, and Laney gave Liam a big hug.

"Welcome to the family," she said, and Evie blushed. They had slipped into a family-esque routine, but that conversation about how much he meant to her still hadn't happened. Something always interrupted them. The kids. Sex. Her ridiculous habit of falling asleep as soon as she was horizontal. Work, and not just hers. Liam had offered his tenants a cut in their rent to move into the smaller but newly renovated flat below his, and now he was mad at work turning the other half of the house into two more units to rent out. He had someone moving in January first.

She was so proud of how he'd buckled down and done what he'd set out to do. It pained her that she was the only one in his corner. She'd curved her body around his earlier today, pressing their daughter into his back as he had a stilted conversation with his mother. She thought it was bizarre that he didn't want to visit with his family for the holidays, but he just kissed her hard and promised that he was spending it with the family that mattered.

"Okay, Ted should be bringing your mom by any minute, how about we get some dinner going?" Liam pushed Evie toward the living room. "Don't you have a Christmas present to wrap for me or something?"

"Should I be concerned with what you're planning?"

"Absolutely." He winked and pointed at Kyle. "Beer, man?"

Kyle shrugged and patted Laney on the ass. "Sounds

about right."

Her sister rolled her eyes, but sauntered over to the couch. "Well, if they're going to cook, I'm going to get comfy."

"I can't believe you're only here for three days this year, you're going to miss..." Evie wasn't sure how far the secret-sharing circle extended, but... "Can you keep a secret? For reals?"

"Evie! I'm a doctor. Of course I can keep a secret."

She rolled her eyes. "Whatever."

"Well, you asked." Laney stuck her tongue out.

"I regret it already. So...New Year's, at the winery? This year, it's going to double as a secret wedding for Karen and Paul."

"Wow." Laney's jaw dropped. "That's freakin' brilliant. I wish we'd thought of that!"

"Have you guys come to a decision about what you want to do?"

Laney shook her head. "Kyle's adamant about wanting to go somewhere, just the two of us. And then let the moms throw another party or whatever next summer."

"But..." Evie felt a pang of sadness at the thought of missing her sister's wedding.

"Yeah, I know. I've suggested that we do a city hall service here, so our families can come, and then immediately drive to the airport. We'll see. We're not in any rush."

"Really?" Evie shook her head. "I'm not judging that, at all." She pointed to her belly. "Hell, I'm obviously not the poster girl for how to do relationships."

"I don't know, it seems to be working itself out now." Laney snuggled closer and wrapped an arm around the baby bump. "Maybe getting married is overrated."

"Oh, I definitely want to—" *Oh, shit.* Evie blinked at her sister.

"Does he know that?" Laney asked in a whisper.

"I don't know." Man, what a mess she'd made. "We're in a really good place, Lane. I don't want to upset the cart again."

"Oh, sweetie. From what I've seen and what you've told me, I don't think you're going to upset anything."

Evie pursed her lips. Yeah, that would need to get talked about. But not at Christmas. "How about you guys? Still not sure about doing this yourself?" She pressed Laney's hand into her belly, right where Little Girl McIntosh's butt was.

Laney smiled and let out a happy sigh. "Oh, I love that! Did I ever tell you I considered obstetrics? It was my favourite clerkship rotation, but then in fourth year I fell in love with reconstructive surgery, and I never looked back. But my goodness, it's a wonderful thing that our bodies can do, eh?"

Evie laughed. "Careful. I'm drifting into the last month, also known as the *this sucks* phase."

"Still amazing. I don't know…maybe in a year or two we'll revisit that conversation. But right now, I just don't feel that urge. And Kyle…he's swamped with school." Laney's boyfriend had moved to Chicago to live with her, and in doing so, had to set aside his teaching career briefly. He was one semester into his Master's degree in Education. "But if he can't find work when he graduates, maybe we'll look into moving back here."

Evie's heart leapt into her throat. "Really?"

Laney groaned. "Don't get excited, and you *can't* tell Mom."

"Okay." She took a deep breath. "Where would you work?"

"London or Detroit." One or two hours away. Still, a big improvement. "And I'll need to set up locums, convince a practice or a hospital there to give me a chance. It's not just a matter of saying I want to work somewhere."

"My lips are sealed." Evie squeezed her sister's hand. "But right now, you're happy?"

"Ecstatic. Once the baby has arrived and is up for a road trip, you need to come and see our new house. We're across the street from a great park that the boys will love." Laney rolled up to a sitting position. "Now, before Mom gets here—are there any presents that need to be wrapped still?"

They were going to open the majority of their presents the next day, when Connor and Max were with them, at the farm, but Evie and Liam were going to exchange tonight before bed. She'd ordered him a Settlers of Catan gel skin for his iPad, and a picked up a World's Best Dad coffee mug at the mall. Those were both wrapped already, but his last present had arrived just this afternoon: a sporty black baby carrier. She hoped he liked it. She'd taken the ultrasound picture to Mari, who had a scanner, and Mari gave her a sturdier print out of the picture, which she wrapped in a swaddling blanket and tucked into the carrier.

Laney watched this production with curiosity. "You got him baby gear?"

"The man already has everything he needs," Evie whispered. "And I think he'll like this."

"Yeah, I'm definitely missing that hormonal thing that drives this whole business. I like shiny and/or sexy things for Christmas."

Their guests didn't leave until almost eleven, and Evie was dead on her feet, but as Liam steered her toward the bedroom, she protested and pointed to the tree.

"Presents," she mumbled through a yawn.

"In the morning, sunshine."

"No, the boys will be here at eight. Let's do it now. Bring them to bed, okay?"

She brushed her teeth and was pulling on a tank top when his hands closed over top of hers.

"Let's sleep naked tonight," he whispered in her ear.

"Is that part of my Christmas present?" She pulled off the tank top and returned it to her dresser drawer. As she moved to crawl into bed, he tut-tut-tutted her and pointed to her underwear.

"All of it, off it goes."

She blushed.

"Come on, seriously? That makes you turn pink?" He stood on the other side of her bed, buck naked himself, and she couldn't help but glance at and then hold her gaze on his sex. He was effortlessly good-looking, and that area was no exception. Trimmed dark hair at the base, silky soft skin that stretched over what felt like steel when erect. Even now, with no expectation of sex from the tired pregnant lady, his cock looked proud while at rest. "Like what you see?"

She nodded as his almost-erection bobbed slightly in her direction, and then he leaned across the bed and flipped back the covers. "Come on, hop in."

His arms wrapped around her, pulling her tight, then he reached back to the bedside table and presented her with a small, wrapped gift. "First one is yours."

It was a bag of red raspberry leaf tea in an oversized cup printed with Connor and Max's picture. She laughed and directed him to open his own mug.

The next round, she told him to go first, and he loved the gel skin, and had a knowing glint in his eye as she pushed herself upright before opening the heavier package he passed her.

When she saw the Apple logo, she pushed the wrapping paper back in place. "No, Liam, it's too much."

"Oh, whatever. Pretend it's for you *and* the boys, then." He pulled the wrapping paper off of her very own iPad, and she gave in to her joy, turning it on and squealing like a little girl when she realized he'd already programmed it with apps she might like. "This one is a contraction monitor, you press a giant button on the screen at the start and stop of each contraction, and it'll generate a spreadsheet…"

"Honey, we're not going to care about a spreadsheet…" And she pushed the gift aside and crawled into his arms, bare skin against bare skin. His hands found her hips, then her breasts, and as his palms teased back and forth over her nipples, she almost forgot about the last gifts. Drunk on his touch, she hummed against his mouth, and he broke the kiss long enough to ask her if she wanted to turn over. Spooning had become their favourite position, a gentle coupling that didn't stress her hips. Evie was looking forward to the energetic sex of the future, but right now, they were limited in their options.

"Yes, but let's finish our presents first." She pushed up onto all fours and reached across for the last gifts, but there was only the one she'd just wrapped. She glanced down at Liam, who wore a look of confused innocence as he lay beneath her. "Was that it? This one can wait if you didn't get me anything else."

"I had a number of ideas for a third gift." He lifted one hand to cup a breast. "These are really nice, by the way. I really like it when you dangle them in my face."

"Mmmm, glad to hear it." She rocked back and forth as a wave of pleasure pulsed from her chest to her core. "Presents?"

"I thought about buying you a car more appropriate for three kids." He chuckled as she stilled.

"Liam, you don't have that kind of money anymore."

"I know. It would have been a really ugly minivan." He laughed as she dropped her head to his shoulder. "So I shit-canned that idea. Then I considered just carseats, because there are these European designs that will fit three across—"

While he was talking, Evie took advantage of the feast of naked man flesh in front of her, and started nibbling her way across his chest. When she reached his left nipple, she swirled her tongue around the tight, dark brown nub, cutting him off mid-sentence. She murmured for him to keep going, but he groaned and laced his fingers around her head, holding her in place. With each swirl and suck, his cock flexed and stretched between them. With a gasp, Liam pulled her up. "No, Evie, hang on. This isn't how this was supposed to go."

"I'm pretty sure this is how you've trained me now. It's a Pavlovian response, I see your body and I think sexytimes."

He clapped his hands to her hips, a light double spank that sparked something naughty inside her. How lucky she was to have gone to the hotel bar, and taken a foolish chance with the young man with the gorgeous voice. What luck to have made such a wonderful mistake, and ended up with someone who loved all of her dirty thoughts.

"Fine, if that's how it's going to be," he growled, and flipped her over to her side. He smoothed her hair into a ponytail and gripped it with one hand, and he curved the other over her hip and between her legs. "Clearly, you've gotten overtired and a little silly, and you need an orgasm to refocus."

She laughed, but it died into a happy sigh as he teased his way into the folds of her sex, and buried his face in her neck. She lifted her top leg, notching it back and over his, opening herself to his probing touch.

"God, I love your pussy," he whispered. "You're so responsive, so wet and willing."

"I thought about shaving it bald for your last present, that was the backup plan if the other thing didn't arrive."

"Mmmm, I'd like that." She didn't tell him that it would probably have to wait until long after baby arrived, because she'd lost all sightlines to that area a while ago. Like many other things they talked about when wrapped around each other, it was still hot just as talk. Another wonderful gift he'd given her. "Maybe I could shave you, would you like that?"

She felt a gush of moisture, and he groaned. "Yeah, I guess you do. Oh, Evie, my Evie, come on my fingers."

He slid two fingers around her clitoris, one on either side, up and down and over, being careful not to apply too much direct pressure, just enough to coax her up the mountain, step by step. And as she got closer to the peak, and her hips started moving as if they had a mind of their own, he picked up his pace, matching his words to his touch. He was quickly becoming a master at this, learning what she liked, what worked and what didn't.

"Tell me. Tell me what you want," he panted in her ear, his hand sliding faster still, her sex too slick to gain traction, but she didn't need that, she needed......

"In me, Liam. With your fingers. In me, please!" She writhed next to him, and he smothered her cries with a kiss, not because he needed to, but because this simple act of kissing had become so central in their lovemaking, a grounding that freed Evie to be whatever she wanted to be in the moment. And as they kissed, his tongue stroking hers, his fingers slipped into her body, finding the magic spot that would send her flying.

CHAPTER TWENTY-TWO

"Wow."

"Proud of yourself?" Evie teased, slowly rolling over.

"Should I be?"

"I'd say yes." She cupped his face, his stubble scratching her palm. "I love you."

He held her gaze for a moment, then slid his lips across hers. "I know."

"I'm sorry it's taken so long to say." She smiled. "I've been meaning to say it for a while. But I wanted it to be a special moment. I'd say this counts."

"That's...well, it's the best possible segue I could imagine." He cleared his throat. "I want to move in here. Before the baby arrives."

She pressed her head against his chest. "Is it awful that my first concern is where will you put all your stuff?"

"I have a plan." He outlined his thoughts for putting on a modest addition, right through her bedroom window. The work could all be done on the outside of the house, and the last step would be joining the two spaces through the window, which would become a doorway.

"And this room would be what, a hallway?"

"Yeah, of sorts. I was thinking a library." She could see it, but the thought of how much it would cost was daunting.

"It would be cheaper than buying a new place, and really, we just need two more bedrooms and a bathroom. Since I didn't buy you a minivan, we can handle that."

"I'm pretty sure it'll be more than a van."

"I'm pretty sure I'm a certified project manager with an MBA."

"So I shouldn't worry my pretty little head about it?"

"Hell, no. So I can show you the spreadsheets and budget analysis, sunshine."

She relaxed against him. "Okay, but I have one condition."

"What is it?"

"Maybe we should talk about it after the holidays."

"Evie, I want to break ground after the holidays. What's the condition?"

She sighed. "The thing is, I thought I'd be okay with the co-parenting plan. And I would be. And living together will be great, particularly since you've proven that you're a hell of a cook. But…"

He stroked her arm, then her hair, then tipped her chin up to look straight in his eyes. "Evie, have I given you any reason to doubt that you can be honest with me about what you want?"

"This is a really big want."

"Try me." He smiled gently.

"How would feel about getting married?" She took a deep breath. "It doesn't have to be soon. To be honest, I'd rather get my figure back, and wait until this baby is old enough to wear a little dress to match mine, but the idea of renovating a house together without some sort of formal plan…"

She realized she'd drifted her gaze away from his, and when she snapped back, he was still smiling. "Was that so hard?"

"No, I suppose not." She relaxed and let out a little laugh. "So, will you think about it?"

He shook his head. "'Fraid not."

"What?" She jerked back as he laughed.

"Good god, I love that little temper of yours." He rolled up to a sitting position, then helped her do the same, and after she was settled, he reached for her ear. "Hang on a second, you've got a little something here…"

It took her a second to focus on the shiny band that he drew from behind her head, and when she realized what she was looking at, she started to cry. "Seriously?"

"Yes."

"Why did you make me ask you, then?"

"Because that's what I want our life together to be, Evie. I want you to always tell me what you want, and I'll move heaven and earth to make it happen for you."

She blinked back the tears that obscured her vision of the ring. White gold, yellow diamond solitaire. "Wow."

He grinned. "Evie Calhoun, will you, at a time that is convenient to you, in front of your three children and whomever else you want to invite, do me the immense honour of becoming my wife? Will you wear this little piece of sunshine from now until the end of time as a symbol of my love, and will you always trust me with your dirty little secrets?"

"Oh, hell, yes." She threw her arms around him, and he squeezed her tight before easing her back and sliding the ring onto her finger.

They slid under the covers together, and Evie wrapped her newly bedazzled hand around her future husband's cock, eliciting a lovely groan. "Your turn."

When Liam slipped out of bed to clean up a little while later, he noticed Evie's last present still waiting for him to open. He set his cell phone alarm for an hour before the boys were due to arrive, and after visiting the washroom, crawled back into bed with his woman. Her soft naked body shifted against his, and he fell asleep truly happy for the first Christmas he could remember.

In the morning, he made tea and oatmeal before waking Evie up. The first thing she did was bring her hand to her face, really close, like she wasn't sure it had really happened. Then she ran for the bathroom, and came back for some heavy duty kissing after she'd brushed her teeth. He hadn't had a chance to ask her about the present when Connor thumped on the door, and she dashed away, eager to sweep her boys into her arms. She and Dale alternated the holidays, so the boys had opened their stockings at their dad's place already—stockings Evie had mostly filled, which Liam didn't quite understand, but it made her happy, so he didn't question it. She listened to the boys update her on what they received and what they did over the last two days, and once they were all around the table, digging in to oatmeal topped with maple syrup, she took a deep breath.

"Connor, Max...Liam and I had an important conversation last night." She smiled across the table at him, and Liam waited for the boys to bust him.

"Oh?" Connor asked with a total straight face.

"Well, you know we're having a baby, and I think you know by now how important Liam is to me—" she shot him a quick grin "—almost as important as you two."

Max looked up from his cereal. "Is this about you getting engaged?"

Connor shushed him, and Evie wrinkled her brow. "How did you know?"

"Because Liam asked us last week how we'd feel about that." Max shrugged. "I suggested a new PlayStation instead of a ring, but he seemed to think the ring was the right way to go."

Liam had learned that sniffles, particularly in pregnant women, were very hard to read. Connor had apparently learned the same lesson. He took one look at his mom, and leaned over to ask Liam if those were good tears or bad tears.

"Damned if I know, but she's not yelling, that's a good sign." He looked at his future bride, who rolled her eyes at him.

"You try living with these hormones, you goof! Of course they're happy tears. You asked them?"

"Of course. If they weren't ready, I'd have waited."

"And you guys are okay with this?" Evie looked from Connor to Max and back again. They nodded in tandem.

"Plus, he's bringing his iPad to live here." Max looked at Liam sagely. "You might need to buy yourself a new one. I think yours might get lost."

CHAPTER TWENTY-THREE

Another glance at his watch. They still had time, but at this rate—

"Stop worrying about parking spots."

"I wasn't."

"You were." She swept into view and even though he had been, parking was now the last thing on his mind. "Do I look okay?"

She wore crazy tall heels, the shiny black patent a saucy counter to her bouncy red chiffon dress. The soft swell of her belly was disguised under the floating layers that seemed to dance as she moved toward him. "Wow. You look stunning."

"Yeah?" She allowed herself a small smile. "It was hard to find something that fit. I don't have an appropriate maternity dress. This is Laney's."

"You'd rock a paper bag, sunshine."

"Hush. Will you do up my necklace?" A glittering strand dangled from her outstretched hand.

He moved closer and reached past it to trace a finger along the inside of her forearm. "You don't need jewels to shine."

Evie rolled her eyes. "Nice line."

"It's not a line. You seriously take my breath away."

"Liam…"

"Okay, okay. Give me that." He took his time sliding the necklace from her fingers, relishing the last little bit of contact. The last week had been a flurry of family and community events, and early bedtimes. No school meant no time for afternoon fun, either. "Turn around."

She spun slowly, revealing her back. All of her back. The loose fabric of her dress sat low enough to reveal dimples below the tuck of her waist. All the blood drained out his head. Not a surprise. It was all needed in his groin.

"Evie—" Her name came out in a strangled hiss. She cocked her head to the side, glancing back at him over her shoulder. "You can't wear this dress."

"You don't like it?"

"It's indecent. I love it." To prove his point, he placed his finger right between those dimples and trailed his hand up her spine. The goosebumps that pebbled under his fingertips confirmed she was as affected by his touch as he was by her skin. By all of her. He fastened her necklace, then dipped his head to whisper in her ear. "And if you wear it tonight, then the entire town population is going to be scandalized, because I'm going to have my hands all over you. And anyone who comes near—and, sunshine, they will try, abso-fucking-lutely—is going to get a face full of me instead of you."

"I don't think anyone is going to be paying attention to me tonight."

"Then you clearly haven't seen the back of this dress in a mirror." He was tempted to slide his hands through the gap in the fabric and test just how naked she was underneath, but he didn't want to test his luck. Or his restraint.

"I promise, all eyes are going to be on Karen tonight." She'd spilled the beans a few days earlier.

He thought it was brilliant, but Evie was quick to dissuade him of the same idea for their wedding. "How many people is this actually going to be a surprise for?"

"Karen seems to think her mother still doesn't know."

"Well, then this should be fun."

Sexy jazz music swirled through the air as Evie walked

into the glittering winery. As Liam had suspected, parking was a nightmare, so he dropped her off and went to find a spot near the back of the lot.

She spotted Beth immediately. The other woman had a discreet ear piece and an obvious clipboard. "Evie!" She stopped for a moment and made gushing noises about Evie's dress, and Evie returned the compliment sincerely. Beth was tall and curvy, with exceptional taste, and she'd outdone herself tonight, wearing a little black dress that walked the line between guest and professional.

"Are you the unofficial Vegas coordinator tonight?"

Karen had started using that as the actual code word for the wedding, and Beth knew exactly what Evie meant. She lifted her hands in a "what can you do" gesture. "I wasn't going to let someone else come in and muck up the place, now was I?"

They shared a laugh, then someone talked to Beth in her ear and she excused herself after whispering that Vegas would happen in about thirty minutes. Evie glanced around for the happy couple. She knew Karen and Paul planned to be here for the whole evening, and not make a special entrance. It was thrilling, knowing what was about to happen.

She saw Paul first, handsome and grinning like a fool in a sharp tuxedo. He had Megan on his arm, and at first Evie didn't recognize her. She was wearing an almost strapless ball gown, but as Evie moved closer, she saw thin metallic bands dancing over the girl's shoulders. She'd obviously gone to the salon with Karen earlier, and her hair was twisted and curled into an up do.

Before she reached them, she heard her name, and spun around to find the bride herself.

"Look at you," Evie breathed. As soon as the justice of the peace announced the nuptials, it would be obvious that Karen was a bride, but her dress was subtle enough to blend in to the wintery party until then. Pale blue, a few shades lighter than Megan's dress, and under the lights on the dance floor it would look white. A diamond necklace glittered around her neck. Her hair was half up and half down, and adorned with dozens of tiny sparkles.

Beside her, Carrie appeared out of nowhere and together they pressed in, sharing a secret squeal about Vegas actually happening.

"Beth has us on a tight timeline. Once she has a visual on everyone on my secret guest list, we'll do this thing, and then it'll be dancing and drinking all night." Karen glanced at Evie. "You can dance and drink Perrier."

"I don't know how much dancing I'll do, but heck ya!" She looked around for Liam, and spotted him in line at the bar. He waved, and she pointed to a table that Ian was staking out.

Before long, two staffers carried a small dais to the center of the dance floor, and once it was in place, Evan escorted a distinguished looking gentleman to the platform and raised his hand. Quiet descended, and he lifted a microphone.

"Welcome, everyone, to Go West Winery's fourth annual New Year's Eve gala. On behalf of myself, my brother Ty, and all of our staff, we're thrilled to have so many from the Wardham community with us tonight." A murmur of mutual appreciation went through the crowd. "Now, some of you were pressed into attending tonight, and I'm going to introduce a special guest to explain why that was a good decision on your part. Ladies and Gentlemen, His Worship Jason McAuley."

The justice of the peace accepted the microphone, and Evan took a seat at a nearby table, where Evie noticed Karen's parents and siblings were sitting. Consummate professional, Evan would want to make sure the reaction was managed to best effect.

"On this most special of nights, I've been asked to lead you all in a celebration of marriage."

This time, it was more of a roar than a murmur, and it took a few minutes for the crowd the settle down. The justice waited patiently, a smile playing across his face. Once he had the rapt attention of the room again, he lifted his hands.

"Constable Paul Reynolds and Ms. Karen Miller would be honoured if you would bear witness to their vows tonight."

Evie watched, with tears in her own eyes, as Karen's mother realized what was about to happen. She shrieked and leapt out of her chair, and then Karen and Paul were right in front of her, with a hug and a whispered word.

And then they were on the dais, and there weren't many dry eyes in the room as Paul took Karen's hand in his and repeated the vows the justice prompted to him.

"Karen, with all that I am, and all that I have, I vow my life to you.

I will be faithful and honest with you;

I will respect, trust, help and care for you;

And I will share my all with you, through whatever may come."

Her own voice warbling with emotion, Karen repeated the same vows back, and then the justice of peace announced that as the couple had signed the registry earlier in the evening, the next part of the service was a pledge to Megan.

Evie had trouble hearing the words, as she sobbed through it, and Liam passed her at least three tissues before she composed herself, just in time to see Megan shyly pass her father a velvet bag containing the rings. As Paul wiggled out the precious contents, his daughter linked hands with her new step-mother, and Evie thought she just might lose it again.

"You going to be okay, sunshine?" Liam shifted his chair closer, his legs spread wide, so she could lean back against him.

She sniffled. "There's just so much love up there."

"And right here, too." He pressed a small kiss to the curve of her outer ear. "You thinking about involving the boys in our wedding?"

She nodded.

"I think they'll like that. I'll like that." He nodded to the platform. "I'll like this next part, too."

"Ladies and gentleman, it is my most sincere pleasure to introduce for the first time as husband and wife, stepmother and step-daughter, a trio of Reynolds, the newly married Paul and Karen and their daughter Megan. Paul, you may now kiss your bride."

The entire room erupted in cheers, and everyone raised their glass high as he did just that, dipping Karen low and holding her there long enough for the whoops to start. When he pulled her upright again, they both looked flushed, glassy-eyed, and ridiculously happy.

Liam stopped at the bar and grabbed a beer for himself and a glass of lemon water for Evie before finding her at the edge of the dance floor. He stopped beside her and ducked his head to her ear, wanting the warm murmur of his voice to be for her alone. "You're enjoying yourself."

She glanced coyly at him out of the corner of her eye and laughed. "Yes, I am."

Between them, her fingers were tapping along with the smooth jazz, and her hips were twisting almost imperceptibly, like she was trying to restrain herself from just letting go and dancing on the edge of the party.

"Then we should go out there and dance."

"I'm fine right here." She gazed at him for a moment, her face softening but still full of joy. "I'm not sure my feet are up to it. They're already swelling."

"There you are, I've been looking for you all night. So glad you came. Are you guys going to dance?" Evan glanced between them, mis-reading their hesitation. "If you don't care for it, I'm happy to twirl Evie around the floor once or twice."

"We're having fun just watching, Evan, thank you." How many times had Evie had to say the same thing to cover for her ex-husband? From the tightening of Evan's jaw, Liam knew more than once. And once would have been one time too many.

"No, you should dance with Evan." He nodded at the other man.

"No, Liam, it's okay—"

He slid one palm over her belly and the other across the back of her neck. He pressed a quick, hard kiss to her temple before twisting his lips to brush against her earlobe. "Sunshine, after you do a twirl with him, it'll be our turn. And at the end of the night, I'm taking you home. I'm going to enjoy watching you. Go."

She twisted in his arms, and all of a sudden he was holding her, their baby squirming between them, and he was tempted to drag her back to her house that very second. "We'll dance together?"

"Absolutely." He brushed his lips across hers.

"Do you two want a room?" They glanced as one toward Evan, who was sporting a shit-eating grin. "Cause I can go..."

"No." Liam pushed Evie toward her ex-boyfriend. "We've got all the time in the world."

CHAPTER TWENTY-FOUR

"You aren't concerned that you're having regular contractions?"

"No."

"Why not?"

"Because they're ten minutes apart, and not getting any closer."

"They've been ten minutes apart for twenty-four hours now. I thought the third labour was supposed to be quick. I was worried about having an unexpected home birth, not having days of early labour."

"Honey, with all due respect, can you not talk about this labour like you're going through it?"

"Unlikely, sorry, sunshine."

"Hey, did you buy me a Valentine's Day present?"

"Maybe, why?"

"Because it's possible that I might give you a child, and I think that'll be hard to top."

Evie wasn't wrong. Their daughter arrived nine hours later, at five minutes to three in the morning on the fourteenth of February. And there was no way that the pendant he bought her, with the birth stones of each of her children in it, could compete with the perfection of holding his little seven pound bundle of love in his arms.

He'd been blown away by Evie's strength during labour. When she cried and begged for drugs during transition, and

Donna quietly told her there probably wouldn't be time for anything other than a bit of gas, she harnessed an inner strength that made *him* want to cry. When she sagged back against him between contractions, and then surged forward again, curling over her belly, he couldn't do anything but hold her and feel humble.

And when baby Ava slipped into the world, it was Evie's hands that reached down and pulled her home, to her mother's chest, and Liam knew his face was wet with tears. He'd tell no one, but he'd never forget that feeling. "You're amazing," he whispered, as he held his woman, who held his daughter.

They were home by mid-morning, and as soon as his girls were settled, Liam called Claire and she and the boys came to meet the newest member of the family.

"Where did the name Ava come from?" Claire asked him quietly as the boys joined their mother and sister on the bed.

"Evie liked the name Anna when she was pregnant with Max. I like the name Evie. I pushed the two together."

"Does she have a middle name?"

Liam didn't tell her how close their little girl had come to being named after her grandmother. "Her full name is Ava Delaney Calhoun McIntosh."

When Claire gasped and rushed to Evie's side, he knew his bride-to-be was right—that was the perfect name. He left Evie to her fan club, and went and made tea.

When he came back a few minutes later, Ava was nursing, the boys had drifted off to their room, and Evie was telling her mother about the birth. "He was amazing, Mom. A total rock, especially when it all got to be too much for me. You remember, with Max? How I sobbed and begged for drugs?"

"No epidural this time?"

Evie shook her head. "No time. Whew, that was a thing, I'll tell you. I guess I don't have to, eh?"

"Oh, sweetheart, luckily that was so long ago that I've forgotten."

"Mom, I hope I never forget."

"Maybe you'll get to do it again."

Evie laughed. "I don't know. Maybe. That'll be up to Liam."

That was his cue. "Who wants tea?"

"Oh, yes, thank you, Liam, that would be lovely." Claire patted her daughter's leg. "I'll help myself in the kitchen."

Evie waited until after her mother was safely on the other side of the house. "You heard?"

He nodded. "You'd have another?"

"Today? I say yes. Don't ask me again for a year, okay?"

"You've got a deal, sunshine."

As much as Liam felt like he'd won the lottery that day, the days that followed were a challenge. The third and fourth days were low points, with midwives and lactation consultants coming and going, and many, many tears. But then the next day was a bit better, and the day after that again so, and by the beginning of March, Evie was whipping the boys to school with Ava strapped to her chest, and then checking in with Stella at the studio before coming home for a morning nap.

Liam finally finished the last two rental units and found tenants, and then it was time for him to call the Wests. He put on a suit for the first time since New Year's, and set off for the winery. Three hours later, he brought home a bottle of sparkling wine and a six month contract for part-time consulting. While Ava had an afternoon nap, Liam and Evie had their first shower together since the birth.

Evie extended the invitation, but then scurried into the bathroom ahead of him. By the time he joined her, steam had successfully obscured her from his vision.

"Sunshine, you want to tell me something?"

She sighed. "It's going to take a while for my body to bounce back."

He reached for her hand and brought it to his raging hard-on. "What does this tell you?"

"I've missed you, Liam." She pressed against him, and he

held her, savouring the connection. "I'm not sure about sex, but the midwives gave me the go-ahead."

That was his kind of challenge. "Now, how many ways do you think I could make you come without us having intercourse?"

She shivered. "I don't know, uhm, maybe two or three?"

He reached for the body wash and slowly lathered her up, from tip to toe, pausing in a few key middle spots to demonstrate the first way. Then he rinsed her clean of suds, and dropped to his knees, pressing kisses her to belly, then her mound, and after he lifted one leg and draped it over his shoulder, to her very core. That provided orgasm number two, and when his fingers got involved again, number three as well.

They took turns drying each other off, and when they lay down on their bed together, Liam reached for a bottle of lubricant and a condom he'd stashed in a drawer. "Just in case," he whispered, as he touched and teased and stroked her through numbers four and five, and finally she reached for the lube and gave them each enough to prepare the other.

"I want to try," she said, and so they did. It wasn't magical for her, as she'd warned him, but it was wonderful in an unexpected way. When she started to cry, Liam moved to pull out, and she begged him not to. "Please, don't. I just need a minute."

He gave her one, and then another, while he whispered how much he wanted her, how beautiful she was, how good she tasted. And slowly, she began to grind against him, which felt out of this world for him, and he had to grit his teeth and hold on for dear life as she slowly figured out what worked the same and what was different. He wouldn't know, it all felt pretty awesome on his end, but he got that this was an important step for her.

And when she reached for his hand and pressed his thumb to her clitoris, he gave her some help, because he knew that asking was as big a challenge as doing for her.

And both were conquered that afternoon, by her.

He was a mere attendant in the presence of a goddess reborn.

THE END

Dear Reader,

Thank you for finishing this first Wardham trilogy with me! If you fell in love with Liam, please write a review. Reviews help other readers decide to give a book a try, and there's nothing I want more than for new readers to discover Wardham. Have you read the other books in the series? If not, go back and check out *Between Then and Now*, *What Once Was Perfect*, and *Where Their Hearts Collide*.

Two notes about Evie and Liam's story:

1. A few early readers from the Wardham Ambassador's Facebook group noticed that I didn't write an epilogue. I usually do, but I think Evie and Liam deserve more than a tag on chapter. The plan is to write them an erotic novella follow-up in early 2015, touch base with them a year after their daughter is born, and find out how they're keeping the passion and love alive in their relationship.

2. American readers may have noticed that Thanksgiving happens before Halloween in this book—I promise, that's not a timeline error! Canadian Thanksgiving is held right in the middle of harvest season in October. Celebrate it with us...twice as much turkey could only be a good thing. Australian, British and New Zealand readers...you're missing out on both holidays. Good excuse for a trip to Southwestern Ontario.

Speaking of Wardham, there will be more stories from this little Canadian beach town...Chase, Ty and Evan all have happy-ever-afters to discover. Look for those books starting in Fall 2014. And there will be a summer novella to tide you over as well, *Beyond Love and Hate*, which will come out in June 2014. Beth Stewart meets her match in Finn Howard, the maddeningly delicious marketing consultant who pushes all of her buttons. Can one night of passion change everything?

But before that book comes out, I'm shifting gears a little, and introducing a brand new series. Welcome to Camo Cay, a Caribbean haven for Rik Amundson and his new

American bride, Calli St. James. We'll first visit Camo Cay in a Navy SEAL novella, *Fall Out*, which will come out as part of a SEAL romance super-bundle, and then Rik and Calli's story, *Fall In*, will be published Summer 2014.

To keep up with all of this, subscribe to my newsletter today! Subscribers are always offered a first chance to read my books as review copies before they come out.

From the bottom of my heart, thank you for joining me on this journey.

~ Zoe

ACKNOWLEDGMENTS
aka The People Who Put Up With All My Bugging

This book has been a long time coming. Evie and Liam's story came to me while I was writing the first Wardham book, What Once Was Perfect. But then Karen and Paul's story started a little sooner, and while I was writing that, Carrie and Ian poked their heads up and…now it's been a year since I first sketched the outline of Evie's unexpected pregnancy! Time flies.

First and foremost, I need to thank my critique partner, Molly McLain, who put up with months of chatter about Evie and Liam while she was putting the finishing touches on her own debut novel, Can't Shake You. Cora Seton, Cate Baylor and the rest of the Romance Divas who talked shop and did writing sprints with me also deserve gold stars.

My street team, the Wardham Ambassadors, who make checking in on Facebook a complete joy. Mona, Bette, Shari, Allison, Holly, Tricia, Lori, Betsy, Vikki, Sue, Fawnia, Keri, Shelly, Sadrina, plus my sister, Molly and my Uncle Matt…can you imagine a better crew? I can't.

Julie D, for sharing her personal experiences as a mother of a child with diabetes. It was hard to capture the rawness of having a child in the hospital within the scope of a romance novel, and I freely admit my bias toward the positive moments in life…Evie and Max, and their entire family, had their lives turned upside down with his diagnosis, and any failings in talking about that experience are my own.

JK Harper, for her brilliant blurb writing skills, which helped me see the spark when I'd run out of words. If you like shifter romances, check out her books! Hot wolf action!

Jennifer M.K., who was the first person to message me on Facebook eight months ago, asking about this crazy book-writing plan I had, and who provided the code word between Karen and Evie in this book…I'd already written a line about running off to Vegas, it's like she read my mind! A wonderful friend and a lovely fan from the very beginning.

Marie Force and everyone on the Yahoo self-publishing loop, who keep me focused on the business of writing and publishing. I click on those email digests the second they hit my inbox, knowing there's a wealth of knowledge inside.

Noelle Adams and Samantha Chase, who included me in their Christmas box set, and introduced me to a whole new set of readers. I will be forever grateful for the opportunity. And all the readers who bought Love for the Holidays, read What Once Was Perfect, and subsequently joined my mailing list and connected with me on Facebook and Twitter. It was that outpouring of love that spurred me on to finish this book.

My in-laws, who still can't quite believe that I write books that people buy, but support my crazy plans anyway.

My friends, who veer in the other direction, God bless them...their confidence that I'm on the right track is inspiring.

My sister, who cuts right down the middle, and puts up with more bugging than anyone else.

And finally, my Vikings. I promise this will be worth it. The late nights of writing and the quick dinners. Me disappearing for hours on the weekend to write at Starbucks. The inappropriate pictures you sometimes see on Pinterest. It's all for you.

ABOUT THE AUTHOR

Zoe York lives in London, Ontario with her young family. She has an English degree and works at a university, so it was probably a foregone conclusion that she'd write a romance novel one day. She's currently chugging Americanos, wiping sticky fingers, and dreaming of happy-ever-after endings.

www.zoeyork.com

CPSIA information can be obtained at www.ICGtesting.com
Printed in the USA
LVOW10s1430260416

485401LV00003B/154/P

9 780993 667527